Dear Luke,

I wrote this down all right and proper with the lawyer over in Cody, but I wanted to explain why I went against your wishes and left you the ranch. Isabelle's just a girl—she couldn't keep a place like this running. You've put your heart and soul and blood into it, you've been a son to me, as much as Bella's been a daughter. Hell, even more so. I never did understand women, and at this point it's too late to start trying.

So the ranch is yours. I've left a couple of pieces of worthless land to Bella, and some stocks that she can cash in. She's better off where she is, in a city, not stuck out on a horse farm in the middle of Wyoming.

You don't have to tell her the truth if you don't want to. She's been gone a long time, and I don't expect she'll be coming back. Tell her you earned the ranch. Tell her I'm sorry I never was much of a father to a motherless little girl, but I loved her. As I love you, son.

Hoyt Romney

Please address questions and book requests to: Harlequin Reader Service
U.S.: 3010 Walden Ave., P.O. Box 1325, Buffalo, NY 14269
Canadian: P.O. Box 609, Fort Erie, Ont. L2A 5X3

**WESTERN** *Lovers*™

# ANNE STUART

## RANCHO DIABLO

*Harlequin Books*

TORONTO • NEW YORK • LONDON
AMSTERDAM • PARIS • SYDNEY • HAMBURG
STOCKHOLM • ATHENS • TOKYO • MILAN
MADRID • WARSAW • BUDAPEST • AUCKLAND

For Judith Arnold (aka Barbara Keiler),
a writer and a friend

HARLEQUIN BOOKS
225 Duncan Mill Road, Don Mills,
Ontario, Canada M3B 3K9

ISBN 0-373-88543-1

RANCHO DIABLO

Copyright © 1990 by Anne Kristine Stuart Ohlrogge

# Chapter One

It was probably her total inability to cook that caused all her problems, Isabelle Romney decided, sitting cross-legged on the narrow little cot in the Sun Glow room of the Basho Meditation Center somewhere north of the Canadian border. If she'd just been a little more blessed with the housewifely arts, maybe she wouldn't have had to resort to manipulating other people to get what she wanted. Maybe she would have found someone who was so entranced by her cooking that he would have married her, and she'd be living somewhere in the Midwest, with three kids demanding her attention, instead of alone at the advanced age of thirty, hiding out from someone she should have had the brains to keep away from in the first place.

Of course, with her fondness for eating, it was just as well she couldn't cook. If she'd been able to boil water without burning it she probably would have weighed three hundred pounds, and then she wouldn't have to worry about whether Martin Abruzzi wanted to have her quietly murdered. She never would have gotten past his kitchen in the first place, much less into the sanctified premises of his Boston town house.

She wouldn't be able to manipulate her Cousin Becky anymore, either, the way she was counting on doing. Becky had always been in awe of the incomparable Bella, and cooking skills or the lack thereof had nothing to do with it. Becky had envied Isabelle's effortless ease in getting what she wanted, using nothing more than her dazzling smile and her congenital charm.

Not that she'd gotten everything she wanted, Isabelle thought, shifting on the cot, listening to the grating, maddening sound of ancient springs creaking. She hadn't gotten the one thing she'd most wanted in her life, and all the charm in the world hadn't brought it any closer. She hadn't gotten Luke Cassidy, and she'd lost her father and her home in the process.

That wasn't what she needed to be thinking about, she reminded herself, running a hand through her lustrous mane of blond hair that not even the rough detergent shampoo supplied by the meditation center could dim. She needed to be thinking about how she could get her Cousin Becky to do exactly what she wanted.

She could see it all so clearly. The parking lot outside filled with rusting Volkswagens, antique Saabs, a camper or two and occasional luxury car, including her own bright red Ferrari. Becky would drive up, probably in something sedate and unimaginative. An Oldsmobile, perhaps, or a Buick. No, a Ford Escort. Something economy and spotlessly maintained. She'd look up at the imposing gray edifice of what had once been a mental hospital, and wonder what her colorful Cousin Isabelle was doing inside. And what she wanted from her.

She'd make it past the visitors' desk in record time—Isabelle had already thought to prime Sister Elizabeth. She'd walk down the sun-splashed corridors with their bizarre murals, down to Isabelle's demure cell, and she'd hesitate before knocking. Becky always hesitated. That was why she'd never gotten into any trouble in her twenty-nine years, while Isabelle had never been out of it.

It was going to be ridiculously easy. Isabelle was used to wrapping people around her beautifully manicured fingers, and Becky had always been one of the most receptive. She'd looked up to her older cousin since they were sixteen and fifteen, respectively, and had spent the summer at Isabelle's father's ranch in north Wyoming. They hadn't seen each other since Isabelle had run away, but back then, Becky had been willing to lay down her life for Isabelle. She was counting on her to feel the same, even after so many years.

Not that Isabelle would be asking that much of a sacrifice of her. She'd be offering her excitement, adventure, the chance of romance and a happy-ever-after ending. And if Becky was frightened of the prospect at first, it would take no time at all to talk her into it. Isabelle could talk anyone into anything.

And if the Fates were particularly kind, Becky might have given up some of her persnickety ways and taken up smoking in her old age. Isabelle had finished her last hoarded cigarette butt three days ago, and her lungs craved the taste of smoke. She'd tried inhaling the ever-present incense and nearly choked herself. If she could just get Becky to agree to her plan, then maybe she'd manage to survive another week or two of clean living, brown rice, green tea and no cigarettes. But she would have killed for a gin and tonic. And it didn't even have to be Tanqueray.

She looked down at her saffron robes, kicking at them with one long leg. If Luke Cassidy could only see her now, she thought with a trace of amusement. He wouldn't believe how his nemesis had fallen.

Fortunately he wasn't going to see her in her current predicament, any more than he'd seen her at all in the past thirteen years. And that was where Becky came in. And after her first panic, she'd agree to Isabelle's plan. She simply had to.

Isabelle flopped back on the hard little bed, kicking her legs out and nesting her arms behind her head. She could feel the tension, the restlessness, prickling through her veins. It was the first time she felt alive since she'd taken refuge at the center, and if things went as smoothly as she knew they would, she wouldn't have to sink back into that apathy again. When had Becky ever been able to hold out against her? When had anyone? With the lone, frustrating exception of Luke Cassidy.

She listened for the sound of sensible flat shoes on the linoleum hallways, knowing Becky too well to expect anything else. The sharp click of spiked heels didn't elicit a moment of interest. Becky had never worn heels.

The knock on the door was sharp, almost demanding, and Isabelle swung herself off the bed with a muffled curse. It wasn't Becky—Becky's knock would be shy and hesitant, the first one inaudible. Something must have held her up, damn it all. And Isabelle didn't know if she could stand the delay.

She almost snarled, "Who is it?" to her tightly shut door, but at the last minute she brought herself under control. It wouldn't do for her fellow pilgrims to realize that Sister Isabelle wasn't the meek, devoted soul she appeared to be. With her usual ease she plastered a saintly, faintly witless expression on her face, and opened her door to her unexpected guest. And found herself looking into a reflection of her own unmistakable face.

Isabelle stood in shock for a moment, blocking the doorway, staring at her Cousin Becky. It shouldn't have come as a surprise. After all, it was her resemblance that had made Isabelle first think of her current plan. But she hadn't expected that resemblance to grow.

All her life Isabelle had been the beauty, Becky the pale copy. Isabelle was tall, Becky was just average height. Isabelle had a glorious golden mane of hair, Becky's was one shade drabber. Isabelle's complexion was glowing, her silver-blue eyes wicked and mysterious. Becky had had pimples, and her myopic eyes were plain blue behind her unremarkable glasses. Becky was always ten pounds heavier, ten times shyer, a hundred times less interesting. While Isabelle, or Bella to all and sundry, burned brightly, a thousand watts of incandescence, Becky was a twenty-five-watt closet bulb.

"Bella?" Becky said, staring at her in apparent disbelief. The voice that had always been flat, somewhat nasal, now sounded throatier, sexier. More like Isabelle's. The extra ten pounds were gone, the pimples had disappeared and her mousy blond hair was a stylist's recreation of Isabelle's natural shade. Even her eyes were a brilliant shade, brought about by tinted contact lenses. Becky wouldn't need Isabelle's expertise to impersonate her. She was already doing a creditable job of it.

Without hesitation Isabelle grabbed Becky's arm and dragged her into the cell, slamming the door behind them, her calculations shifting rapidly. "You haven't started smoking, have you?" she asked, getting her priorities straight.

"No," Becky said. "Isabelle, what in heaven's name are you doing here? You don't belong in a place like this."

Isabelle quickly pulled her serene expression back around her face. Despite the improved makeup and clothes, Becky was still a far cry from the incomparable Bella. And she was still just as gullible. Or so Isabelle hoped. "Actually, I do," she said mildly, sinking down on the narrow pallet as if she actually found it comfortable. "It was so sweet of you to come visit, Becky. It's been so long. You look wonderful."

"Of course I came," Becky said, taking the single, straight-back chair the room boasted. "The moment I got your letter. I..."

"What kind of car are you driving?" Isabelle asked abruptly, still staring at her transformed cousin in amazement.

"I beg your pardon?"

"You used to drive a Nova. What are you driving now?"

"I don't see what that has to do with anything," she said with a trace of irritation. Something new, Isabelle thought, adjusting her calculations rapidly. The old Becky would never have shown irritation for Isabelle's abrupt questions—she would have been grateful for the interest.

"Trust me," Isabelle said in dulcet tones, smothering her own pang when it didn't appear as if Becky was ready to do any such thing.

"A Ford Escort," she said finally. "Why?"

Isabelle breathed an imperceptible sigh of relief. Becky hadn't changed that much. "Just curious. Becky, I need your help."

Becky immediately looked wary. "I assumed you did," she murmured. "I'll do anything I can, Bella, but I have to find a job. I wasn't expecting the layoff, and I can't afford a vacation right now."

"If you go along with my plan you won't have to worry about affording anything ever again," Isabelle said, crossing her legs under her saffron robes and hoping it looked like the lotus position to her cousin. "I'm sorry you're out of work, but really, things couldn't have worked out more conveniently."

"For whom?" Becky said tartly.

"You're the only human being I know who actually says 'whom,'" Isabelle said with a trace of admiration. "And this is going to work out for both of us. It'll be just like the old days, when we were teenagers and too young to know better. I have this wonderful plan, and if everything works out as I know it will..."

"Does it involve money? Because let me tell you right now, Bella, that I haven't got a penny."

"When have I ever asked you for money?" Isabelle demanded, affronted. She'd forgotten Becky's compelling fondness for money.

"You haven't," she agreed. "Just don't start."

"As a matter of fact, this involves making money. And living happily ever after. I have the perfect man for you, Becky. Someone devastatingly handsome, brilliant, strong, sexy and unattached."

"Sounds too good to be true. I've given up looking for true love, Bella."

"But wouldn't you like to find it? Wouldn't you like to settle down on a ranch in Wyoming and raise little cowpokes?"

Becky held herself very still, and her flat blue eyes stared at her cousin. "You're not talking about Luke, are you?"

"You were in love with him when you were sixteen, admit it. No one ever gets over their first love."

"You were in love with him, too," Becky pointed out.

"Yes, but I was seventeen, and believe me, he was far from the first person I had a passion for."

"He was probably the first person who wasn't interested."

Isabelle resisted the urge to kick Becky. Instead she plastered her saintly smile on her face. "Probably," she agreed. "And he might have been the last. But that has nothing to do with the price of oranges. I'm offering you a chance to go back to Wyoming, to Rancho Diablo, and see Luke again. And if my instincts are right, and they always are, you two are going to fall in love at first sight.''

"Why do you want me to go there?"

Now came the tricky part. This wasn't going nearly as well as Isabelle had imagined it would, but then, life had a tendency to fall short of expectations. She still had no doubt whatsoever that she'd be able to talk Becky into it. Eventually.

"I want you to go out there and talk to Luke about selling Rancho Diablo. He has a small parcel of land for sale, and he needs my signature. I want you to go out there, refuse to sign it and try to talk him into agreeing to let me put the whole place on the market."

"I wouldn't be able to talk Luke Cassidy into anything," she said flatly. "And why in heaven's name would you want to sell the ranch? And for that matter, why does he have to agree? Isn't the ranch yours?"

Isabelle shrugged. "It's mine. I just don't want to have to get into endless arguments with Luke over it. After all, I haven't been back there since I was seventeen, not even for Daddy's funeral. It's never meant that much to me, you know that."

"No, I don't. When we spent that summer together you adored the place."

"Well, my father didn't think I was worthy of it," she said carelessly. "He wanted a son, and when my mother died before giving him one he went and found Luke Cassidy. Lucky for Hoyt that Luke's father was an abusive drunk who had the decency to die and leave Luke free. Speaking of love at first sight, you should have seen Daddy. The moment he brought the scrawny, bedraggled little hoodlum home he didn't have a moment to spare for me."

"Bella, he loved you."

Isabelle smiled brightly. "Of course he did. He loved me almost as much as he loved Luke and the ranch. The point is, Luke hasn't seen me since I was seventeen."

"So?"

"So he won't have the faintest idea that you aren't who you say you are."

Becky stared at her in blank confusion for a moment, and then horror dawned on her face. "You're out of your mind! You want me to pretend I'm you?"

"Exactly."

"Why? Why can't you go out there and confront him yourself? Simply tell him you want to sell the place, not just a tiny piece of it. If you think I could hold out against him you've forgotten what little you know about me. The first strong breeze and I blow right over. And Luke Cassidy, if I remember correctly, is a very strong breeze."

"True enough," Isabelle agreed. "And all I really want you to do is stall for time. I already have someone who might be interested in buying the place, but they won't be back in this country for another two weeks. I have the right to sell the ranch, with or without Luke's agreement, but I'd rather not have to deal with him. I just need two weeks, Becky. That's not asking so much, is it?"

"Why do you have to do anything? Why not just sit tight and wait?"

"Because Luke said if I don't sign those papers in time for the sale by Friday he's going to come East and drag me back by the hair." She tossed her heavy mane over her shoulder, and Becky tried to do the same. The permed copy didn't have quite the bounce Isabelle's had, but it was a creditable attempt.

"That still doesn't answer my question. Why don't you sell the piece of land? After all, you're planning to sell the entire place—why not go ahead and get Luke off your back for now?"

"I'm not signing anything until I know what Mr. Takashima's corporation is interested in. Anyway, Luke hates me. He always has and he always will."

"So he'll hate me if I pretend to be you."

"I don't think so," Isabelle said reflectively. "It's not so much the idea of me, it's more instinctive. Hormonal, maybe. We're like two hungry timber wolves, circling each other. If we met under completely different circumstances, with nothing in common, we still would have despised each other. But he was always sort of sweet to you."

"He scared me half to death," Becky said.

"But he wasn't trying to. He was trying to scare me, and not getting very far. If you go out and pretend to be me he'll just think he's gotten over his hatred of me. And I think he's going to fall in love with you."

"Now that really is crazy."

"Maybe. You know what a romantic I am," Isabelle said.

"I know what a lunatic you are. Why can't you go?"

"I've taken holy orders," she said glibly.

"What?"

"I told you, I've taken holy orders. I'm a nun. I can't leave this place, and I really don't want to. The world has finally gotten too much for me. I need peace and tranquillity, the repose I can find behind these four walls." She smiled sweetly, aware of Becky's expression. Her cousin wasn't sure whether to believe her or to laugh in her face.

"If you don't need the world, why do you want to sell the ranch? Surely you wouldn't need the money in a place like this?"

"It's all going to charity, Becky," Isabelle said with a soulful little sigh. "To needy children. Those poor little tykes need it more than a big strong man like Luke does. Besides, he doesn't even make a profit from the ranch. It'll have to be sold sooner or later, and right now is when it can do the most good. You love children, don't you, Becky? Doesn't it grieve you to think of them going hungry at night, crying for food?"

"Yes."

Isabelle could feel the ready tears sparkling in her silver-blue eyes, and she fastened a tremulous smile to her mouth. "Then you'll do it, Becky? For the children's sake?"

And Becky, her obedient, awe-struck cousin, said, "Absolutely not."

LUKE CASSIDY STORMED inside the kitchen door, threw his Stetson down on the scarred table, followed it with his worn leather gloves and began to curse. The hat landed in a plate filled with the remnants of bacon grease and pancake syrup, and the gloves knocked over the pitcher of milk that had been left out since morning. He watched the pitcher break, the thick milk spreading over the dusty, littered floor, and he continued his cursing, with volume, fluidity and color. No one was close enough to hear him, and he didn't give a damn if they were. He'd just spent the worst damned day of his whole damned life, and if things didn't improve right quick he was going to start breaking more than a pitcher of milk.

Scooping his battered hat from the table, he ran it under the sink, shoving dishes out of the way to reach the faucet. And then he tossed it toward the rocker by the old wood stove and began cursing again when it landed in the dog dish.

He could hear the phone ringing, and he didn't move. He was damned if he was going to answer it. It was probably the bank, wondering when the land sale was going to go through and they were going to get their money. Or it was the vet, with more bad news about Telly. Or the power company, or the gas company, or his ex-mother-in-law, or that hot-blooded teenager who'd been sniffing around his heels all last summer and looked set to do it again.

Or maybe, just maybe, it was good news. An offer on the old Foley place, the other piece of useless land he wanted to sell. Or maybe it was some poor fool interested in keeping house for the ornery widower and feeding another three bachelors of varying age and description. Or maybe, just maybe, Isabelle was planning to send her signed purchase and sale agreement back by express mail. That, or bring her pretty little butt back to the place she'd forsaken.

That was the least likely of all the possibilities, and he wasn't sure whether that would count as good news or another disaster. Probably the latter. But whoever was calling was the persistent sort, and once again he thought of Isabelle. He headed for the phone, taking his own sweet time about it, and when he picked it up he was ready for anything.

"Yeah," he said, his voice no more than a dry snap.

"Luke? Is that you?"

He hadn't heard that voice in a long time. "Isabelle," he said flatly. "Yeah, it's me. You finally decided to see reason?"

"Uh...er...I thought I'd come out there."

He froze. Definitely disaster, he thought. "All right. You're half owner of the place, it's your right. When are you coming?"

"Day after tomorrow. Can someone meet me? I'm flying in to Cody on the 7:00 p.m. flight."

"Someone can meet you. Why?"

"I don't want to rent a car . . ."

"No, I mean why are you coming?"

"I wanted to talk to you about the ranch."

"What's there to talk about?"

"You're trying to sell off pieces . . ."

"I don't have a choice. You got any other suggestions?"

"I might."

Great, Luke thought. This damned rotten day only needed the return of Isabelle Romney to cap things off. "Well, you can make a list when you get here," he drawled. "It's been a long time."

"Too long," Isabelle said to him.

Not long enough, Luke thought grimly. "See you Friday."

He hung up before she could say something again in that husky voice of hers. Funny, but it hadn't sounded quite right. Sort of fake. But then, he'd decided long ago that that was exactly what Isabelle Romney was. A phony from the top of that golden mane of hair to the toes of her feet. It was no wonder that husky, sexy note in her voice seemed put on. What was a surprise, however, was the fact that he hadn't responded to it anyway. For the first time in his life Luke Cassidy hadn't felt even a trace of longing for the woman on the other end of the line, a woman forever out of his reach. Maybe today wasn't such a bad day after all.

ISABELLE WATCHED BECKY hang up the pay phone in the cafeteria of the meditation center, and once more she had to reconcile her idea of the old, incompetent Becky with the very efficient liar she'd just listened to. "He believed you, of course."

"I'm crazy to do this," Becky said flatly.

"No, you aren't. For once in your life, take a chance."

"What makes you think I haven't?" Becky said.

"Have you?"

"Not very many. Is Luke still as handsome as he was when he was Cassidy's bad boy and we were teenagers?"

"I don't know. I told you, I haven't been home in thirteen years."

"That doesn't mean you haven't been in touch with someone, anyone. Like Mildred Howell. That old bat always did like you."

"She wasn't an old bat. She was a good teacher, even if she was a little strict. And yes, she's been in touch. She says Luke's handsomer than ever, and that all the women in the county are chasing after him, married or not."

"He doesn't have anyone?"

"Not since Cathy died. The grieving widower is waiting for the right woman."

"The right woman isn't Isabelle Romney," Becky said. "Or someone who's impersonating her. When he finds out who I really am he'll never forgive me."

"You just have to make sure he's in love with you before he finds out. Then he'll just yell a lot and get over it," Isabelle said with her usual confidence. "You know you can do it, Becky."

Indeed, it surprised her that Becky had succumbed so fast. For all her demurrals and feet-dragging, it hadn't taken more than another half hour to get her to agree. If Isabelle didn't know Becky so well she would have thought her cousin had ulterior motives. But what could those motives possibly be? She was offering her Luke and a new life, if Becky was smart enough to win them. What else could she gain?

"Can I call you here?" Becky said as Isabelle escorted her to the front hallway.

"Not really. I'll call you."

"Won't Luke get suspicious?"

"I'll just say I'm Cousin Becky," Isabelle said with a grin. "I can't tell you how much I appreciate this."

"And the children," Becky said. "Don't forget the poor starving children."

"I never do," Isabelle said soulfully, stifling a sudden pang of guilt. "Be careful, Becky. Don't talk to strangers."

Becky's expression held an uncharacteristic amusement. "I promise. I'll be in touch."

Isabelle stood by the door, watching Becky leave, wondering if she should have warned her cousin. Becky knew almost as much about Luke and Rancho Diablo as Isabelle did. When Becky had gone back to her father's city apartment at the end of the summer, Isabelle took off, and neither of them had been back. There was no way Luke would ever guess that the woman calling herself Isabelle Romney wasn't the girl he'd despised for most of his life.

Still, she couldn't rid herself of the notion that she should have told Becky a couple of things. One, that the last time she'd seen Luke Cassidy she'd been lying stark naked in his bed.

And the other thing that was of almost equal importance. That Martin Abruzzi probably wanted very much to kill her. And anyone who passed themselves off as Isabelle Romney might, just possibly, be in danger, too.

# Chapter Two

Luke Cassidy stared at the telephone, wondering whether he should call Isabelle back and tell her not to come. He'd done everything he could to keep the creditors off his back—he had no choice but to sell that tract of scrubby land or go under. It wasn't as if it was of any use to Rancho Diablo. But he hated selling even the smallest portion of the place he'd poured his blood and heart and soul into. And the damnable thing of it was, he had to have Isabelle's signature on that worthless tract of land, a fluke of Hoyt's damnable will. Some of the prime land to the west he could have gotten rid of without Isabelle ever being the wiser. But Hoyt had left her a share of two of the worst pieces of acreage, along with those stocks. He'd left her the most disposable assets, and if Luke was going to come up with some desperately needed cash he was going to have to risk everything and go through Isabelle.

He didn't want to see her again. For the past thirteen years he'd run the ranch, keeping it going despite drought, flood, farm crises and even a tornado. He'd been able to wrest a profit from its stubborn soil, but not enough of one. There was no money to plow back into the place, no money for improvements, expansions, no money for a new truck when the old one was barely running, no money to buy that promising new colt that Murphy was offering at a steal. And Telly's stud days were nearing an end. He didn't know what the hell he was going to do when that happened.

God, he didn't want her in his house, smelling of that damned perfume she always wore. Maybe she'd changed her brand in the intervening years. He still couldn't pass a woman wearing the stuff without setting his hormones into an uproar. Compulsion, it was called. Aptly named.

He'd made the major mistake of buying some for Cathy during the short time they were married. It was soon after she'd lost the baby, and she'd been so mournful and depressed that he'd wanted to cheer her up. So he'd bought her a bottle of perfume when he was in Jackson, not even bothering to see what it smelled like. It wasn't till she put it on, her gentle brown eyes lighting up with pleasure, that he realized it was Isabelle's signature scent. And there was nothing he could do about it. Cathy had been such a delicate, fragile soul that he couldn't explain his mistake. And he couldn't not respond to the first sexual overture she'd ever made in his direction. He'd had no choice but to make love to her in the darkness she preferred, his head filled with Isabelle Romney's scent. And for the first time Cathy had believed he really loved her, that he hadn't just married her because she was pregnant.

He didn't know whether they would have stayed married if she hadn't died in a car crash. He wasn't a man to admit mistakes. He had a duty to her, and he would have stuck by it. And she, poor soul, had loved him. But maybe sooner or later she would have gotten tired of the love going in only one direction. Or maybe he would have learned to love her back.

He'd never know the answer to that. And since Cathy's death, some seven years ago, he'd learned to be very careful whom he got involved with, and what sort of expectations he raised. He had no intention of living with that kind of guilt ever again.

Hell and damnation, he thought, stalking over to the overflowing sink and turning on the water. Just one good year, that was all they needed. Just one year where they made so damned much money he could do some of the things he'd planned to do and never been able to afford, like fixing the roof on the west barn, like fencing in another couple of corrals, like increasing the small beef herd. Maybe, just maybe, if some sort of miracle happened, if he could buy Murphy's foal and he turned out to be something extraordinary, maybe he could start to turn things around, and Isabelle would never have to do anything more than cash the checks he had the bank send her. While he could survive with her staying half a continent away, he would have liked her gone completely, out of his life, out of his dreams, out of his blood.

He began washing dishes, haphazardly, keeping an eye out the back door to make certain none of the men saw him up to his elbows in soapsuds. Not that he really cared. The first man that walked through the door and laughed would end up with dish detail for the next week.

He'd simply have to make life as unpleasant as he could for Isabelle when she showed up. Enough to make her leave as quickly as possible, and to think twice before she decided to come back again. For starters, she could take her turn doing dishes, just like everyone else. For another, he had no intention of giving up the best room in the house, simply because it used to belong to her. He'd gotten rid of the frilly four-poster bed and replaced it with a king-size one. He'd put her pink curtains and dressing tables and wardrobe in storage, and if she thought he was going to get them out for her she was in for a rude awakening. She could make do in Hoyt's no-nonsense bedroom upstairs, or the smaller guest room under the eaves with its narrow bunk bed. Where he used to sleep. Where she'd ended up the last time he'd seen her, taunting him as usual.

The dish slipped out of his hands, shattering against the chipped porcelain sink, but for the moment he was too bemused to curse. He could remember her shoulders in the moonlight, the thin cotton blanket held up in front of her, her glorious tawny mane of hair flowing around her, her eyes full of promise and something he couldn't quite fathom.

For a moment he'd been tempted to believe. For a brief moment he'd been tempted to take her, to lose himself in that beautiful, teasing body. Whatever her hidden agenda had been, by morning he would have made certain she was aware of only one thing. Him.

But old habits, old doubts, had died too hard. He'd looked at her, sitting in his bed, her mouth pale and soft, her eyes huge and luminous, her body like pale silk, and he'd turned around and spent the night in the barn. And the next day she was gone.

She hadn't even come to Hoyt's funeral. That was what had galled him most. It wasn't Hoyt's fault that he didn't know how to bring up a girl. He was a man used to the outdoors, to horses and cattle and other men. The hothouse flower he'd managed to sire was as foreign to him as caviar and champagne. He'd done his best by her, but it wasn't his fault that he always felt like a stranger around his own daughter.

Still and all, he'd loved her, Luke knew that better than anyone. He just hadn't known how to show it, and it wasn't Luke's place to tell him how. Besides, if Luke had been fool enough to love Isabelle Romney, he would have shown it in far different ways. Starting with not walking out on her that night.

He'd been too damned quixotic as it was. When Hoyt had drawn up the new will he'd wanted to leave the ranch to Luke entirely, and simply settle some money on Isabelle. After all, Hoyt had argued, Isabelle was bound to get married, and a woman with her charm and looks would marry well. Marry money, marry some poor rich fool who'd have no other interest than to make her happy.

But Luke had told him not to do it. He'd remembered the look on Isabelle's face one summer day when she thought no one was watching. She was looking at her father with a combination of hope and exasperation and love, and Hoyt had never even noticed her. Even if Hoyt was a blind old fool, Luke couldn't live with being part and parcel of her father's rejection of her.

But in the succeeding years he'd learned to. If he'd just managed things, if they hadn't had a couple of bad years, he never would have had to get involved in trying to sell that chunk of land, he never would have had to ask Isabelle to get involved. He never would have had to risk his own precarious peace.

He was going to regain that peace, and get rid of Isabelle as quickly as possible. Of course, he might have no trouble at all, he thought, dumping the soapy dishes in a draining rack and tossing a cup of clear water over them. Her voice had left him cold. Maybe her witch's power had vanished with age. Maybe that old stirring he felt inside was nothing but a lingering nostalgia for being nineteen years old and in love with life. In love with the beautiful, spoiled, willful daughter of the man who'd given him hope. Maybe he'd finally grown up and learned better.

Maybe. And maybe not. He wasn't going to count on anything but getting Isabelle Romney out of Wyoming as fast as her long legs would carry her. And then maybe he would work on getting this ranch in order.

ISABELLE COULD SEE it all clearly. Luke had never trusted her, and when he met Becky at the plane he'd be withdrawn, wary, ready to bite her head off as only he could. But Becky would charm him, as Isabelle never could. She'd look up at him, shyly, she'd be deferential, sweet, just forceful enough to fool him into thinking she was the real Isabelle. A toned-down, milder, meeker Isabelle, ready to listen to his wisdom and do what he told her.

It would be a match made in heaven, just like his first marriage. Isabelle remembered Cathy Parker from childhood. Remembered the pale, gentle girl with her graceful ways, her undemanding adoration of the male of the species in general and Luke Cassidy in particular. And she'd been so pretty, with her softly rounded body, her perfect features, her delicate hands and feet. She'd been the perfect girl for Luke, and the perfect ranch wife.

Becky could fill that role, too. Becky could cook, could clean, could shut up and stare at a man with mute adoration. Clearly that was what Luke wanted in a woman, and Becky could give it to him. Once she sold the ranch, Luke could take his very substantial share and start a place of his own. Not that she was obligated to give him anything. But she felt she owed him some equity, for the years he'd stayed and worked the ranch.

If he didn't want to stay on when Mr. Takashima took over, then he could certainly afford something of his own. Smaller, of course, and maybe without the view of the towering Tetons out the back door. And maybe the stock would have to go with the ranch—she hadn't hammered out those details yet. But still, Luke Cassidy could do anything he set his mind to.

He'd be furious when he found out they'd tricked him. But Becky was turning out to be more devious and persuasive than Isabelle remembered. She had complete faith in her younger cousin—Becky would win him over with her sweet smile and gentle ways. Luke would simply blame Isabelle for leading her astray. After all, he'd been blaming her for everything that went wrong since they'd first met. There was no reason to change.

It would be nice if she didn't have to go out there at all, but even with her usual optimism she thought that was probably a vain hope. At least Becky would buy her enough time to get back in touch with Mr. Takashima. And the longer she could stay hidden in the retreat center the safer she was. By the time she surfaced, in some two or three weeks, Martin and his cohorts might have forgotten she existed. After all, the mob had other fish to fry, didn't they?

BECKY MADE CERTAIN she was one of the last people off the 727. Isabelle would make people wait, and she had to remember she was Isabelle Romney. It shouldn't be too hard. She'd been trying to convince herself she was Isabelle since she was sixteen years old and had first been dazzled by her glorious cousin. It should have become second nature by now.

She was only slightly nervous of meeting Luke Cassidy. She'd had a crush on him that summer, but it was more a required part of being in her midteens than anything lasting. He was older, physically beautiful and just a tiny bit dangerous. She hadn't liked the dangerous part, but Isabelle surely had. And since Isabelle couldn't think or talk about anything but Luke Cassidy, Becky had followed suit.

But now she was simply curious. She didn't really believe there was a chance that he was going to fall in love with her, but she was more than willing to encourage him if he did. A nice, comfortable engagement out here in the back of beyond should pass the time nicely. Even if he turned out to be lousy in bed, he was still good-looking, or so Isabelle had assured her. And even the most stubborn man could be taught a thing or two.

She might even marry him. If Isabelle really managed to pull it off and sell the ranch, Becky could trust her to make a generous settlement, even though she didn't have to. There'd be enough money to live on, quite well, for a year or two. She'd have to decide whether to stay with him long enough to spend it, or leave early and get her share in the divorce settlement. She hadn't checked to see if Wyoming was a community property state—that had been short-sighted of her, but she could take care of that easily enough. She'd have to make sure she married him before they sold the ranch. If she decided it was worth the bother.

The airport terminal in Cody was small and rustic. She didn't really remember much of what Luke looked like, except that he was tall, wiry and blond, and he wore a Stetson and cowboy boots. Almost every man in the place was wearing a Stetson and cowboy boots, and most of them were tall. And none of them were hovering at the exit gate of Becky's airplane.

She stood there for a good five minutes, tapping her foot on the stained linoleum, peering through her tinted contact lenses for a suitable hero to fit into hers and Isabelle's fantasies. She never noticed the small, bowlegged little man heading toward her, and when she did, her eyes slid over him with complete indifference, until he came to a halt in front of her.

His leathery face looked guarded. "Miss Isabelle?" he said, his voice harsh from too many cigarettes. "Don't you remember me?"

Becky had only spent one summer at Rancho Diablo, and she hadn't paid much attention to anyone outside of the immediate family. She focused on the man in front of her, giving him her sweetest smile, the smile Isabelle used to make people her slaves. "Of course," she said warmly, keeping the husky note she'd perfected.

He looked at her uncertainly. "I wouldn't have thought you'd forgotten old Charlie," he said. "I put you up on your first horse."

"I remember," Becky said, breathing a sigh of relief that she'd managed to master horseback riding during the past ten years. Neither she nor Isabelle had been much good at it, but she'd been determined to succeed. "I hope I can ride while I'm here."

"Do you? Got over your fear of horses, then?" horrible old Charlie said. "Where're your bags?"

Becky's smile diminished several degrees. "I imagine they're at the baggage claim section," she said coolly. "Where's Luke?"

"Where do you think he'd be? At the ranch, working. You didn't think he'd drop everything and come fetch you, did you?"

"It would have been polite."

"When has Luke worried about being polite?" Charlie countered. "What's your bag look like?"

"There are four of them. Matched gray leather. You can't miss them."

He stared at her for a moment. "Four of them? How long were you planning to stay this time?"

"It's been thirteen years since I've been home, Charlie," she said, sure of at least that one fact. "I thought I'd stay a couple of weeks, at least."

He blinked. "Thirteen years. That's right, you didn't come home for Hoyt's funeral, did you?"

"You know I didn't," she said irritably.

"That's right," he said slowly. "I know you didn't. Wait for me by the front door over there. I'll be along in a minute."

Becky watched him go, pleased with herself. She'd gotten through that easily enough. The first person she met was convinced she was exactly whom she said she was, and the rest should follow. Bella was the type who'd forget details like people's names. She'd just shrug and smile sweetly as people refreshed her memory. If they were all as easy to trick as old Charlie, she'd have no trouble at all.

And old Charlie, hoisting the heavy bags in his strong arms, stared across the empty terminal and wondered who the hell was pretending to be Isabelle Romney.

MAYBE SHE SHOULD have warned Becky that she'd been back for Hoyt's funeral, Isabelle thought. She'd been so busy denying that she'd gone that it was second nature. She'd come in late, flying into the Cody airport and renting a car, arriving at the deserted ranch in the middle of the afternoon, while most of the county was assembled at the church in town. She hadn't wanted to bother with the hypocrisy of a religious service. Hoyt hadn't had much use for religion during his lifetime. He used to say he and God had made a bargain—he'd stay out of God's house if God stayed out of his.

She knew everyone was going over to the Parkers' ranch afterward, and that was one other thing she couldn't face. She wasn't going to sit there sipping whiskey and watching Luke and Cathy make sheep's eyes at each other. She had enough grieving and guilt to deal with.

She'd come home for one reason, and one reason alone. To say goodbye to Hoyt in her own way.

They hadn't been much of a father and daughter, but there were times when blood would tell. Her best memory of her father was an afternoon she'd spent with him in Devil's Canyon, on a little knoll that overlooked the Devil's Creek that ran through the place. They'd ridden out there together, Isabelle just managing to stay on the horse that terrified her, a few days after her mother had died. It had been a silent ride, but one that held a certain comfort. When they'd gotten to the knoll Hoyt had dismounted, lifting his twelve-year-old daughter down with his work-roughened hands.

"This is where we were going to build, Bella," he'd told her. "Your ma didn't much care for the old ranch house, and I was always intending on building her something prettier out here. Something more fitting. She gave up a lot, coming out here with an old wildcat like me, but she never regretted it. Or if she did, she never said so. Looks like I'm never going to be building her that house."

"You can build it for me, Pa," she said, when she still called him that, and not "Hoyt."

He'd looked at her then, with that usual confused expression on his face. "You like it here then?"

"I love it here," she said, meaning it.

"Well, when you grow up I'll give this piece of land to you. Hell, you'll have everything in the end, but this spot I'll keep special. When you turn eighteen I'll deed it over to you, and you and your husband can build here if you want. Would you like that?"

"I'd love it," she'd said, love shining in her eyes.

And five years later, when he'd brought Luke Cassidy home with him, he'd offered it to him, forgetting that summer afternoon and his promise to his grieving daughter.

That was when she started calling him Hoyt. That was when she started hating Luke, hated him for taking what was hers, her land, her father's love, her place. Hated him for treating her like a useless doll, hated him for hating her.

But that knoll, that perfect clearing that belonged to Luke Cassidy and not at all to her, still held the memory of the best moment she'd ever had with her father. And that was where she'd gone to say goodbye.

Charlie had found her there, bawling her eyes out. Charlie had been with Hoyt since the beginning of time, and he had no truck with church services and phony rituals. He'd gone out on the land to say goodbye, and run into Isabelle.

"I thought you couldn't stay away," he said, his voice flat and unemotional as always. "Didn't want to go to the church, eh?"

"Nope," she'd said, running her sleeve across her streaming eyes. "What about you?"

"Nope. Luke wouldn't have done it, if it weren't for that Parker woman."

"Cathy?"

"Not her. His ma-in-law. She's got strong opinions, and Luke wasn't sure what was right. When you said you weren't coming he just decided to go with what was easiest."

She nodded, staring out at the mountains she'd missed so desperately. "I don't mind. I just didn't want to deal with it. I don't want anyone to know I've been here, Charlie. I'll be gone before they're back. I just wanted to come on my own. To say goodbye."

"I understand. They probably won't be back till after dark. Cathy's pretty dependent on her mother, and Luke likes to please her."

"The Luke I know never went out of his way to please anybody," she said flatly.

"People change."

She turned to look up into his weather-beaten face. "Has Luke changed?"

"Not much. But what with the baby coming, he..."

"She's pregnant?" She didn't know why it hurt so much. Why should she care? "They didn't waste any time, did they?" she said with just a trace of bitterness.

"A ranch needs children to help run it," Charlie said gently.

"No, it doesn't. It needs boys," she said, rising. "I'm not coming back, Charlie. Never again."

"You said that five years ago when you left the first time."

"This time I mean it." She looked out over her beloved mountains and hardened her heart. "Take care of this place for me, Charlie."

"Luke does that."

She couldn't help it. "Then take care of Luke for me."

"I'll do that, Miss Bella. I surely will."

ISABELLE FLOPPED BACK on her bed, pulled the hand mirror out from underneath the pile of meditation tracts and stared at her reflection. She didn't look that different from eight years ago. Her hair was still its natural, tawny fall, her eyes hadn't changed color, and even her skin was its usual creamy tone, with no lines or signs that she'd reached her thirtieth birthday. Even though the hideous saffron robe made her look faintly jaundiced, she still looked like Bella, Bella the incomparable. Bella, the girl-woman whom everyone loved. Everyone but those who counted. Everyone but her father. And Luke.

She put the mirror down with a sigh and sat up. She'd never been one for self-pity, and now wasn't the time to start. Though the enforced solitude and introspection that were a staple of the Basho Meditation Center could make Mother Teresa feel sorry for herself, she thought, longing for a cigarette.

But at least here she was safe. At least here no one could find her. At least here . . .

"Sister Isabelle?" A saffron-robed figure poked her head inside the door. "Sister Elizabeth asked me to warn you. There are some men asking for you. And they don't look like the sort who are going to take no for an answer."

For a moment Isabelle didn't move. "Did they give their names?"

"No. But one man called another Martin."

And saintly Sister Isabelle swung her long legs over the side of her narrow cot and said, quite clearly, "Oh, hell."

# Chapter Three

The one window Isabelle's cell boasted was a narrow, horizontal one, up near the ceiling. Sunlight poured in, making the stark confines of the little room look almost cheerful. Isabelle wasn't in the mood to be cheered.

Her messenger had disappeared with a shocked hiss, closing the door behind her, and Isabelle knew she had to think fast. Nothing would stop Martin from finding her, not Sister Elizabeth's stern manner or the whole horde of peaceful meditators. Her only chance was to escape, fast, before Martin cornered her like a rat in a trap.

She peeked out the door, then shut it silently, quickly, as she recognized Martin's well-dressed figure at the end of the hallway. He wasn't looking in her direction, thank heavens, and didn't see the closing of the door. But he would go through every room until he found her, and she didn't like to contemplate what would happen next.

There were no locks on the doors of the Basho Meditation Center. The flimsy orange crates that served as tables wouldn't slow down Martin and his henchmen for more than a millisecond, and they wouldn't support her weight if she used them to climb to the window. In less than a second she'd dragged her narrow iron bed over to the outside wall, tipping it up on its end and tossing the thin foam mattress on the floor. The sagging springs served as a makeshift ladder as she scrambled up, sliding sideways over the window ledge. She hovered there a moment, as she realized she was a good twelve feet above the paved parking lot. Already she could hear the voices moving closer to her room, and she knew she had no choice. Closing her eyes, she dropped down, landing first on her sandaled feet and tumbling sideways onto the cracked macadam.

Her Ferrari was still parked where she left it when she'd set foot inside the center six endless weeks ago. Every now and then she'd peer outside at it, mourning the effects of the bright northern sunlight on its gorgeous red finish. If she'd had any sense at all she would have put it in storage while she hid out. If anything had brought Martin to her hiding place, the flashy car was probably responsible.

She took off across the parking lot at a sprint, wincing slightly at the pain in her hip. Martin's conservative Lincoln was there, but no one was in sight. As she ran she pulled the key from around her neck, ready to fit it in the lock and get out of there as fast as her Ferrari could take her. Her hand was already on the door handle when she realized her car wasn't empty. Sitting in the passenger seat, calm and elegant as always, was Martin Abruzzi.

She froze. No one else was in sight—his little entourage was still searching the center for her. Maybe, if she took off into the underbrush, she could hide out until they gave up looking for her. After all, they were all city boys, born and bred in the heart of Boston's south side. Their fancy suits and city shoes wouldn't take them very far in the rough Canadian countryside.

Neither would her sandaled feet. It was late June— blackfly season, and even if her voluminous yellow robes could cover most of her, and even if Martin and his boys were helpless in the woods, neither they nor the insects would give up until they'd finished with her. And she wasn't quite sure which nasty little bugs she preferred.

Martin leaned across the driver's seat and opened the door. "Get in, Bella," he said affably. "We have a lot to talk about."

He wasn't pointing a gun at her, that was something. As far as she knew, Martin never carried a gun, preferring to have someone else take care of the dirty work. She still didn't move, wondering whether she had a chance of escaping him. "Get in," he said again, a slight edge beneath his flat Boston voice. "Or I might possibly lose my temper."

Martin's temper was long gone, but Isabelle got in anyway. "What do you want?" she said, slipping behind the steering wheel and staring straight ahead at the front entrance.

"Don't be stupid, Bella. You know exactly what I want. I want those photographs."

She turned to look at him, then, fluttering her eyes with mock innocence. "What photographs?"

He growled an obscenity, low in his throat. "You know perfectly well what photographs, Bella. The ones that were in my safe. The ones of me and Mario Delanty. I had a hard enough time getting them in the first place. I want them back."

"They're not really very flattering, Martin," she said. "I can't see why they're all that important. You and the most notorious white-collar criminal having a nice little meeting is not my idea of art photography. Neither of you look all that good."

"Now that Mario's taken a fall I don't want to be dragged down with him," he said flatly.

"Then why did you have the pictures taken in the first place?"

"Insurance. I learned years ago not to trust anyone, including some pretty little socialite who shows up looking for a job. I had those pictures taken as protection, in case Delanty might decide he didn't need me anymore."

"But since he's already been convicted, why do they matter?" she asked.

"Because I don't want to go along for the ride," he growled. "I made a nice little packet of money on that insider trading scam. I don't want to give it back. That was the first semilegitimate money I ever made. I'm fond of it."

"But Martin." Her voice was sweetly reasonable. "If I give you back those photographs, how will I know you won't decide to make me disappear? I need them for my own insurance."

He rolled his eyes heavenward. "You know, you are one pain in the butt, Bella," he said. "You've seen too many movies. The mob isn't a bunch of uncouth hoodlums anymore. We're professionals, with certain standards. We don't get rid of nosy young women who know too much."

"What do you do with them?" she asked, momentarily distracted.

"We marry them."

"I beg your pardon?" She stared at him in blank astonishment.

"You heard me. We marry them."

"That isn't an offer." She was horribly afraid it might be.

"Maybe," he said. "Where are the pictures?" He reached out and took her wrist. His grip wasn't painful, and she was once again aware of the softness of his skin, the perfection of his manicure. The sheer, polished, protected elegance of the man. "They'll find them, you know."

"Then you won't have to marry me," she said rashly, wishing he'd go away. His citrusy after-shave filled the tiny cockpit of the car, augmented by the heat of the sun, and she felt a little dizzy.

"It's not necessarily a question of have to, Bella," he murmured, bringing her wrist to his mouth and kissing it lightly. "I've never had a woman run away from me before. I've never had a woman I've wanted so much. Even in that horrible yellow dress, you're still the most desirable woman I've ever seen."

"You wouldn't think that if I'd gone to bed with you in the first place," she pointed out, wishing he'd stop licking her palm.

He looked up at her, his flat brown eyes suddenly narrowed. "That's where you're wrong," he said. "I don't think I'd ever get tired of you. Just tell me . . ."

Three dark-suited figures appeared at the entrance of the meditation center, signaling to their well-dressed boss in the Ferrari. Martin reached for the door, snatching the keys from her nerveless hand. "Stay here, Bella," he ordered. "I'll be right back."

She leaned back against the leather seat, her eyes narrowed in the sunlight as she watched him stroll over toward his three neatly dressed employees. Hit men, she thought, not sure if she was overreacting. For a moment she let herself admire her erstwhile employer. He was something to admire. Never in her life had she seen a man more impeccably dressed. Nothing was ever out of place, not a lock of his perfectly cut brown hair, not a speck of lint on his priceless linen and wool suits, not a scuff mark on his handmade leather shoes. She always felt rumpled around him, no matter how well-dressed she was. It was no wonder she couldn't give in to temptation and embrace a life of organized crime.

She reached up under the dashboard, withdrew the magnetized box and took out her spare key. Martin's elegant back was turned to her, supremely confident in his power. The Ferrari started and accelerated so quickly that he barely had time to whirl around before she'd made it out of the parking lot. She glanced in the rearview mirror, long enough to see Vito, the plump one, raise a large, nasty-looking gun in her direction. She swerved the car, then realized with surprise that Martin had knocked the gun out of his hand. Maybe he really did want to marry her. At least he didn't seem to want her dead.

Or maybe he already realized he didn't have those incriminating pictures. Any organized crime don worth his salt would wait to rub out a witness until after he'd retrieved the proof. Though Martin probably wasn't quite a don yet. What did they call a minor-league don? A donny? A donette?

If she was lucky she'd never have to find out. She knew that Lincoln, knew it didn't have anywhere near the power her Ferrari did, and she patted the leather seat beside her with real affection. "I knew such an extravagance would have its practical side," she murmured aloud, reaching for the glove compartment as she drove, too fast for those roads in eastern Canada. The only pack of cigarettes left inside was empty, and she cursed as she stomped down harder on the accelerator, wondering if she dared stop for some on the way to the border. It might almost be worth being captured by Martin if she could just have a cigarette. Didn't they usually give a prisoner one before an execution?

She'd waited six weeks, she could wait a little longer, she thought, making a sharp right onto the gravel road and spinning her wheels slightly. For now she had to get out of sight, go to ground where not even Martin could find her. Her apartment would be watched, her friends would be monitored. There was only one safe place she could think of, and that was where she was headed. Becky's apartment would be empty, and if her neighbors happened to spot Isabelle they'd merely assume Becky was back. She could hide there for the next two weeks while she waited for Mr. Takashima to be in touch, and by the time she was ready to surface life would have shifted and settled. Martin would have given up on his quarry. Mr. Takashima would have a signed purchase and sale agreement for an outrageous sum of money, enough to shut up even Luke Cassidy. And Luke and Becky would be planning their honeymoon.

Yup, Isabelle thought glumly. Things were going to be just dandy. All she needed was a little time.

RANCHO DIABLO wasn't quite what Becky had remembered. Surprisingly enough, it seemed bigger than it had when she was sixteen, and a great deal less hospitable. It might have to do with the fact that she was arriving at night, and there were no lights on in the long, low ranch house. It might have to do with the taciturn driver beside her and the uncomfortable ride in the ancient pickup that smelled like sweat and horse manure. Or it might have to do with a guilty conscience. But of those possibilities, the last was the least likely. She hadn't been burdened with second thoughts in years.

"Where's Luke?" she asked, opening the sagging door of the pickup after several tries. Charlie was busy dragging her luggage to the porch, but he paused, long enough to spit in the dust, and shrug.

"Dunno. You'll be in your daddy's old room. Top of the stairs," he added, looking at her strangely.

"I know where my father's room was," Becky said sharply, remembering Uncle Hoyt with a singular lack of affection. "If you see Luke tell him I want to talk to him."

"I'll tell him," Charlie said, his voice making it clear that he didn't expect much reaction. "Welcome home, Miss Bella."

If she didn't know better she would have thought he'd sounded sarcastic. But her memory was coming back— Bella and old Charlie had always been friends. Maybe this was just the code of the West, or something. Maybe people out here didn't go for manners or small talk. And maybe she'd get out of here as soon as it was safe, and to hell with Bella and her intricate plans.

By the time she'd dragged her last suitcase up the narrow flight of stairs she was covered with sweat. No one had bothered cleaning the room, making the bed, or doing anything to make her feel welcome. The bathroom was a crime, the dust bunnies wafting along behind her as she stomped down the narrow hallway to stare out into the pitch-dark night. She hated the countryside, hated the West, hated everything around her. And most of all, she hated her golden Cousin Bella, and the mess she'd talked her into. If it hadn't suited her very well to disappear at the moment, nothing on earth would have made her do it. The police wouldn't find her out here, would they? Were they even looking for her?

She'd stay as long as she needed to, and not a second longer. Unless Luke Cassidy was even better looking than she remembered, she was going to make tracks as soon as possible. And if there was anything of value in this dilapidated old house, anything portable, she'd take that with her, as her due compensation for even spending one night in such a godforsaken place.

BY THE TIME Isabelle managed to park her car in an underground garage and sweet-talk her way into Becky's high-rise apartment she was ready to drop. It had been eight hours since she'd taken off from the meditation center, eight hours of looking over her shoulder, not daring to stop for a bite to eat, for a bathroom, for the greatest necessity of all, cigarettes. By the time she reached Burlington, Vermont, she was too tired to care. All that mattered was finding Becky's apartment and getting safely inside.

It had turned out to be surprisingly easy. While the maintenance man looked askance at Isabelle's floor-length saffron robes, he didn't bother peering too closely into her face, assuming she was who she said she was, a weary Becky Romney who'd left her keys someplace.

He unlocked her door, and she stepped inside, over the pile of messages on the floor, and wondered if Becky had any money around to tip the man, when he turned away, apparently used to Becky's parsimonious ways. Then he paused. "'Bout time you came back," he said. "People been looking for you."

Isabelle felt a moment's panic, until she realized that it was Becky people were looking for, not Bella. Sweet, quiet Becky couldn't have done anything so awful that Isabelle needed to worry. "Really?" she said, only faintly interested.

"The police," the doorman said flatly, turning away. And it took all of Isabelle's natural optimism to tamp down the sudden feeling of doom.

Becky's apartment was small and sparsely furnished. She had an answering machine, its light flashing insistently, but for the moment Isabelle controlled her curiosity, prowling instead around the apartment. It didn't look like Becky's sort of place at all. It was too unfrilly, too stark, too depressing.

At least Becky appreciated decent gin. The bottle of Tanqueray in the kitchen was such a welcome sight that Isabelle almost burst into tears. She would have preferred cigarettes, but those could wait. The tonic water in the almost empty refrigerator was flat, the tiny section of lime had a trace of mold, but Isabelle didn't care. She kicked off her sandals, slid out of her saffron robe and took her drink over to the utilitarian sofa, sinking down with a groan. It wasn't much more comfortable than her cot at the meditation center, but the gin and tonic was a huge improvement over green tea and she took a long, delicious swallow.

She leaned her head back for a moment, blinking away the tears. She shouldn't waste her time feeling sorry for herself. She should simply be glad she was temporarily safe and sound, away from Martin, away from brown rice and endless silence. She couldn't help it if the thought of Becky filled her with sudden, irrational jealousy. After all, she didn't want to be in the warmth and friendliness of Wyoming, tucked up in her big old bed. She didn't want Luke Cassidy looking at her with those dangerous green eyes of his warming with helpless attraction. That was for Becky. Becky was the right woman for Luke, and for Wyoming. Not Bella. Never Bella.

"SHE'S ASKING for you," Charlie said.

Luke looked up from the winning poker hand he was holding. "Yeah?" It shouldn't have come as a surprise to him. Why did he think he'd know the moment she set foot back on the place, why did he think some sort of sixth sense would tell him she'd come back? Just because he'd known that other time, after Hoyt's funeral, didn't mean he'd always be so aware of her. Hell, maybe the spell really had been broken after all this time. His palms weren't even sweating.

"She can wait," he said, staring down at his three kings and the pair of nines. The pile of money in the center of the table was a hefty one. He didn't usually like to play poker with the boys—it didn't sit right when he'd win their paychecks back from them in a single evening. But nowadays, with money so tight, he couldn't afford to be too picky in his ideas of niceness. And tonight of all nights, he couldn't sit in that house and wait for Isabelle to show up.

"I think you oughtta see her," Charlie said.

"Eventually."

"I think you oughtta see her now," the old man insisted. "It's been thirteen years. You might find she's changed."

Luke's eyes narrowed as he looked up at him. Charlie knew as well as Luke did that it had only been eight years. The other two men were relative newcomers to Rancho Diablo—Jimmy had finished high school a couple of years ago and Johnson had been around a few years longer. Neither of them knew Isabelle, except as a shadowy figure who once lived there and still exerted some sort of influence over the place.

"I'll play your hand," Charlie said, coming up behind him.

Luke dropped the cards down on the table. "That's all right. I was losing anyway." He rose, towering over the table in the bunkhouse. "Guess I'd better go."

"She gonna cook breakfast tomorrow, Luke?" Jimmy was young enough to ask.

"Don't count on it, boy," Charlie said. "Women nowadays don't like kitchens. And Miss Isabelle never could cook to save her life."

"Anything's got to be better than what Luke dishes up," Johnson, a taciturn man in his early fifties, muttered.

"You'd be surprised," Luke said. "See you in the morning."

The kitchen lights were on as he crossed the yard. He moved slowly, wishing Charlie had come with him, wishing someone would be around to run interference for them. He hadn't looked in her eyes since she'd sat naked in his bed, and for thirteen years he hadn't stopped wishing he'd thrown caution to the wind and done what he'd always wanted to do.

Well, she'd been running ever since, and he'd been doing some running of his own. Looks like the running was just about over. He could see her moving about in the room, could see the way the electric light shimmered in her long, thick hair. It wasn't quite the brilliant tawny shade he remembered, but that was probably because he'd romanticized her like the hormone-crazed nineteen-year-old he'd been.

He moved silently, a skill he'd developed years ago, and stepped inside the kitchen without a sound. "Isabelle," he said, his voice deep and surprisingly steady, even as his stomach was churning.

She whirled around, her hair whirling with her, and stared at him, her soft mouth open in fright, her silver-blue eyes wide.

Except that her mouth wasn't really soft at all—it had a slight hardness to it, like it had been pursed too often. And the eyes weren't quite the same—they didn't have that magic, that enticing, bewitching stare. Maybe he'd finally outgrown the effect she had on him. Or maybe not.

She managed a nervous smile. "Hi, Luke," she said in that throaty voice of hers.

He found the knot in his stomach had disappeared. He looked her up and down for a long moment, then nodded, half to himself. "Hi, Bella," he said. "Welcome home."

ISABELLE SAT UP, knocking over her half-finished drink. She'd fallen asleep without realizing it, and she'd been dreaming. Dreaming about Luke.

She thought she'd gotten him out of her system after so many years. It must be the thought of Becky, out there charming him, fooling him, winning his love. She shook her head, sitting up and staring about her at the unfamiliar room. She needed to go to bed, she thought groggily. She needed to stop dreaming and start planning.

She got up and headed for the bathroom, then stopped by the desk on her way to the bedroom. The answering machine was still blinking, and on impulse she pushed the message button.

Five minutes later she finally turned the damned thing off, sinking down in the uncomfortable chair and staring blankly at the desk. No wonder Becky gave in so easily to Isabelle's grand scheme. She was in trouble. In the kind of trouble that was just as real, just as serious, as Bella's trouble. Except it looked as if Becky had brought it on herself. That is, if she really had embezzled one hundred and twenty-three thousand dollars from the investment company where she worked.

At least the police wouldn't put Becky in a cement overcoat and drop her in Lake Champlain. Martin would do that to Isabelle, for all his quixotic, unbelievable proposal. Or at least have Vito and the boys do it. And he'd find her. If he didn't, Becky's accusers would. Either way, Isabelle was in the wrong place at the wrong time.

She had no place else to run to. No one she could turn to, no one she dared risk. There was only one place, one person who wouldn't be cowed by the likes of Martin Abruzzi, if he happened to be lucky enough to find her. She was going to Wyoming, as fast as her Ferrari would take her there.

She paused for a moment, wondering how Luke might react to the deception. Not well, if she knew Luke, and she knew him far too well. She didn't know for certain if Becky actually had turned out to be an embezzler. Maybe she was just as much a victim of circumstance as Isabelle was. She still thought there might be a future for Luke and Becky. Besides, once she sold Rancho Diablo Luke would have enough money so that Becky wouldn't need to steal.

No, Isabelle had no choice but to make her way to Wyoming. But she was going as Becky Romney, not Bella. And she had no doubt whatsoever she'd be able to trick everyone as easily as Becky herself had.

LUKE STEPPED OUT on the back porch, looking up at the stars overhead, at the jagged edges of the Tetons in the distance. The woman had gone to bed in a cloud of Compulsion, and he'd watched her go without a twinge. Sinking down in one of the old rockers, he propped his booted feet up on the railing, tipping the chair back and folding his hands over his flat stomach. He waited, knowing it wouldn't take long.

"You seen her?" Charlie said, appearing out of the shadows.

"Yup."

"And?"

"And what?" Luke said lazily.

"You tell me, boy," Charlie snapped.

"If you mean, tell you who the hell she is," Luke drawled, "I expect she's Isabelle's cousin. You remember—she came to visit that last summer. But I really don't care. As long as she signs the papers she came to sign she can be anyone she pleases. She's even offered to cook breakfast for the boys."

"Isabelle can't cook."

"This one can," Luke said.

"Don't you care where Isabelle is?"

"Not in the slightest." Luke rocked back gently, staring at the stars. And for a moment he almost believed he meant it.

# Chapter Four

Even in a Ferrari the trip from Burlington, Vermont, to the northwest section of Wyoming was endless. The Ferrari was in sore need of a tune, but Isabelle couldn't afford the money or the time. Becky, cheapskate that she was, hadn't left a red penny behind in her austere apartment, and if she believed in credit cards she had them all with her. That left Isabelle with no alternative but to use her own credit cards, despite the fact that her credit was up to the max, and Martin would have no difficulty whatsoever in tracing her. Her only hope was to choose small, out of the way places to test her poor, abused VISA card and pray the mom and pop stores would take a while to send in their bills.

On top of everything else, Isabelle couldn't tell whether Becky really had such abysmal taste in clothes, or whether she'd stripped her closets of anything colorful to further her masquerade. All that remained in the apartment were drab, shapeless clothes that were better consigned to a trash bin. It took Isabelle only a few moments to realize that there was a very good reason there was nothing of value in the expensive apartment. Becky had no intention of coming back.

Isabelle took a baggy pair of jeans and a couple of shapeless sweaters anyway, desperate to get out of the saffron robes and sandals that had been her thankless lot for the past few weeks. To add insult to injury, Becky's shoe size was unmanageably smaller. The only pair of discarded shoes that Isabelle could cram onto her narrow, size-ten feet was a pair of black spiked heels. Not the sort of thing to go with shabby jeans or saffron robes, but one of the straps on her sandals was broken and she had no choice.

Not too much longer, she told herself as she sped across New York State, heading west. In a few more weeks she'd get herself out of this mess. She'd have money, or the reasonable promise of it from the sale of the ranch, she'd have Luke safely married off, or on his way toward that happy eventuality, she'd have decent clothes and shoes and time to catch her breath. She'd even have cigarettes again.

It must have been an oversight that she'd forgotten to buy some at her first stop for gas. By the time she stopped again, she realized it had been almost three weeks since she'd last had a delicious lungful of nicotine. Maybe, just maybe, now was the time to give them up. At least, for the time being.

The problem was, it gave her even more time to think. To remember. As the highway stretched endlessly in front of her, even the country music on the radio couldn't keep her mind off the past. And the future.

Funny, she hadn't listened to country music in years. It was the thought of Wyoming, of wide-open spaces and spiky Teton mountains in the distance, of Stetsons and boots and, heaven help her, horses that started an unconscious longing for pedal steel guitars and high, lonesome voices singing about cheating and drinking and pickup trucks. She'd grown up listening to that kind of music, instead of rock and roll, and she still felt an unconscious tightening inside when she heard Merle Haggard sing.

She didn't even dare go much above the speed limit, and New York, dammit, still had a high of fifty-five. She didn't dare court any police attention by speeding up, and by the end of the first day on the road she felt worn out for the strain of holding back the powerful engine of her Ferrari.

She picked motels that closely resembled something out of *Psycho*, kept out of the shower and watched game shows on TV until she fell asleep. By late morning of the third day she was halfway across South Dakota and thinking she just might change her mind about the cigarettes.

Maybe it wouldn't be as bad as she expected. Maybe Luke would have mellowed over the years. Not if the terse notes that accompanied her quarterly checks were any guide, but maybe he just didn't like to write letters. Maybe he'd have a beer gut, maybe he'd already be in love with Becky, maybe he was looking for a chance to get out from under the burden of the ranch and settle down in a mobile home outside of Caspar. Or he might just head for the yuppie tourist mecca of Jackson Hole. Becky would probably be happier there, and they could run a bed and breakfast...

"No," she said aloud, shaking her head at her reflection in the mirror. He wouldn't do that, any more than he'd run a dude ranch like she'd had the gall to suggest a few years back when the profits from Rancho Diablo had begun to dwindle. Luke wasn't a man who liked to take orders from anyone. He'd rather eat rattlesnake than baby-sit a bunch of tourists.

No, she was fooling herself. He'd be as mean and ornery as she remembered, and that lean, tough, youthful fire would be gone. He'd be weathered, cynical and of no more interest to her than her father's friends had been. It had been youth and proximity and hormones that had made her vulnerable. After thirteen years her only enemy was nostalgia.

Still, she couldn't help but remember those summer nights, sitting on the back porch, studiously ignoring Luke just as he ignored her. It was no wonder she'd fallen in love with him back then. He was tall, taller even than her father, and whipcord lean. During the long, hot days of summer he seldom wore a shirt, and his smooth-skinned chest had turned the color of burnished bronze. She'd wanted to touch his chest, but she never dared. She contented herself with brushing up against him when they were in the kitchen together, bumping into him in the stable, putting her hand on his arm on the few occasions she had to talk to him.

She didn't know what drew her to him, whether it was that reckless aura he carried with him, or his mesmerizing green eyes, wide mouth, high cheekbones or stubborn jaw. It might have been the blond hair he'd worn too long, or the surprising contrast of his dark brows. Or it might just have been the fact that he'd been a bad boy, and he was young and healthy and living in the tiny bedroom above her, sharing the same bathroom, eating the same food, sneaking looks at her out of those defiant green eyes when he thought she wouldn't notice. It might have been the fact that he acted as if he didn't like her, and used every opportunity to display that dislike and contempt when he thought he could get away with it. Or it might have been the fact that he had touched her.

She wasn't used to people being mean to her. The hired hands around the ranch had spoiled her, protected her. Madeleine, the cook-housekeeper, had kept her under her wing, and her father, while he'd never understood her, seemed to dote on her. And Becky had arrived for the summer, following at her heels like a devoted puppy dog.

But Luke's young eyes hadn't been filled with devotion and admiration. They'd been cool, cynical and daring, and any conversation he'd spared for her had been brief to the point of terseness. If she hadn't surprised those occasional secret glances she might have thought he'd hated her.

They were alone in the kitchen one afternoon in early August. He'd come in late, throwing a shirt over his darkly tanned body, and she'd just been finishing her lunch. For some reason she'd lingered, pouring herself another cup of coffee when she hadn't yet acquired much of a taste for it, helping herself to a second serving of pie. She lingered, while Madeleine finished the dishes and went off to town with Becky to do some shopping. She lingered as Hoyt and the hired men rode out to check on some strays; she lingered until Luke looked up, his fierce green eyes boring into hers, and said, "Does your daddy know you look at me like you're a mare in heat?"

She hadn't been close enough to slap him. She'd felt the color flame into her face, and she'd run, out the kitchen door slamming it behind her, fury and embarrassment washing over her as she cursed him under her breath. She headed straight for the west barn, seeking a comfort she couldn't even begin to understand.

She loved horses. Always had, always would. She just didn't like to climb on top of them, didn't like to ride them and especially didn't like to fall off them. Crescent, her favorite, was a sweet, docile mare who loved turnips and being curried. Isabelle would spend hours grooming her, but it would take an act of God to get her up on Crescent's broad, sturdy back.

Isabelle had raced through the deserted confines of the barn that afternoon, straight for Crescent's stall. She wasn't out in the corral with the others, and Isabelle had slid into the stall beside her, putting her arms around the mare's neck and burying her face against her smooth hide. "Damn him," she muttered, feeling unaccustomed tears spill against Crescent's side. "Damn him, damn him, damn him."

The afternoon sunlight was streaking through a gap in the barn siding, and dust motes danced on the beam. The familiar smells of the barn began to ease the knot of anger and pain in the pit of her stomach, the smell of leather and horses and hay. Maybe she'd been a fool. Maybe she ought to leave Luke Cassidy as alone as he clearly wanted to be. Maybe...

She never expected him to follow her. Crescent lifted her head and made a soft sound, one of pleasure, and she blew through her nose, as Isabelle felt a presence behind her, just outside the stall. She lifted her head, knowing her face was wet and hoping against hope he'd feel guilty.

If he did, his cool, implacable face didn't show it. "Sorry," he said briefly, and turned to leave.

She slipped out of the stall, running after him, and without thinking she caught his arm. "Luke..."

He whirled around, and his face was no longer impassive. It was ablaze with hot, dangerous emotion. "Don't," he said fiercely. "Don't look at me out of those blue eyes of yours, don't chase after me, don't touch me. Leave me the hell alone, girl."

She didn't release him, and for some reason he didn't pull away. "Why?"

"Because your father's a good man. The best thing that's ever happened to me. And I won't repay him by taking his daughter and doing to her what she's been begging for ever since I set foot on this place."

"I'm not..." she began hotly.

"You are." This time he touched her, breaking free only to catch her slender arms in his hard, work-roughened hands. "You come twitching around me smelling like flowers and money and the kind of life I'll never have, and you watch me. You watch me when I eat, you watch me when I clean up after work, you watch me when I'm sitting in front of the TV or talking with your father. I want you to stop it. I want you to stop watching me and stop touching me."

"Why?" she said again, her voice husky, confused, curiously hopeful. His sudden outpouring of anger was more emotion than she'd seen from him since he first appeared, and it was all directed at her. Anything was better than the unfeeling contempt she'd sensed from him. He was far from immune to her. Far from unfeeling. "Why?" she said again.

She didn't know what she'd expected, but certainly not what happened. He yanked her into his arms, roughly, hard against his body, and he kissed her.

She was tall, but he was a lot taller. She was strong, but he was stronger. And she wanted him to kiss her, had wanted it since she couldn't remember when.

It wasn't the kind of kiss she was used to. She'd necked with the clean-smelling, dressed-up sons of the neighboring ranchers. She'd kissed bankers' sons and doctors' sons, and enjoyed herself. But nothing had prepared her for the feel of his bare chest against hers, the strength in his arms as he held her, the raw hunger of his mouth as it covered hers, forcing hers open.

That hunger frightened her. Alone in the barn, with no one around, no one but the oblivious Crescent as witness, she was entirely at his mercy. She knew she should push him away. Should run. Instead, she slid her arms around his waist, inside the shirt hanging loose around him, and clung tightly, never wanting to let him go.

His hand reached up between them and touched her breast, and she didn't push him away like she had with all the ranchers' sons. She wanted his hand on her breast, she wanted his skin against hers, she wanted him. She belonged to him, he belonged to her; she'd known it from the moment she'd set eyes on him, and it had just taken him longer to realize it . . .

He pulled away, with a shocking suddenness, and moved out of her reach. She swayed slightly, realizing with numb surprise that her shirt was unbuttoned down to her waist, her breasts hard and tingling beneath the thin lace bra. She looked up at him, expecting love and bewilderment, and met his usual stony contempt. Her shy smile vanished.

"Get it from someone else if you're so hot," he said. "Your father brought me here to give me a chance, and I'm not going to throw it away providing stud service for a spoiled brat. I've told you before and I'll tell you again. Leave me the hell alone!"

She sank down into a comforting pile of straw as he stormed out of the barn, his flannel shirt flapping around him, his tall, lean body vibrating with anger and other emotions she could only begin to guess at. She was shaking, shocked beyond tears, and it took her less than ten minutes to put her own self-absorbed slant on what had happened. He was in love with her, and afraid to do anything about it.

If he expected a scene at dinner she didn't give it to him. For the rest of the summer she kept her distance, maintaining a sweet, friendly attitude that left him as bewildered as she wanted it to. She didn't confide in anyone, even Becky, of her certain knowledge. Luke wouldn't have been so angry, wouldn't have kissed her like that, if he didn't know, deep down inside, that they were made for each other.

She was supposed to be heading East for college at the end of August. She didn't really want to spend four years in the cold climate of Massachusetts, even if Smith was supposed to be a wonderful college; she didn't want to be away from Wyoming, and the ranch, and her increasingly distant father. And she didn't want to leave Luke.

She had it all planned. Becky had already left, gone back to her newly divorced parents in Maryland, and Isabelle was due to fly out first thing in the morning. Old Charlie was driving her to the airport the night before and setting her up at the airport motel—Hoyt and Luke had some problem with a fractious mare and couldn't spare the time. When her father had first told her he wouldn't be seeing her off her reaction had been hurt and jealousy. And then she realized she had no reason to be angry. She wasn't going to be on that plane.

She'd reckoned without Charlie. He wasn't interested in her schemes, even if he didn't want to see her go any more than she wanted to go. "You've got to get an education, Bella," he'd said, driving the pickup with a set expression on his face.

"Why? I don't intend to do anything spectacular with my life. I want to be a rancher's wife," she said smugly. Luke's wife, she thought.

Charlie had snorted. "That doesn't sound like the Bella I've known all my life. I thought you had more gumption than that."

"What's wrong with ranching? You're a rancher, and so is Hoyt."

"Nothing's wrong with ranchin'. You didn't say you wanted to be a rancher. You said you wanted to be a rancher's wife. Your ma was a rancher's wife, and she was miserable every day of her married life. You've got to make your own life, your own way. Not just follow some good-looking stud who'll get you knocked up in two seconds flat.''

Isabelle's eyes had widened. "Why, Charlie. I do believe you're a feminist."

"Hell, no, I ain't no wimmen's libber," he'd shot back, deeply affronted. "I just don't want to see my best girl throw her life away without making damn sure that's what she wants to do."

Isabelle had leaned back against the bench seat in the pickup and pictured Luke in her mind. "I'm sure," she said softly.

He'd lingered, far too long, getting her settled in the motel and warning her about any possible danger in the big outside world of the decadent East Coast, a place he'd never seen. When he finally headed back to the ranch it took her another half an hour to find a taxi who'd take her that far for half the traveler's checks her father had given her, and another couple of hours to make it home.

It was past midnight when the taxi had pulled up in front of the west corral, far enough away from the long, low ranch house to keep alert fathers at bay. The pickup was back in its usual place, but there was no sign of the station wagon her father used. She hadn't expected there to be. Her father usually spent Friday nights at Elsie Marley's, though he was naive enough to think his daughter didn't realize it. She'd known for years, and hoped this Friday wouldn't be any different. It didn't appear to be.

The house felt deserted when she tiptoed inside, slipping off her shoes and leaving them in the shadows on the porch. She moved past her open bedroom door, noting with faint surprise that it already felt abandoned. She knew which step to avoid as she climbed the stairs, but she needn't have worried. Her father's bedroom door stood open, empty. As was Luke's tiny little room, at the far end of the hall.

She kept the lights off when she stepped inside, closing the door most of the way. She wondered whether Luke had found someone to visit, then dismissed the idea. He was in love with her, which he'd realize if he just wasn't so damned angry and stubborn. She, the proud, strong, Isabelle Romney, was going to throw herself at his feet. Once he realized how much she was willing to give, he'd be unable to fight it anymore.

She was never one for folding her clothes neatly, and tonight was no different. She tossed her jeans, her shirt, her lacy underwear on the unused top bunk in the little room and slid between the covers of the lower one. The sheets were cool, crisp, wonderful against her bare skin. She imagined them against Luke's tanned skin, and her heart began pounding.

She could see his faded blue flannel shirt hanging over the back of the one straight chair the room boasted, and for a moment she was tempted to get up and put it on. There was no need. The night was warm, the small window open to the night air, but she wanted to wrap herself in his shirt the way she wanted to wrap herself in his skin. Leaning back against the one pillow on the sagging, narrow bunk, she spread her thick blond hair out behind her, closed her eyes and waited.

LUKE MOVED OUT onto the back porch, a glass of neat bourbon in his hand, and sank down into a chair, tipping it back and setting his booted feet on the railing. The woman calling herself Isabelle had been there for three days, and he wasn't any closer to figuring out why she was there than he had been at the beginning. He didn't really care, except for a few nagging moments of curiosity. Becky, if that's who she was, certainly was a better cook than Isabelle had ever been, and seemed determined to prove herself a perfect little housewife. He wasn't about to object. If she wanted to clean his kitchen and cook for him and the boys, he wasn't about to argue. Sooner or later he'd find out what she wanted, what happened to the real Isabelle. For now he was content to let things be. If he found out what was really going on, it might precipitate the return of his nemesis. And that was the last thing he wanted.

As long as someone safe and domestic was taking her place, it suited him just fine. The only fly in the ointment was the fact that he still couldn't close on that parcel of land. Isabelle's stand-in seemed to have no qualms about committing forgery, and he was half tempted to go ahead and have her sign, but he didn't dare. If something happened to foul up the deal he'd be up a very toxic creek without a paddle, and he couldn't afford to let that happen. So he'd wait a few days, come up with a few more lame excuses and see what happened. He knew, whether he liked it or not, that Isabelle couldn't be far behind her.

He remembered the last time he'd set eyes on her. He'd been all of nineteen, full of anger at the world in general and Isabelle Romney in particular. He thought he'd finally gotten her out of his hair, off to college where she'd no longer be such a miserable, gnawing temptation. Even then his feelings had been mixed—he hadn't been able to sleep the night she'd left, and he'd gone for a long, solitary ride up into the mountains, not coming back until the moon was high and it was well past midnight. Come back, climbed the stairs to his lonely bedroom and found her waiting for him, lying naked in his bed, her big blue eyes shining, her luscious mouth vulnerable as she looked up at him and said simply, "I love you."

What kind of fool turned his back on that? What kind of fool turned his back on everything he could ever want, on what he'd been dreaming about, longing for, night after night after endless night?

A stubborn nineteen-year-old fool who couldn't trust anything, and most particularly that a spoiled, beautiful brat like Isabelle Romney could ever really care about someone like him.

He hadn't said a word. He hadn't trusted himself to. The moonlight was streaming through that tiny window, throwing a pool of light around her, and he would have given ten years off his life to pull that cover away from her, to take what she was offering.

But he couldn't. He couldn't throw away the trust and love of the man who'd befriended him when he'd had nowhere else to go, a man who'd rescued him. He couldn't tell the girl lying in his bed that he loved her. Because he didn't. He didn't know how to love anyone, and he didn't know if he ever could.

He simply stared at her for a moment, then turned and left. Walked down the stairs, out to the bunkhouse and threw himself into an unoccupied bunk. Old Charlie had woken up for a moment and peered at him in the dark. But he'd said nothing, sinking back into a snoring stupor. Luke had lain awake, all night long, listening to that snoring, thinking about the girl upstairs. And when he got up the next morning, when the sun first came up and Hoyt returned from his sheepish assignation with the Widow Marley, she was gone. Never to return, except for that one secret visit when Hoyt died.

He still wondered what would have happened if he'd handled it differently. If he'd just said to hell with it and gotten into bed with her. Hell, he could have told her he loved her. He'd learned to lie early, when faced with the prospect of his father's drunken rages.

He might even have managed to knock her up, and then marry her. He'd been through that since, and survived. What if it had been Isabelle he'd gotten pregnant?

There would have been no question of who inherited Rancho Diablo. They would have been married, straight away, Hoyt would have seen to that. Maybe he shouldn't have been so damned noble.

But he would have had to face Hoyt, the first person who'd ever believed in him, and told him he'd betrayed his trust.

No, he made the right decision, walking away from all that temptation years ago. The question was, if that temptation were offered again, would he still be smart enough to keep away?

ISABELLE LIFTED HER FOOT off the accelerator when she realized she was edging toward ninety as her Ferrari soared over the Wyoming border. She didn't have that much farther to go—she'd be a fool to blow it now and get stopped for speeding. She'd been a fool to start thinking about Luke, thinking about the withering embarrassment of throwing herself at someone who didn't want her.

She'd never done that again. Her few relationships had been brief, equal and ultimately unsatisfying. But at least she'd never had to suffer that kind of humiliation again.

She wouldn't think about him. Wouldn't think about that awful night, hitchhiking back to the airport with tears streaming down her face, catching that miserably early flight and suffering her first and only bout of airsickness during the entire flight. She'd think about Paris. About the clear, warm blue of the Caribbean. The noise and excitement of New York. The deadly boredom of the Basho Meditation Center.

And despite her misgivings, she'd think about home. About the place she'd loved and turned her back on. As the wide, flat spaces started reaching toward the spiky Tetons, she felt a familiar tightening inside her. For whatever reason, she was home. And no matter if it was a haven or a disaster, she was suddenly very happy.

# Chapter Five

Charlie appeared out of the darkness, climbing onto the porch and sinking down beside Luke. "Got any more of that whiskey?" he asked as he lit a cigarette, the brief flare of light illuminating his impassive old face.

"In the kitchen."

Charlie didn't waste more than a glance over his shoulder at the door. The woman was moving around, cleaning things, humming something tuneless under her breath, and Charlie shook his head, leaning back against the rocker. "I'll pass. Give me a slug of yours."

Luke passed his half-full glass over without hesitation, feeling only a faint regret as Charlie drained it. "You don't like her?"

"I don't like cheats and liars," he said flatly. "She can smile all she wants, cook all the pies and cakes and stews she wants, she can take over kitchen detail so that I never have to wash another dish. I'll eat the food, leave the dishes and be polite. But I don't want to spend any more time around her than I have to."

"The others must like her." Luke phrased it as a question. He was curious whether his mild antipathy was simply a dislike for dishonesty, or something more ingrained. "They don't know she's not Isabelle, do they?"

"I haven't said anything, if that's what you're asking," Charlie said with great dignity. "Besides, none of them knew Bella—Johnson's been with us the longest and that's only seven years. They take her at face value. Jimmy seems taken with her, but then, he's only nineteen. You know what it's like when you're nineteen. You think with your zipper."

"Yeah," Luke drawled. "If you don't know any better."

"That's right, you were nineteen when Bella left here, weren't you?" Charlie said, but Luke wasn't fooled. Charlie knew perfectly well how old Luke had been. He hadn't brought up Jimmy's age as idle conversation.

"Yes," Luke said.

"Have anything to do with it?"

Luke turned to stare at him, but Charlie was looking no more than idly curious. "It's been thirteen years, old man. Why are you asking now?"

"Stands to reason. Someone shows up claiming to be Isabelle. Makes me wonder why Bella didn't come herself. It's not me she wouldn't want to see."

Luke squirmed in the chair. "Maybe she hates Wyoming. Maybe she feels more at home in Paris or New York or someplace like that. You know she never settles in one place for very long."

"And whose fault is that?"

"Are you saying it's mine?" Luke asked, a dangerous edge to his voice.

As usual, Charlie wasn't fazed. "Is it?"

"Isabelle made her own choices, and it hasn't a damned thing to do with me. I haven't seen the woman in thirteen years, and I didn't have much to do with her when she was around."

Charlie appeared to consider that for a moment. "I believe you."

"Good thing," Luke said. "If you called me a liar I'd have punched you."

"I've got twenty years on you," Charlie said.

"You've got thirty-seven years on me and we both know it. Let's talk about something else."

"Like what?" Charlie demanded. "The weather?"

Luke opened his mouth to respond with suitable profanity when the screen door opened. The woman calling herself Isabelle stood silhouetted against the light, and he had to admit her shape was everything it should be beneath the frilly gingham apron. "Luke?" she said, her voice with that husky note that somehow rang false.

"Yeah?"

"I thought I'd go on up to bed now. Unless there was something you wanted. Maybe we could go over the books..."

He'd caught her snooping in the office a couple of times, and it was all he could do to keep from snapping at her. He had to find the key for that room, or invest in a padlock. "Some other time," he said, his drawl faintly sarcastic. "You don't need to worry your pretty little head about men's work."

The real Isabelle would have handed him his own head. Her stand-in simply nodded. "Whatever you say, Luke."

The real Isabelle would never have been so politely acquiescent. He considered trying to irritate her, then realized he simply didn't care enough to bother. "Good night," he said instead, his voice brief and dismissing.

"Good night." Her voice was soft and caressing and intensely irritating. "Good night, Charlie."

"Night, Miss Isabelle," Charlie said. "Maybe tomorrow we'll see about getting you something to ride. Maybe

Diabolique would suit you. He's got a lot of fire, but nothing more than you can handle."

"I'd love that," she said with real enthusiasm, and Charlie and Luke exchanged glances. He almost said something then, but the phone rang, and he bolted out of his chair, brushing past the attractive woman standing in the kitchen door as if she were nothing more than a stray cat. He hated the smell of her perfume, hated her soft, sexy voice, hated her very presence. And he couldn't understand whether it was because she was a cheat and a liar, as Charlie had said, or simply because she wasn't Isabelle. And for some unknown reason he wanted her to be.

"Yeah?" he barked into the phone, irritation ready to spill over onto the first hapless victim.

There was a pause on the other end of the line, and Luke knew, with sudden, shocking clarity, that it was the real Isabelle. He didn't know how he knew it, but his stomach tightened as if he was a kid of nineteen again, and he felt his heart begin to pound.

"Hello," the voice said, the voice with its unforgettable husky note. "Is Isabelle Romney there?"

"Yeah," he said again, the terseness covering his sudden, overwhelming tension. "Who's asking for her?"

Another pause. "A friend."

He spun around, stifling his fury. "It's for you," he said, holding out the phone to the pretty woman in his kitchen.

It didn't take a fool to see that her tension matched his, and he strode back out onto the porch, slamming the screen door behind him and sinking back in his chair.

"Who...?" Charlie began.

"Shh. It's her." Luke didn't need to explain further. The two of them sat there in total silence, eavesdropping on the one-sided phone conversation.

"Don't you dare!" It was a muffled shriek, and the husky note had disappeared completely from the impostor. "No one will believe it. You can't..." Her voice dropped, and the two men leaned closer to the door. "No," she said. "Absolutely not." And they heard the slamming of the phone, the hurried sound of footsteps racing upstairs.

For a moment Luke stared at the door, willing Isabelle to call back. This time he'd tell her he knew. But the old black wall phone remained silent, and he turned back to Charlie. "Let's find that bottle, old man."

"Sounds good to me," Charlie said somberly.

ISABELLE STARED at the pay phone in mute frustration. Damn Becky and her lack of spirit. If she'd managed to fool everyone into thinking she was Isabelle, Isabelle would have no trouble playing Becky. She was a better actress any day, and all she needed was to wear those baggy, shapeless clothes, scrape her hair back, and she'd fool anyone who even vaguely remembered Isabelle's pale cousin.

She didn't dare call back, however. For one thing, she really didn't fancy talking to Luke again. She'd spoken to him over the phone any number of times in the past thirteen years, but she'd never grown comfortable doing so. Even though the conversations had been entirely about money, about the ranch, she always felt a peculiar tightening in her stomach at the sound of his laconic drawl.

It would do her a world of good to actually face him again. To banish old demons, and get on with her life. And while she'd like nothing more than to put off that reckoning, at least until tomorrow, she was out of cash, her credit card had been refused at the last convenience store she'd stopped in and she was so tired she was afraid she was going to drive into a ditch. Rancho Diablo was less than forty miles away. She was damned if she was going to risk spending the night in her car when home was so nearby.

Ranchers went to bed early. She'd get there sometime around midnight, and the place would be dark. Even if Luke had gotten paranoid in his old age and locked the place, she knew how to get in. The first thing she'd do was head straight for her old bedroom and wake Becky up. She needed a few answers to a few questions, like whether Becky really had embezzled all that money from the brokerage house where she worked. Like whether there'd been any sign of Martin Abruzzi and his henchmen. Like whether she'd been able to broach the subject of selling off the ranch.

It hadn't sounded as if Cupid had done his work too well. Luke's tone of voice when he'd passed the phone to Becky sounded less than warm, but maybe they were in the midst of a lovers' quarrel. Or maybe she'd been foolishly optimistic in hoping she'd be able to manipulate the situation that completely.

She'd deal with that when she had to. What she needed right now was a place to hide out for a few days. And while she was at it, maybe she could face some of the things she'd been hiding from, and start to make her peace with her past. If she could just convince Luke that selling was the best thing for everyone, just make sure he wouldn't do his damnedest to queer the deal, then she'd be off in a few days, with the promise of a huge amount of money to support her wanderings.

After all, that was everything she wanted, wasn't it? Except that, looking around her as she climbed back into her car, she couldn't help thinking that she might be ready to end her wanderings. That she might have finally come home to stay.

THAT WAS NO LONG DISTANCE phone call, Luke thought later as he headed for his bedroom at the back of the first floor of the old ranch house. The respectable amount of bourbon he'd consumed didn't cloud his thought processes or slow his progress one iota, and if he was just a trace more deliberate in everything, well, that was a good thing. He'd unbuttoned his shirt when he suddenly realized that the real Isabelle wasn't that far away.

He sat down on the king-size bed, hard, and thought about it. The fake Isabelle had been panicked about something, and it didn't take a Ph.D. to figure out that the real Isabelle intended to show up, whether the phony one liked it or not. And if Luke knew Isabelle, and even after thirteen years he still did, then he knew she wouldn't be willing to sit back and wait. She'd show up, as soon as she could. And he had no doubts at all she was going to show up tonight.

The question was, when. And how. Would she stride up to the front porch as if she were a welcome visitor? Would she call again, try to get her fake self to meet her? Neither seemed likely, though the Isabelle he remembered wasn't short on gall.

She was going to try to sneak in first. He wasn't quite sure how he knew it, but he did. And he knew how she was going to do it. The rear window on the downstairs bedroom, the big, spacious one that had always been hers, didn't have a latch, much less a lock. He knew that very well, for the simple reason that he'd spent his nineteenth summer thinking about that unbarred window and the girl that lay behind it. He'd never gotten around to replacing it. It didn't seem to matter much, since he seldom locked the place anyway. Isabelle would know that, of course, and would realize she could walk in the front door with no one the wiser. But she wouldn't do it.

He kept his double-aught shotgun, the one he used to scare away varmints from the henhouse, in a gun rack in the hallway. He rose from the bed and fetched it, making sure it was unloaded as he'd left it. Kicking the door shut behind him, he sank down in the creaking old rocker he'd rescued from the kitchen porch. He didn't finish undressing, just left his shirt hanging unbuttoned, his feet bare, his jeans zipped but unsnapped, as he held the big shotgun across his lap and waited. There was more than one kind of varmint out to rob the henhouse, and he planned to scare the hell out of the female one about to invade the male-dominated environs of Rancho Diablo.

ISABELLE COULD SEE it all quite clearly in her mind. She'd pull up outside the ranch house sometime before midnight. The doors would be locked, so she'd head directly to the back bedroom, to the window that never had a lock. Becky had shown herself to be surprisingly cunning—she'd doubtless be wide-awake in the frilly canopy bed, awaiting Isabelle's arrival. Together they'd hatch their plan, presenting a united front to Luke when he woke up the next morning.

Attitude was half the battle, she thought with her usual optimism. If she and Becky simply assumed everyone would believe them, they'd carry it off. By the time Luke found out who was really whom, Mr. Takashima would be back with a written offer for the ranch, Martin would have given up looking for her and Becky would have managed to give Luke a nice, matrimonial alternative to his widower's life on the remote ranch.

Dwight Yoakum was on the radio, singing some song about fools, and for a moment Isabelle knew a moment's doubt. She wasn't a careful planner, she was an extravagant dreamer. And she couldn't help but wonder whether things were going to explode in her face.

Of course things never went as she planned. The ranch was farther, the roads ruttier, than she remembered, and she had too much appreciation for her poor abused Ferrari to drive at the speeds she was longing to. It was closer to two in the morning when she finally pulled up to the long, rambling ranch house that had sheltered her for the first seventeen years of her life. The only place she had ever called home, a place she'd turned her back on.

She killed the motor, sitting there in the silence for a moment, listening to the sounds of the night around her, the old familiar smells of horses, hay, summer air and the indefinable essence she'd always simply called Wyoming. She sat in the comfortable leather seat of her luxury car and felt tears form in her eyes, felt her throat close up in sudden pain. For a moment all the very good reasons she had for keeping her distance seemed vanished in the night air. Her father's rejection, Luke's cool disdain, her sense of helplessness, were far away, and she wished with all her heart and soul she was seventeen again, and that she could make her father love her best.

She slipped on the high-heeled black sandals and slid out of the car, brushing back her thick tangle of hair and the tears from her eyes in the same gesture. She'd spent too many years as the incomparable Isabelle to fall prey to childish emotions. She knew, as well as Thomas Wolfe did, that you can't go home again.

She didn't bother with the front door. She'd parked behind the familiar silhouette of the house, and she headed straight for the back window of her bedroom. She'd crept in and out of that window any number of times over the years, when she didn't want her father to hear her. She snuck out to go skinny-dipping with her friend Elly; she'd snuck out to go to a dance with David Granger when her father had forbidden her. He'd been right, too. Davey Granger had the fastest hands in the West, and the certain belief that because his daddy owned the biggest spread in the area, not to mention the bank, any girl would fall at his feet. Isabelle hadn't been impressed, and she'd made it home with a torn blouse and dignity intact. Until she'd met the contempt in Luke's eyes the next morning, and known that he knew what she'd done.

Dammit, she thought, moving as silently as a shadow toward the window. Why did everything always come back to Luke? She spent almost sixteen years on the ranch without him. Why did almost every memory seem tainted by his presence?

She peered in the window, but in the darkness things seemed indefinably different. She couldn't make out the frilly white of her canopy bed, the pale wood of her matching dressers, the white fluffy rug on the old pine floor. Everything was dark inside, and she wondered whether Luke had changed things, wiped out all trace of her existence.

The window slid open with nothing more than a faint creak. It was higher than she remembered, almost four feet off the ground, and she was wearing her saffron robes as a slight protection against the night chill. With a muffled grunt she slung her leg up, through the window opening, and hoisted herself through, pausing for a moment on the sill as her eyes searched the pitch-dark room. And then she dropped down into the room, landing on her rear on the old pine floor with a noisy thud.

She couldn't see a damned thing in the inky darkness. One thing she knew for sure—her canopy bed was gone. She blinked a few times, willing her eyes to grow accustomed to the blackness. "Becky?" she whispered. "Cousin Becky?"

"I figured that's who she was," a deep, unforgettable voice came out of the darkness. A moment later the room was flooded with light, illuminating a man sitting there in an old rocker, entirely at his ease. Across his lap was the biggest gun Isabelle had ever seen, and she was too mesmerized by that lethal weapon to look up at the face of the man. For a moment, that is.

"It's an old western custom to shoot housebreakers," the voice drawled. "The front door wasn't locked."

"So how'd you know I'd come in this way?" she said, still staring at the gun. Staring at the dark, smooth chest and flat stomach behind the gun. Staring anywhere but at his face.

"I know you better than you think," he said, putting the gun aside and rising from the chair. She was still sprawled on the floor beneath the window, and while she cursed her ignominious position, a part of her brain noted that he was even taller than she remembered.

"I hope not," she said devoutly. "Aren't you going to shoot me? It would solve a lot of your problems."

"I fight fair. No lies, no evasions, no people pretending to be someone they're not."

She looked up then, at his face, and could have cried. He was, if anything, even better looking than he'd been at nineteen. The past thirteen years showed in his face, showed in the fine network of lines surrounding his mesmerizing green eyes, showed in the grooves alongside his large, sexy mouth. He still wore his blond hair long, slicked back away from his face, and the planes and lines of his face were harsh, uncompromisingly beautiful.

She swallowed, keeping her face as impassive as his. "It's hard to fight fair when one side has all the ammunition," she said, pulling her saffron robes down around her long legs.

He moved over to her, reaching a hand down. She stared at it for a long moment, not wanting to touch him. If looking at him made her feel that disoriented, what would touching him do to her?

He didn't give her any choice. When she made no effort to take his hand he simply reached down and took hers, hauling her to her feet with more force than grace. She stumbled on the high heels, then righted herself, keeping her distance from him, noting absently that he hadn't released her hand. Noting that he towered over her, even when she was wearing heels.

"You've gotten taller," she said stupidly. "I thought people stopped growing by nineteen."

"You've gotten . . . riper," he said, dropping her hand and taking a step back, away from her, as if she were suddenly poisonous. "Welcome to Wyoming. Welcome home, Izzy."

LESS THAN TWENTY MINUTES later Luke stretched out on his king-size bed, staring at the darkened bedroom. Isabelle was upstairs, settling in for the rest of the night, probably settling in for a round of planning with her co-conspirator, he thought, though he didn't hear the sound of footsteps, footsteps that would surely carry in this old wooden house. She was sleeping in the narrow bunk that years ago had been his, but if she remembered she didn't show it. Her face had been devoid of emotion, of memory. That final confrontation in his tiny bedroom might never have happened. Maybe she'd been lucky enough to forget it. He hadn't.

He shifted in the bed, wide-awake and restless. He was someone who never had trouble sleeping—he worked long, hard hours and his conscience was clean. But the presence of his nemesis, after so many years, was enough to throw anyone off. He hadn't gotten any explanations out of her, but then, he hadn't asked any direct questions. He figured tomorrow would be soon enough.

He'd dozed off in the chair, awaiting her, and when he'd first heard the creak of the window, saw that long, enticing leg slung over the sill, he hadn't quite believed it. Particularly since that leg had been followed by the rest of a body clad in the strangest garment he'd ever seen in his life. He hadn't asked her about that, either. He'd simply wanted to get rid of her, as fast as he could, while he came to terms with her sudden reappearance in his life.

It hit him harder than he would have thought. He'd always suspected he wasn't immune to her, and now he knew it. Much good it would do him. She'd proven herself to be just as flighty, shallow and greedy as he'd always thought, flitting from city to city, country to country, taking the money he sent her and offering nothing in return. And now she was back, and he hated to see what she wanted. Whether the ranch would survive, once she got what she was after. Whether he'd survive.

Idiot, he told himself, rolling over and punching his pillow. That was the sort of thought that came to him in the middle of the night, when his defenses were at their weakest. He wasn't going to let a temptress like Izzy Romney get to him. He was too old and too smart for that.

Still, he could sense the faint whisper of her perfume in the air. He told himself he was imagining it. Just a trace of the scent had clung to her, and he hadn't even noticed until he was standing dangerously close. It smelled different on her. It always had. It always would.

And now it permeated his bedroom, insinuating itself into his senses, doubtless into his dreams. And he wondered what strong breeze could ever blow it completely from his life.

## Chapter Six

By five-thirty the next morning Isabelle figured she might as well forget about sleeping. She would have thought she'd be dead to the world for twenty-four hours at least, given her headlong dash across the country and the few hours' sleep she'd managed to snatch along the way.

But six weeks at the Basho Meditation Center, with their 5:00 a.m. trances, appeared to have ruined her for life. Isabelle Romney, who seldom woke before eleven on a good day, was now so used to predawn risings that it would take all her determination to sink back into her slothful ways.

She swung her long legs out of bed and dropped to the floor. She'd slept in the narrow top bunk in that corner bedroom. Not all the fiends in hell could have gotten her in the lower one last night, particularly since she hadn't come equipped with a nightgown. Sleeping naked in what used to be Luke Cassidy's bed was something she wasn't about to attempt. She wouldn't have had the few hours of sleep granted her if she'd tried it.

She wrinkled her nose at the saffron robes and high-heeled shoes. If only Luke hadn't been so ruthless about stripping her bedroom. Despite his odd comment about her being...riper...she still wore the same size she'd been wearing thirteen years ago, a testament more to good luck than any effort on her part. She generally ate what was put in front of her and forgot to eat when no one fed her. Maybe that was why she hadn't learned to cook.

She pulled the heavy robes around her, dismissed the high-heeled shoes and opened the door into the hall. A thick, oddly peaceful silence had settled around the house. Isabelle knew where Becky was—her father's bedroom at the end of the hall was the only possible choice. She should go wake up sleeping beauty and demand to know what was going on. How she'd managed to botch things so completely, and whether anyone had been after her, either the possibly embezzling Becky or the less-guilty but equally endangered Isabelle.

She should, but she wasn't going to. Becky could wait a few hours. It had been thirteen years since she'd been home—that brief return at Hoyt's death didn't really count—and she wanted to have a little breathing space. Time to say hello to things she used to care about. Time to say goodbye to them all over again. In a few weeks, a few months, whatever the legalities took, this ranch and the two thousand acres would belong to Mr. Takashima's corporation. And her sense of homelessness would no longer be imaginary.

Luke's bedroom door was closed when she tiptoed downstairs. She let out a tiny breath of relief. She wanted to avoid him even more than she wanted to avoid Becky, and she practically ran out through the kitchen door, leaving it open to the cool morning air.

From a distance she could smell coffee. She knew it came from the bunkhouse, a mysterious place off-limits to an adolescent female, and it took her a moment to realize such strictures no longer applied. She headed straight for the little house, entertaining the notion that it might be the equivalent of a men's locker room, with naked cowhands wandering around, ready to be embarrassed. Somehow she doubted it. The cowhands she'd known in her youth had never been overly concerned with cleanliness, and as far as she knew old Charlie wore the same union suit summer, winter, spring and fall.

She paused in the doorway for a moment, her eyes growing accustomed to the room, to the long table and the heavenly smell of coffee. Three men were looking at her, but she had eyes only for one.

"Hey, Charlie," she said softly.

He stood, stumbled for a moment and started toward her. "It's about damned time," he said, his voice scratchy.

She flung her arms around him and held him tight, ancient union suit and all. She thought she could feel something damp against her shoulder, and she laughed rustily. "You aren't crying, are you, Charlie?"

"Hell, no," he said, stepping back and rubbing his eyes. He turned to glare at the others as if daring them to comment. The two men were watching them with varying confused expressions. "This here is Isabelle," he said. "Miss Bella to you boys."

One of the boys, a taciturn-looking man in his midfifties, said, "What's the big deal? She's been here for days."

"No, she hasn't." The one who could actually qualify as a boy spoke up. He looked about nineteen, with sunburned shoulders, an open, freckled face and jug ears. "I don't know who's been hanging around but this one's prettier."

"Trust you to notice something like that, Jimmy," the older man said, looking at her with new interest. "So if you're Bella Romney, who's that been cooking for us?"

"My Cousin Becky."

"That's Johnson," Charlie broke in, making belated introductions. "The kid there is Jimmy Martin—you might remember his pa, Jack Martin."

"Hi," she said, feeling suddenly self-conscious.

"Does Luke know you're here?" Charlie asked.

"He caught me sneaking into my own bedroom," she admitted sheepishly, casting a longing glance toward the coffeepot.

A second later Jimmy Martin was handing her a mug, his sunburned face blushing darker red when she thanked him. The place didn't seem to come equipped with sugar and cream, so she took a cautious sip of the deadly stuff, just managing not to shudder as the caffeine danced through her veins.

"It ain't your bedroom anymore," Charlie muttered. "It's Luke's."

"So I noticed."

"Luke must have been some surprised," Johnson said, his dark face lightening slightly in amusement.

"Not really. He was waiting for me with a shotgun across his lap."

"He wasn't!" Jimmy was scandalized.

"Bet he was," Charlie said with a chuckle. "Bet the gun wasn't loaded, either. He just wanted to put a scare into you, Miss Bella."

"Well, he didn't," Isabelle said darkly, taking another sip of coffee and moving over toward the open door. "Luke can't scare me, gun or no."

"Luke's always scared the hell out of you, Miss Bella. Why else haven't you come back in so long?" Charlie pitched his voice low.

"Maybe I just don't like it here," she said. "Maybe I'm bored with mountains and fresh air and tin-horse towns. Maybe I'm just a city girl at heart."

"And maybe I'm the king of England," Charlie said with a snort. "You don't fool me, girl."

"That's too bad," Isabelle said. "I manage to fool everyone else." She handed him the half-full cup of poison and stepped out into the yard. "What happened to my stuff, Charlie? My furniture, my clothes? Did he burn them or just give them away to the Salvation Army?"

"We don't have the Salvation Army out here, Miss Bella. I guess everything's in the attic. Luke doesn't like to throw anything out, and as far as I know, he never had no problem with you. You were the one with the problem."

"The more things change, the more they remain the same," Isabelle said softly.

"What's that, Miss Bella?"

"Nothing, Charlie." She straightened her shoulders, staring at the old ranch house. It was early, but she didn't dare hope the two inhabitants were still sleeping. "Want to give me a hand getting some of that stuff out?"

"Better ask Luke first."

"I own this place, Charlie. Not Luke. I'll do what I damned well please, up to and including throwing him out of my bedroom if I have a mind to."

Charlie looked troubled. "I wouldn't try it if I were you," he said somberly.

"I won't if he doesn't give me a hard time. But that corner bedroom doesn't have a dresser, and I don't have any clothes. I must have left some jeans behind, some sweaters and stuff."

"Why don't you borrow some from your cousin?"

Isabelle made a face. "I don't think Becky is too generous with her possessions. Give me a hand, and I won't evict Luke from the best room in the house."

"It's a deal," he said. But he still looked troubled.

LUKE KNEW THE MINUTE he entered the kitchen that it was Becky and not Isabelle. For one thing, he could smell freshly baked cinnamon buns spicing the air, and as far as he could see last night, Isabelle Romney hadn't changed that much. Becky was standing at the sink, humming beneath her breath, something tuneless and irritating. She turned when he walked in, flashing her great, phony smile.

"Good morning, sleepyhead," she said. "It's almost seven o'clock. I thought you were up and gone already."

He just stared at her for a minute, assimilating things. Obviously Isabelle hadn't tracked down her stand-in for a session of planning. As far as Cousin Becky knew, her position was still secure.

Luke ambled across the kitchen and poured himself a cup of coffee. "I didn't sleep too well last night," he said, dropping down beside the scarred old worktable.

"Really?" She batted her eyelashes at him, already thick with makeup. "I slept wonderfully. It's this mountain air. I can't imagine why I ever left it."

"Can't you?" He kept his voice neutral.

She moved to join him at the table, obviously encouraged by his lack of hostility. "I always loved this place, from the time I was a little girl," she said. "The clean air, the mountains, the meadows. And the horses."

"You like to ride, don't you?" Luke drawled, noticing the shadow appearing in the kitchen door, behind Becky's back.

"I love it. There's nothing like a brisk ride across the countryside, the wind at your back, a clever, strong horse beneath you," Becky chattered on, for once with real enthusiasm. Isabelle opened the door behind her, standing there for a moment, and he had a chance to compare the two of them.

When seen together the resemblance was less pro-
nounced. Isabelle's eyes were bluer, her mouth fuller, her
skin creamier. Even in that absurd yellow robe her body
seemed more enticing. She looked rumpled, as if she'd just
climbed out of bed, but Luke had no doubt whatsoever
she'd been visiting Charlie and the boys. As far as he knew,
Becky had never set foot near the bunkhouse, and spoke
to the hired men like the Lady Bountiful she imagined
herself to be.

"You thinking of staying, Isabelle?" he asked, his eyes
on the woman in the doorway.

"If you don't mind," Becky said with just the right
amount of shyness. "This is where I belong. I know Daddy
would have wanted me here."

Isabelle made a sharp movement, as if negating the very
idea, but she said nothing, momentarily distracted by the
woman playing her role.

"What about your jet-setting life-style?" Luke asked
idly. "Wouldn't you miss Paris, New York, all those fancy
places?"

Becky hesitated. "Of course not. I've had my fill of
those places. After all, I've been gone for twelve years."

"Thirteen," Luke corrected. "You'd better get your
lines right."

"I beg your pardon?"

"You might as well forget it, Becky," Isabelle said from
the doorway. "Luke knows."

The woman sitting at the table froze, and for a moment
Luke wondered why he'd thought there was any resemblance at all. In her sudden fury Becky Romney was quite
ugly.

And then a moment later that expression was gone, and
she turned to face her cousin. "You might have warned me
before I made a fool of myself," she said mildly enough.

"I expect he's always known," Isabelle said, moving into the kitchen with unconscious grace and heading for the coffeepot. "Haven't you, Luke?"

"Yes."

"And you didn't say anything?" Becky demanded.

He pulled his eyes away from Isabelle to look at her cousin. "Didn't seem necessary," he said. "I figured I'd find out sooner or later what was going on."

"Is that why you kept making excuses about signing those papers?"

"He knew you wouldn't want to add forgery to your other crimes," Isabelle said lazily, sitting down at the head of the table with all the grace of a duchess, her tattered robes draped around her.

"What other crimes?" Becky demanded, her eyes narrowed in sudden panic.

"Oh, impersonation. Accepting food and lodging under false pretenses," Isabelle continued, her own eyes observant.

Something was going on between the two of them. Luke had been around people enough to feel the undercurrents, though he couldn't for a moment imagine what it was. "I don't think impersonation is a crime," he said.

"And the food and lodging belongs to you, Bella," Becky pointed out. "After all, the ranch is yours, and you sent me here."

"So I did."

"Which brings me to the question of why?" Luke said. "Why send someone pretending to be you, why not come yourself? And for that matter, what the hell have you got on?"

Isabelle lowered her eyes demurely. "I was in a convent," she murmured. "I've taken holy orders."

"You're full of holy—"

"Luke!" Charlie appeared at the door, ignoring Becky, flashing a smile at Isabelle. "You'd better come quick. We're having some trouble with that new mare."

"Damn." He was up and heading toward the door without a moment's hesitation. He paused at the door for a moment, looking at the two women, both so full of secrets. "We'll finish this conversation later," he said.

"Yes, sir, boss," Isabelle said, mocking him.

He stood stock-still for a moment, wanting to go back and take her by the arms and shake her till her teeth rattled. Wanting to go back and kiss her until she melted against him.

He must be out of his mind. Though the very thought of what both Becky and Charlie would do if he followed his insane instincts was enough to startle a laugh out of him. "That's the right attitude," he said. "Keep it in mind." And he followed Charlie out into the morning sunlight.

ISABELLE DRAINED her coffee, giving herself a brisk little shake of pleasure. "So," she said. "Did you embezzle money from your employers?"

"You've been very busy in the past few days, haven't you?" Becky said, her expression giving nothing away.

"I've been driving across the country the past few days," Isabelle said. "Did you?"

"Why aren't you still in the meditation center? What about your holy orders?"

"I lied," she said simply. "And things got a little sticky there. I was trying to avoid a messy situation, and unfortunately that messy situation found me. You...er...haven't seen anything unusual around here? No one's been asking for me?"

"I'll tell you what, Bella. You tell me about your messy situation, and I'll tell you whether I embezzled money," Becky said, rising and heading toward the oven.

The odor of cinnamon was so strong that for a moment Isabelle considered learning how to cook, then dismissed the notion as impractical. One might as well try to teach a pig to fly, she thought. "Give me one of those buns," she said, "and it's a deal."

Becky deposited one in front of her, the steam still rising from it. "Who's after you?"

Isabelle burned her fingers, then her mouth, and then her tongue as she devoured the bun. It had been more than twenty-four hours since she'd remembered to eat, and she was suddenly famished. Wyoming always did that to her. She was lucky she had no intention of staying. She'd be fat as a pig within six months.

"A man named Martin Abruzzi," she said, licking her fingers. "Not really the sort of man to run afoul of. He has nasty connections, and lots of people willing to do anything for him for a certain price."

"Are you talking about the mob?"

"I'm afraid so."

"You have the mob after you, and you sent me off to impersonate you?" Becky's voice rose in a shriek, losing its artificial husky note. "You set me up when you had hit men after you? You unprincipled, amoral, rotten . . ."

"Not unprincipled. As far as I know there isn't a contract out on me. No one wants to kill me. They just want something I have. They aren't about to kill me until they get it."

"And you were willing to risk my life on that chance?"

Isabelle tried her melting smile. Becky didn't melt. "If they hadn't been able to track me to the Basho Meditation

Center in six weeks it didn't seem likely they'd trace you to an obscure part of Wyoming in a matter of days.''

"But they did trace you to the center.''

"The next day,'' Isabelle agreed with a sigh. "I promise you, Becky, you were in no danger. If they'd managed to catch up with you they would have taken you to Martin, and he would have known immediately that you weren't me.''

"How?''

"The same way Luke and Charlie did. People who know me aren't fooled. You may look like me, sound like me, wear your hair and your clothes like me, but you aren't me.''

Becky simply stared at her for a moment, and Isabelle told herself she was imagining the waves of hatred emanating from behind that impassive countenance. "Obviously not'' was all she said. "Fortunately your theory wasn't put to the test. They found you, not me. And I hate to tell you this, darling, but I'm not leaving.''

Isabelle shrugged. "I didn't say you had to. After all, this is my place. Anyone I want can stay here. But why would you want to stay?''

"Who's to say your friend Martin wouldn't make a mistake? Our names are similar, our looks are certainly similar. What if he's not as smart as you think? What if he shoots first and asks questions later?''

"I told you, he's not going to shoot,'' Isabelle said patiently. "Anyway, he'd have someone else do it.''

"I'm not going to take that chance. And I have my own messy situation to avoid.''

"Did you embezzle the money?''

"No. Unfortunately I'm going to have a hard time proving it.''

"Why?''

"Because a man I was involved with took it. He's in the Caribbean somewhere, and I doubt they'll ever find him. He wanted me to go with him, but I told him no. I didn't realize he'd set it up so that I'd look as guilty as he was." She took a careful bite into her own cinnamon bun, and Isabelle watched with real admiration. She didn't believe a single, solitary word of what Becky had just told her, but she had no intention of saying so. It wouldn't do any good. Becky's shady financial dealings had nothing to do with her, and besides, her cousin had attempted to do her a favor, even if it hadn't worked, even if Martin had shown up the very next day, even if Becky had had her own hidden agenda.

"All right," Isabelle said. "We both have a nice little vacation until things cool down a bit. I think Luke can put up with that. You don't look as if you've made too much progress in winning his heart."

"He doesn't have a heart," Becky snapped. "And he's not going to fall in love with me when you're around."

"Why ever not?"

"Because as long as you're in the room he doesn't look at anyone else."

Isabelle laughed, genuinely amused. "You've spent approximately five minutes in the room with the two of us and already you've come to that conclusion? If Luke can't keep his eyes off me it's because he's too busy glaring."

"Maybe. But as long as you're around, whatever he feels for you is going to overwhelm any other considerations."

"We'll all be leaving soon enough. Maybe on neutral ground..."

"I don't really care, Bella. He's not my type. I like quiet, gentle men. Men who are a bit more amenable."

"That's one thing I'd never call Luke," Isabelle agreed. "And he might not leave. Mr. Takashima might want to keep him on as manager of the place. After all, no one knows more about Rancho Diablo than Luke does. I don't suppose you had a chance to mention selling the place?"

"Anytime I brought up business he'd either change the subject or walk out on me. He's not much on the social graces, Bella."

Isabelle thought about it for a moment, about the angry, bruised teenager her father had brought home one sunny afternoon, about the reserved, still-angry man she'd confronted last night and this morning. The difference being that now he knew who he was and what he wanted. Now he had control, of himself and everything surrounding him, and if he didn't want to be polite he didn't have to be.

"No, I suppose he's not," she agreed. "Hoyt sent him off to the University of Wyoming but I don't think they taught Manners 101 there. Still, at least he's honest. That's more than can be said about either of us."

Becky rose, clearly affronted. "I'm going upstairs. Do you need some clothes, or are you going to traipse around like a Buddhist monk?"

Isabelle let her eyes drift over Becky's frilly cotton dress. "I think I'll find some of my old stuff. I'm feeling nostalgic."

"Suit yourself. You'd better be careful, though."

"Of what? I thought you said Martin hadn't been around?"

"Martin isn't the most dangerous thing in your life right now," Becky said shrewdly.

"Don't worry about me," she said. "I know perfectly well that I'm not seventeen and he's not nineteen. And I don't believe in happy endings. If we can somehow manage a truce I'll consider it a triumph.''

"Don't count on it. He's not going to like his home sold out from under him. And he's not going to think too kindly of you.''

Isabelle shrugged. "That wouldn't be anything new. I know what I'm doing, Becky. It's what I have to do, to survive. Once this place is sold I'll be able to get on with my life. Without having to look back.''

"It's a nice thought," Becky said. "But as far as I know we're never free of our pasts. Think about it.''

And as Isabelle watched her cousin leave, she knew she had no choice but to do just that. And to hope she'd come up with some answers.

## Chapter Seven

The east barn was cool after the blazing sunlight, and Luke narrowed his eyes, squinting through the shadows toward the troublesome new mare. She was standing in her stall, peacefully munching fresh timothy, her pregnant sides still and calm.

"What's the problem with the mare?" he demanded of Charlie. "She looks fine to me."

"Hush up." Charlie cast an elaborately furtive glance around him, then nodded, satisfied that the barn was empty. "I needed to talk to you."

"I gathered that much." Luke leaned against a stall and waited. It took Charlie a certain amount of time to get to the point, and there was no use rushing him. "I wasn't going to bite her head off, if that's what was worrying you. You don't need to appoint yourself Isabelle's guardian."

"I did years ago," Charlie said. "I don't think anything's going to change that. We've been friends for a long time, Luke. There's not a man I'd trust more'n I trust you. I'd follow you through hellfire and back again if I had to. But I won't let you hurt that little girl."

"That little girl is thirty if she's a day, and she can take care of herself," Luke drawled. "She's certainly had enough practice at it. She doesn't need anyone's protection, and she certainly doesn't need any protection from me. I just want her to sign a few papers and then take her sweet little butt out of here. And take her cousin with her."

"I think she's in trouble, Luke."

Luke froze. He'd had the very same notion, but he'd dismissed it, not wanting to have to worry about Isabelle and whatever mess she'd gotten herself into. But there was no ignoring Charlie's premonitions. He knew things, and no one ever figured out why, but they'd learned to pay attention when Charlie came out with one of his warnings.

"Got any idea what kind of trouble?" he asked carefully.

"Johnson said some people have been asking for her in town. City people. East Coast people, in dark suits with dark faces. He didn't like 'em, and when Johnson doesn't like someone he doesn't do much talking."

"Johnson never does much talking anyway. What were these people asking?"

"If Miss Bella ever came home. If we'd seen her recently. If we were expecting her."

"Men in dark suits with dark faces, eh?" Luke said. "Sounds like the mob or the IRS."

"Not much difference between the two of them if you ask me."

"How would you know? You don't pay your taxes as it is."

"Hell, you don't pay me enough to owe taxes," Charlie scoffed.

"And whose fault is that? I've offered..."

"Listen, we've been through this before. Hoyt left me taken care of, and if you pay me any more they'll start docking my social security. I want to get everything I can out of the government before they start wiping out Central America."

"You're too old to be so liberal, Charlie."

"And you're too old to be such a damned conservative. And we've had this argument a hundred times over the past ten years, and neither of us are going to change our minds. That still doesn't solve the problem with Miss Bella."

"If she's gotten herself into trouble then she can damn well get herself out of it," Luke said, wishing he really meant it. "If she owed back taxes she can figure out some way to pay it."

"You're forgetting one thing."

"What's that?"

Charlie grimaced. "If she needs money then to her mind there's only one major asset to be liquidated. I think she's planning to sell the ranch."

"Oh, hell," said Luke, disgusted. "That's all I needed."

ISABELLE WAS INTERESTED in finding more than her old clothes, but she hadn't bothered to tell Charlie that. He knew she used to keep a diary, but he'd probably forgotten all about it. Isabelle hadn't. She'd poured out her heart and soul that last summer, committed it all to paper, and she'd left it behind when she'd taken off.

Problem was, she'd had several hiding places. She'd been so paranoid about someone finding the diary that she'd moved it every few days. She hadn't even gone back in the house when she'd snuck back after Hoyt's death, but she couldn't ignore it any longer. Not when she was actually back in residence, at least for a few weeks.

Luke couldn't have found it. If he had, he wouldn't be treating her with the same old hostility. He'd be pitying and contemptuous instead, and she would have headed straight for Martin Abruzzi rather than face that.

Therefore the diary must still be in one of its many hiding places. In the back of her dresser. In the hidden pocket beneath her old mattress. Or beneath the loose floor-board in what was now Luke's bedroom.

That was the very last place she was going to check. Once she got out of these blasted robes she'd head for the stables. She'd avoided them so far, not out of her old fear, but something deeper. She didn't want to face Crescent's empty stall.

She'd have to, sooner or later. That was the problem with animals. You gave them your heart and soul, and they died before you did. Maybe she'd have to get a parrot. At least they outlived their masters. Though if her current streak of bad luck held out she'd end up with a geriatric one.

Nevertheless, she had to say goodbye to Crescent, just as she'd said goodbye to Hoyt. She hadn't been able to bring herself to ask Charlie about the old mare, afraid she'd cry. Maybe she'd just manage to sneak into the west barn, sit in the grass and have that cry she'd promised herself. And then she could make herself hunt for the diary.

She was damned if she was going to check with Luke before she went foraging for her own possessions in her own house. If he hadn't simply tossed everything out, they should be in the attic. And she wasn't going to wait for Charlie. In the cruel light of day she realized he'd aged, more than she'd imagined he could, in the past few years. He didn't need to go scrambling around in hot, narrow places. And he didn't need to be the one to find her diary. Charlie could be discreet when he had to, but he could also be damnably bigmouthed if it suited his sense of right-ness. Isabelle and Luke's enmity had always troubled him. If he thought the diary might put an end to that enmity, he wouldn't be above using it.

Which meant that Charlie hadn't found it, either. Therefore either it was still safely hidden, or it had disappeared long ago, never to be seen again. And the sooner she went looking for it the sooner she'd know the answer.

The access to the attic was through a trapdoor in the ceiling in the closet of Becky's bedroom. Isabelle had no idea where Luke kept a stepladder, and she wasn't about to ask. Becky was somewhere outside, and it wouldn't really matter if she came back and found Isabelle rummaging through the attic. As long as she didn't find the diary first.

With ruthless determination Isabelle pulled the small dresser over into the closet, shoving Becky's lace-and-gingham clothes out of the way. The dresses looked like someone's idea of what the well-dressed ranch wife would wear, not Becky's or even her own style at all. Becky must have decided to dress the part when she agreed to come out here, and Isabelle realized she was much more adept at lying than she ever would have imagined.

She balanced a straight-back chair on top of the dresser and then climbed up, shoving the trapdoor out of the way.

The heat up there was tremendous, suffocating, and for a moment Isabelle had second thoughts. She dismissed them, hoisting herself up, her long legs following, and peered through the shallow gloom.

Everything was up there. Her four-poster princess bed, still with its powder-blue hangings, her white-and-gold furniture, her frilly lamps; even the lacy curtains were piled in a dusty corner. The dolls that Hoyt loved to buy her and she seldom played with were sitting at drunken angles against one wall, and even her old bicycle was stuck away in a corner. She didn't know whether Luke had some latent feeling for her, that he couldn't throw out the accumulations of a lifetime, or whether he was simply too stingy to toss something that might come in handy. Either way, at least her things were still there, including her neatly folded jeans and sweaters in the old dresser drawer.

But no diary. Not in the dresser, not in the old trunk that held quilts and sweaters, not in the mattress that had proven a warm haven to a family of mice. If the diary still existed, it didn't exist up there.

"What are you looking for?" Becky poked her head up, staring about her in fastidious distaste.

"Just some old clothes. I think they'll still fit me." Isabelle jumped back from the box she'd been ransacking with an elaborate show of nonchalance.

"Really? It looked to me as if you were searching for something," she said shrewdly.

"Nothing of value, Cousin," Isabelle replied. "Besides, why should it matter to you?"

"Just curious," Becky said. "Luke's looking for you."

For a moment, Isabelle didn't move. She was covered with sweat and grime, the attic felt like an oven, and yet she had no desire at all to climb down and face anyone, particularly Luke. "Why?"

"I've told you, he doesn't say much to me. He just told me to tell you he was looking for you."

"To which you said, 'Yes, sir, boss.'"

"I leave that stuff up to you," Becky said. "I've found you catch more flies with honey than vinegar."

"You've been using saccharin, Becky," Isabelle said, swinging her long legs down through the opening and landing on the chair, just as Becky pulled out of the way. "Luke doesn't trust you for a moment, and neither do I."

Becky smiled sweetly. "That's your problem, isn't it? You're the one who sent me here."

"And I've been regretting it ever since," she muttered beneath her breath as she headed for the door.

"Aren't you going to put my furniture back?"

"Why bother?" Isabelle shrugged. "You're going up there to search through everything yourself. I'm just saving you the trouble of moving everything over again." And she closed the door behind her with a satisfying click.

The shower in the upstairs bathroom was worse than ever, the hot water nothing more than a thin, rusty trickle, the side of the stall flaking white paint onto the pitted tile beneath, but Isabelle managed, using half of Becky's shampoo and every speck of hot water the old heater could provide. By the time she emerged, one threadbare towel wrapped around her torso, another around her head, it had been more than an hour since she'd started. And emerged to run smack into a very tall, very angry man.

She'd always half hoped, half dreamed that Luke maintained a well-hidden attraction to her. If so, he certainly didn't show any sign of it as his cool green eyes swept over her sparsely clad figure with no more interest than if she'd been a new brood mare he'd been considering. No, scratch that, she thought. He'd be a lot more interested if she were a brood mare.

"Where the hell have you been?" he demanded roughly.

"Stupid question," she shot back, unable to resist. "Where does it look like I've been? In the shower."

"You used up all the hot water."

"You need a bigger hot-water heater."

Luke ground his teeth. "Didn't your cousin tell you I wanted to see you?"

"She did."

"And?"

"I wasn't ready to see you. I'm still not. If you'd be so kind as to allow me a little bit of privacy, I'll get dressed and meet you downstairs."

"In how long? I have things to do around here," he growled.

"Let's see. First I'll have to blow dry and curl my hair," she said, knowing perfectly well her hair would drip-dry into its usual tawny mane. "That'll take about twenty minutes if I hurry. Then makeup. Can't rush that. Say another forty-five minutes. Then I'll have to decide what to wear. Why don't we make it two hours?" she suggested sweetly.

"Why don't we make it right now." His big hand closed around her upper arm and started hauling her toward her room.

She clutched the towel around her as she felt the one around her hair start to slip. "My, how masterful," she said somewhat breathlessly. "What are you going to do to me when we get to my room?"

"Not what you're hoping for," he said crudely.

"What I'm hoping for," she said, "is for you to let go of me and let me get dressed in peace. If you don't stop mauling me my towel is going to fall off at your feet, and I expect you'll be a hell of a lot more embarrassed than I will."

He stopped outside her door, but he didn't release her. "You mean you're used to parading around naked in front of strange men."

"You're not exactly strange. No, let me amend that. I think you're very strange. But you're no stranger to me. And I don't happen to be uptight about my body. Somehow I get the impression that you are."

He released her then, just in time, as the towel ends began to part company. She grabbed it, pulling it back around her with a sassy smile. "Thanks. And as a reward for your kindly forbearance I'll meet you downstairs in the office in fifteen minutes. A deal?"

He was grinding his teeth again in silent rage. "A deal," he agreed finally. "And when you get down there, you can answer a few questions for me. Like why you're really here."

Isabelle didn't let her bright smile waver for a moment. "Certainly," she said. "And you can tell me why you're afraid of having me here. Been cooking the books, Luke?"

Once more he ground his teeth in rage, and she reached up and caught his strong jaw in her hand. "Bad for the bite," she said, like a chiding mother. "Try counting to ten when you're feeling frustrated."

"I'd rather get rid of the source of my frustrations. Unfortunately they don't have hired guns in Wyoming anymore."

Isabelle thought of Martin Abruzzi and his henchmen. "I sincerely hope not," she murmured, releasing him.

Fifteen minutes later she was standing on the threshold of her father's office, fighting a sudden rush of ancient grief she thought she'd dealt with. It looked and smelled almost the same. Leather and dust and cigarettes, though she hadn't actually seen Luke smoke since she'd gotten back. The battered manual typewriter was still there, but so was a fancy new computer. The curtains were the same, sagging and grimy and probably never been washed since they were first put up, and papers littered the huge scarred oak schoolteacher's desk, the bookcases, every possible surface. It was as if her father had just stepped out for a moment, and the sight of Luke sitting behind that desk, her father's desk, acting as if he belonged there, brought a sudden surge of fury to Isabelle's already unsteady temperament.

She banked it down, stepping into the room and shaking back her still-damp hair. "This room hasn't changed much," she observed, sinking into the cracked red leather armchair opposite the desk, trying to forget the hours she used to spend curled up in that chair, watching her father work on the ranch accounts.

"There was no reason to change it," he said, his voice neutral. She could almost read his mind—he'd decided to control his irritation with her, probably in the vain hope that if he didn't fight with her she'd leave sooner. "Where'd you get those clothes?"

Isabelle looked down at her faded jeans and worn flannel shirt. "The attic. There aren't many women who can still wear the same jeans after thirteen years." It was deliberately provocative of her, and he responded immediately.

"Neither can you. They're too tight."

"I can still breathe," she murmured. "Just keep your eyes off my backside and you won't have to worry about it."

"I'd like to apply something else to your backside," he muttered. "Listen, Izzy, what are you doing here?"

"What do you mean, what am I doing here? You asked . . . no, you demanded I come."

"So you send your cousin in your place to lie? That's just the sort of harebrained thing you'd think of. And I didn't need you to show up here. I needed you to sign some papers so I could sell some land. If you'd just simply done as I'd asked it wouldn't have had to turn into this . . . this . . ."

"Sweet reunion?" she suggested. "Wonderful homecoming?"

"Damned fiasco," Luke growled, leaning back in his chair. "I don't want to play games with you, Izzy. Sign the papers, get back in your fancy red car and go back where you belong."

She held herself very still. It shouldn't have hurt so much. Luke didn't have the power to reject her, and it was nothing more than she'd chosen years ago. And yet it sliced through her like a knife.

"Who says I don't belong here?" She kept her voice level.

"You know it and I know it. Your father knew it best of all. You belong in big cities with lots of noise and excitement. You know that Rancho Diablo drives you crazy with boredom."

"I haven't been home in thirteen years," she said. "How do either of us know what bores me?"

"You haven't been home in eight years," he corrected her. "I know you came back when Hoyt died."

"Damn Charlie."

"Charlie didn't have to tell me. I knew you would. Someone saw you driving through town. Why didn't you come to the service? Why didn't you at least show your face?"

Isabelle shrugged. "I figured you were busy. What with a new wife and in-laws and stuff." She allowed herself a furtive glance at his shuttered expression, to see whether the mention of his wife brought any emotion to his impassive countenance. It didn't.

"People wondered."

"I don't spend a whole lot of time worrying about people's opinions. You never used to."

Luke shook his head. "I grew up."

"And I didn't?"

"You still remind me of that half-wild seventeen-year-old." There was a disconcerting softness in his voice, one that vanished almost immediately. "You still haven't answered my question. Why are you here?"

"To sign the papers."

"Why didn't you come in the first place? And don't give me any bull about holy orders in a Buddhist monastery."

"Convent, please," she corrected lightly.

"The only religion I see you joining is a local coven."

"Is there a local coven?" she asked, momentarily distracted from her self-appointed task of irritating him.

"Not that I know of. If there is, I'm sure they'll be in touch. It takes one to know one. Why are you here? Why did you send Becky here if you were so damned eager to revisit your roots?"

She shook her head. "You got me on that one, pardner. You're right. The last place in the world I wanted to be is Wyoming, in particular at Rancho Diablo or anywhere near you. I was hoping Becky would manage to fool you long enough to keep you off my back."

"Why?"

She grimaced. "I'm in a little bit of trouble. Nothing that I can't handle, of course. I'm used to taking care of myself."

"Does it have anything to do with a couple of dark-suited East Coast types asking impertinent questions?"

Isabelle had never actually seen anyone turn white, but she suddenly knew exactly what it felt like. "They're here?" she asked faintly.

"I'm afraid so. Now who the hell are they?" he demanded, and if she hadn't known better she would have thought there was concern beneath the gruff anger in his voice.

"Oh, no one of importance," she said lightly. "Just the hired guns we were talking about earlier." She smiled brightly. "And you'll be happy to know they're after me."

# Chapter Eight

Luke seemed to freeze. "What are you talking about?"

"The mysterious men who are after me happen to work for a man named Martin Abruzzi." There was no reason not to tell him the truth, Isabelle thought. There might come a time when she needed his help. She devoutly hoped not, but she had enough imagination to know that anything was possible. "Martin's involved with organized crime back in Boston. He's in the white-collar branch of the mob, involved with computer theft, insider trading and the like."

"How did you happen to get involved with someone like that?" There was no missing the deep censure in his voice, and Isabelle wished she hadn't been fool enough to give up cigarettes.

"You don't smoke, do you?" she questioned hopefully.

"I quit years ago. You didn't answer my question. What are you doing hanging out with the mob? Your father would be turning over in his grave."

Isabelle froze. Somehow the very mention of her father brought a raging shaft of pain slicing between them, a pain so fierce that she couldn't even begin to confront it. Instead she took a deep, calming breath. "I wasn't hanging out with the mob," she said in a deceptively even voice. "I was attempting to work for a living."

"You?" he scoffed. "What would a woman with a fat inheritance from her father and a new Ferrari be doing working for a living?"

"My fat inheritance, as you call it, doesn't go as far as it used to," she said. "As a matter of fact, I wanted to talk to you about that..."

"I'm not interested in discussing the ranch right now. I want to know why hit men are after you."

"Don't you wish?" she murmured. "No one wants to kill me. Except maybe you."

"I don't want you dead," he said. "I just want you gone."

"Thanks."

"You still haven't answered my question. Were you sleeping with this mobster?"

For a moment Isabelle just stared at him. The question was so unexpected all she could do was blink. "What has that got to do with anything?"

"Just wanted to get a sense of what was going on. Were you?"

"No, darling," she said with her sweetest smile. "I was saving myself for you."

His eyes met hers then, for a brief, charged moment that almost took her breath away. The moment passed, as quickly as it had come, and once more the veil of polite irritation was between them. "You shouldn't have bothered," he drawled. "I'm not interested."

The hell you're not, Isabelle thought, fighting her own astonishment. She had no idea whether he'd ever been as immune to her as he'd pretended to be thirteen years ago, but he was immune no longer, no matter how hard he tried to hide it.

All the urge to taunt him vanished. She wanted to get away from him, as quickly as possible, to sort out this new revelation and her reaction to it. "You want 'just the facts, ma'am'?" she said, straightening from her comfortable slouch. "All right. I got a job as administrative assistant to a man named Martin Abruzzi. It was more sort of social secretary than anything else. As you know very well, I'm not trained in anything practical like shorthand or typing or computers. I arranged his business meetings, his social gatherings, took care of his shopping, decorated his house..."

"Decorated his bed," Luke interjected.

"With black satin sheets," she mocked. "After all, it's the only thing I'm good for. A perfect courtesan, wouldn't you say? I just haven't found the right man to keep me in the style to which I've become accustomed."

"You managed to buy the Ferrari."

"Actually Martin gave it to me for my thirtieth birthday." She tossed her still-damp mane of hair over her shoulder, noting with veiled interest the absolute fury with which he accepted that bit of information. "Anyway, because I had so little to do with the business side of Martin's life, I didn't realize that he wasn't on the up and up. I'm not such a bigot that I assume anyone with an Italian last name and Sicilian heritage is connected with organized crime, even if they have a small army of humorless men following them wherever they go. But I stumbled across something I wasn't supposed to, and I realized I'd be better off out of that situation."

"And this man doesn't agree?"

Isabelle shrugged. "Let's just say he's not accustomed to taking no for an answer. I happened to take something for insurance, and he'd like to retrieve it."

"So you were hiding out from him in your monastery?"

"Convent," she corrected.

"And you sent that woman to take your place, knowing she might run into your ex-boss?"

"Yes."

"Still the same old Izzy. Don't you care what happens to anyone besides you?"

"I don't have to justify my actions to you, Luke Cassidy. I knew Becky wasn't in any real danger. Martin's men aren't into shooting first and asking questions later. If they happened to catch up with her they'd have known almost immediately that she wasn't me. After all, she didn't fool you for very long, did she?"

"Not for an instant. And I imagine your friend Martin knows you a hell of a lot better than I do. At least in the biblical sense."

"I don't know why you're harping on that," Isabelle said. "Whether or not I slept with Martin Abruzzi doesn't have anything to do with the real situation."

"Really? I'd have thought a man would think twice before killing a woman he'd slept with."

"Would you?"

"Not if the woman was you." The last was bitten off, as if he regretted it the moment he said it. "Look, I didn't want to spend the morning fighting with you."

"You could have fooled me," she said, keeping her face impassive. "You don't need to be so angry with me. Becky's more than capable of taking care of herself."

"I don't give a damn about your cousin. She got herself into this mess, she can get herself out. I'm worried about the ranch. What are these men planning to do? Do we expect an all-out assault? Or can I just hope they'll kidnap you and get you out of my hair?"

"No such luck," she said, not exactly sure if she was telling the truth. Kidnapping was just the sort of thing Martin might do. Especially if he was egocentric enough to believe he could simply marry her to shut her up. "I imagine I'll have to give them what they want and hope Martin meant it when he said he wasn't planning to harm me."

"How are you going to manage that?"

"If his men have already showed up in town I imagine they'll be in touch." Her voice was laced with irony. "I may as well just wait."

"For how long? How long were you planning to stay, Izzy?"

"As long as I want. You seem to forget, Luke. I own this place."

"I haven't forgotten," he said briefly, his face impassive. "Just don't start getting any ideas."

"What about? You?"

"No. You're too smart for that. I mean about the ranch. I don't want you interfering with the way I run things. Your father left me in charge, and I, by God, am going to stay in charge."

"I guess we'll see about that," Isabelle said.

He moved so fast she wasn't expecting it. One moment she was sitting lazily in the big old chair, in another he'd yanked her out of it, towering over her in a truly impressive rage. "We won't see about anything, Izzy. Leave me well enough alone. Or you might wish you had."

"Is that a threat, Luke?" She didn't flinch. He was dangerously close, so close she could see the tiny flecks of gold in his green eyes, could smell the warmth of his skin. Suddenly she felt like she was seventeen years old again, and all she wanted to do was melt against him.

But she didn't. She was older, wiser, and she'd been rejected once too often. "Is it?"

"Not a threat. Call it a friendly warning. I don't want to hurt you, Izzy. But it might not be up to me." And on that enigmatic note he walked out of the room.

She didn't move for a moment. She looked down at her long, slender hands and realized with a sense of bemusement that she was trembling. Her heart was racing, her face felt flushed and her skin tingled all over. Hell, she wasn't seventeen, she thought in disgust. A seventeen-year-old would have at least a bit more self-control. She was acting like a young girl in the first giddy flush of puberty, and she was old enough and jaded enough to know better.

"Hey, Miss Bella." Charlie's cigarette-roughened voice broke through her abstraction. "What'd you say to Luke to put him in such a state?"

She turned and looked at him lounging in the doorway. "I don't need to say much to get him worked up."

"That's a fact," Charlie said. "Did you tell him you weren't coming to the dance?"

"Which dance?"

"Down t' Grangers'. They always have their summer barbecue and square dance this weekend. Thought you'd remember."

"It's been a while. The last time I went to one of those I was seventeen years old. It was just before Hoyt brought Luke home."

"I remember. We're all going in the pickup. Even your cousin, if she's a mind to. What about you?"

Isabelle shook her head. "I don't think so. I wasn't invited."

"Don't need no invitation to the Grangers'. Open to everyone. You know that."

"I think I'll pass this time, Charlie. Somehow I don't feel like dancing."

"Suit yourself," Charlie said. "We'll be leaving around six, if you change your mind. Or you could always drive yourself. You remember how to get there, don't you?"

"Davey Granger used to be one of my beaux," she said. "Of course I remember."

"Let me know if you change your mind."

"Not likely," she murmured. Davey Granger had some of the busiest hands in the state of Wyoming. It didn't matter that he was probably married and a father by now—the Davey Granger she'd grown up with wouldn't know the meaning of the word faithful.

And she didn't want to relive any part of that summer, or that particular night. She didn't want to stand around and watch Luke dance with every single female but her; she didn't want to remember thirteen years ago when the notorious bad boy, Luke Cassidy, had showed up at Grangers' barbecue, drunk, wild and looking for trouble.

He'd danced with her that night. He'd gone up to her, locked safely in Davey Granger's arms, and simply waited. And she'd gone to him, a move she'd regretted the rest of her life.

She'd never even spoken to him. She'd been warned away from him. None of the other girls there would even look at him, half fascinated, half terrified by his wildness and fury. But Isabelle had never been able to resist a dare, and Luke's green eyes had dared her. And she'd never been able to resist a wounded creature, and Luke's green eyes hid terrible wounds.

But if she hadn't danced with him then he wouldn't have waltzed her out behind the stables and kissed her. And she wouldn't have been surprised enough to try to push him away. Just as Davey came looking for her, and jumped to the wrong conclusion, precipitating a brawl that was probably not forgotten to this day.

Hoyt had heard about it, of course. He'd gone looking for Luke, but Luke had already left. So Hoyt went out to the ramshackle old Cassidy place the next morning, the place Luke had lived alone since his mother had run off and his drunken father had taken a final tumble down a flight of stairs.

And when he'd come back to Rancho Diablo, he'd brought Luke with him.

You'd think she'd have learned not to be so headstrong, she thought. You certainly couldn't prove it by the way her life had been going since she'd left Wyoming, culminating with her idiotic involvement with Martin Abruzzi.

But she was turning over a new leaf. She was going to be sensible, safe, levelheaded and mature. She wasn't going to the Grangers' barbecue and risk setting something unpleasant in motion. She was going to stay in her little room under the eaves, Luke's old room, and think about her sins. And if that didn't keep her busy, she'd try to call Japan and see what was keeping Mr. Takashima's corporation from putting their final offer in writing.

She spent the rest of the day avoiding people, including her so cheerful and busy Cousin Becky. It wasn't until sixthirty that hunger drove her down to the kitchen. She'd waited until she heard the old pickup drive off, the sounds of voices and laughter drifting on the night air. She decided she'd feel sorry for herself, so she went down searching for the whiskey she knew Luke kept somewhere about. She would have preferred a nice chilled chardonnay, but she could imagine the reaction if she'd asked for such a thing. Whiskey would do her just fine.

The kitchen was deserted, spotless, cleaner than anything Isabelle had seen in her entire life. Maybe that was why she didn't trust Becky, she thought. Anyone that clean had to be hiding something.

The refrigerator was full of plastic containers, all neatly labeled and dated. Isabelle hung on the door, sipping her dark glass of whiskey, and then shut it with a sigh. Her self-pity seldom took the form of eating—she was more likely to forget about food entirely when she was feeling maudlin. And right then she was feeling about as maudlin as she could get.

She heard the sound of a car with sudden foreboding. While she'd half expected Martin to show up here, she didn't know if she was in the mood to face him right now. Maybe she'd just go lock herself in Becky's closet and wait until the others got back. After all, he couldn't know for certain she was still here. Though the fire-engine-red Ferrari might just tip him off.

She peered out the kitchen door, then backed away abruptly. She didn't recognize the late-model pickup truck, but she knew it couldn't belong to anyone remotely connected to the fastidiously upscale Martin Abruzzi. She was just racing for the hallway when the back door was slammed open, and Luke stood there, filling the doorway and positively bristling with rage.

"What the hell," he snarled, "are you doing here?"

She stopped where she was, the whiskey bottle in one hand, her glass in the other, and hoped she didn't look as foolish as she felt. "Haven't you asked me that before?"

"I still haven't got a straight answer. Why aren't you at the barbecue? Didn't Charlie tell you about it?"

"He told me about it. I just didn't feel like going."

"You're going, all right," he said grimly. "People are busy enough asking questions. I don't want them thinking I have you locked up back here while your cousin sashays all over the place.''

"You never used to care what people said about you."

"I was nineteen years old. The only thing I cared about at the time was fast cars, getting drunk and getting—"

"Never mind," she interrupted him. "I get the picture."

"I imagine you do. Go upstairs and get changed. I'll wait for you." He snatched the bottle of whiskey out of her hand before she realized his intent, and she knew it would be a waste of time trying to get it back. If she reached for it, she'd end up touching him, and that was a very real danger, though she wasn't quite sure why.

"You'll wait for me?" she echoed instead. "Why, Luke, is this a date?"

"Don't count on it. Get your tail in gear, Izzy, or else."

"Or else what?"

"Or I'll dress you myself, toss you over my shoulder and dump you in the pickup."

"My, you are a savage brute," she mocked him. "Speaking of trucks, where did that fancy rig come from? How come you make the men drive that decrepit old rattletrap?"

"Because that's the only truck we can afford. The fancy rig belongs to Marcy Parker."

"Your mother-in-law," Isabelle said flatly. "Don't tell me she has an eye for you herself?"

"You're really asking for it, Izzy."

"Marcy always had an eye for a good-looking man. She's not that much older than you anyway, maybe ten years at the most. She was Cathy's stepmother, not her real mother. I bet she's just itching to take Cathy's place."

The expression in Luke's usually cool face was a combination of rage and sheepish embarrassment, the latter informing Isabelle that she'd guessed right. The knowledge didn't happen to please her. "Get your mind out of bed, Izzy. Marcy's fond of me. Besides, we're the two people who loved and miss Cathy the most. It's no wonder we'd get along well."

"You know, I'd almost forgotten you were a grieving widower." She'd gone too far. The moment the words were out of her mouth she knew it, and she didn't need to see the sudden darkening of Luke's green eyes. "I shouldn't have said that," she admitted immediately. "I'm sorry, Luke, I don't know what gets into me sometimes."

He didn't say a word for a moment, just simply stared at her with remote contempt. And then he turned away. "Five minutes, Izzy," he said, his voice flat and distant. "Or I'll come and get you myself."

HE LISTENED to her footsteps as she climbed up the creaky front steps. She was always so damned light on her feet, big as those feet were. He moved to the cupboard and poured himself a glass of whiskey, dark and neat, ignoring the adjacent sink and the water he should have added. He'd already had a couple of drinks at the Grangers', and this would put him over his limit, but he needed a drink right now, and needed it bad.

"Women," he muttered out loud, raising his glass in a mock toast. Damn Isabelle, for a thousand things, not the least of which was being right about Marcy Parker. He'd never even noticed her hovering solicitude, never noticed the heavy perfume, the too-frequent touches, the soulful expressions, until tonight. Maybe Marcy had never indulged in that sort of behavior before, but the message had been coming across loud and strong since he'd set foot on Granger property.

He knew why, too. Marcy had as good as told him. Her sole topic of conversation had been the return of the prodigal daughter, preceded by her near twin.

He didn't know how Marcy knew about his weakness. Probably Cathy had told her; Cathy had told her everything. They were more like sisters than stepmother and stepdaughter, and he knew, he just knew, that Cathy had informed Marcy about absolutely everything in their private life, up to and including his performance in bed.

And Cathy had known about Izzy. He'd always refused to discuss her with his erstwhile wife, but Cathy had known anyway. She was tuned in to things like that, and she'd known she'd never held his heart, his soul.

Not like Izzy did, damn her, with her painted fingernails wrapped around him like a claw. He had to break free of her. Thirteen years was too long to be thinking about a spoiled brat of a woman. Thirty-two years old was too old to be carrying a torch for someone like Izzy.

He drained the glass of whiskey, turning back and leaning against the counter. Hell, he could do it. He wasn't really that susceptible to her, it was just that she managed to irritate him royally every time she opened that mouth of hers.

He'd take her back to the barbecue, dump her and see if he could find a little safe entertainment in the back room. Granger's men always had a poker game going somewhere, and tonight would be no different. He'd hole up with them, and Izzy and Marcy Parker could glare at each other across the sawdust-covered dance floor.

Not that Izzy would glare. Izzy wouldn't give a damn. Not that Marcy would glare. She was too much of a lady to give in to base emotions.

And tomorrow morning he was getting Izzy out of there, and her interloping cousin with her. If he had to tell her the truth, he would. As long as he could get her out of his hair.

It was a lucky thing she no longer had the power to turn him on. A lucky thing that he was an adult, in control of his emotions, his hormones, his reactions. Izzy was like a diamondback rattler, glittering, shiny and absolutely deadly. And he was going to keep his distance.

"I'm ready." Her husky voice broke through his dark thoughts, and he lifted his head, once again cursing the fact that he never heard her coming.

He didn't move. He couldn't. She was wearing a peach sundress that should have been all wrong for her. It was too small, for one thing. The style was better suited for a seventeen-year-old. He knew that, because she'd worn it when she was seventeen years old, at the Grangers' barbecue where he'd first met her.

She filled the dress out a lot better than she had back then. Thirteen years ago she had been all coltish, long-legged beauty, and he'd been just drunk enough and just angry enough to go after her.

Now she was promise fulfilled, a warm, ripe woman who needed to be touched. But he wasn't the one to do the touching, he reminded himself, clenching his fist. And he wasn't going to let himself get drunk, or angry, again.

"Aren't you a little old for that dress?" he drawled.

She didn't flinch. She saw through him, dammit, as he'd always suspected she did. "Oh, I don't know," she said airily. "I thought it looked rather sweet on me. Anyway, why not relive the past, just a little bit? There's nothing wrong with a touch of well-placed nostalgia."

She was taunting him. "I've never seen that dress before," he said, remembering how her body had felt beneath it when he'd kissed her on the Grangers' back terrace. Wondering how her body would feel now.

"Haven't you?" she murmured, and he wanted to wipe that smile off her wide, luscious mouth. Wanted to kiss it away. "Well, some of us have better memories. Are you just going to stand there glaring at me, or are we going to the Grangers'?"

He pushed away from the sink, careful not to move too close to her. The scent of her perfume clung to her, and he had to stifle an instinctive groan. "We're going to the Grangers'," he said. "Maybe Davey will remember the dress."

## Chapter Nine

Isabelle smoothed the peach cotton skirt over her bare legs, hoping Luke wouldn't notice her hands were damp and faintly trembling. It had been sheer cussedness on her part, putting on this dress, and she was already paying for it. While he almost managed to convince her he didn't remember the dress, she was busy reliving every moment, from Davey Granger's hot, heavy eyes, to the irresistible lure of Luke Cassidy's wildness. No decent girl would be seen dead with Luke, no decent girl would dance with him, or even exchange meaningless pleasantries with him. And she'd gone beyond the barn with him, and had lived to regret it.

She glanced over at his profile as he piloted the fancy pickup to a parking spot over by the Grangers' barn. Men were silly about cars, she thought. She knew by the way his big hands held the leather-covered steering wheel, the way he shifted the gears, accelerated and braked, that he loved this flashy red pickup with an almost inhuman passion. Maybe that's where all his emotion went, she thought. Not to human beings, but to inanimate objects that wouldn't betray him, wouldn't hurt him.

And who was she to judge him anyway? She loved her Ferrari with the same intensity. It represented speed, beauty and freedom. Any time, day or night, all she had to do was climb in the elegant cockpit and race away, away from all this tangled history and frustrated emotion.

Soon, she promised herself. She had to start putting her house in order, move ahead with a clean slate, and all those other clichés. First, she had to get Martin off her back. Second, she had to bring Mr. Takashima up to scratch on the sale of Rancho Diablo. Third, and what should have been least important but was steadily looming larger and larger on the horizon, she had to get over Luke Cassidy.

If she'd been fool enough to think she had, a few days in his presence told her otherwise. Maybe her best bet would simply be to get him drunk and crawl into bed with him. Maybe one night of lovemaking would get him out of her system. After all, she'd learned that sex was a messy, overrated business. Maybe she needed to experience it with Luke to break his hold over her.

"What's that expression for?" Luke demanded, swiveling around to look at her.

She could feel the sudden warmth stain her cheeks. So much for fantasy. Much as she liked the idea of playing Mata Hari, she'd never be able to carry it off. Besides, she had the gloomy suspicion that lovemaking might not be overrated with Luke.

"What look?" she countered, reaching for the door handle, prepared to slide off the high bench seat of the truck.

He caught her arm, forestalling her departure, and she froze. She could hear the noise of the crowd, smell the wood smoke and sizzling meat from the barbecue, the hot air of summer and the scent of whiskey and perfume on the gentle wind, and she wished to God she was seventeen again.

"Like you were planning a battle."

She laughed, the spell broken, and easily pulled out of his grasp. "I am. Tell me, is Davey Granger married?"

"He just got his second divorce."

"And does his daddy still own the bank?"

"Nope. Jase Granger died three years ago. Davey owns the bank. Thinking of casting your lures in his direction? You'll find you have competition."

Isabelle flung back her mane of hair and gave Luke her sultriest smile. "I never let a little competition stand in my way. It just adds spice to the quest." She dropped down on the ground, her high-heeled sandals sinking slightly into the soft dirt.

"You're going to have to start with your cousin. Last I saw she'd draped herself over Davey."

"Why didn't you stop her?"

"Why the hell should I care?" he demanded, reaching her side and putting a steadying hand under her elbow. "She's your cousin, not mine."

"I thought the two of you might make a nice couple," she said.

His reaction was explosive and profane. "God deliver me from matchmakers. If I want a woman I'll find my own. I certainly don't want a second-rate version of you."

What about the real thing, she thought, saying nothing. I've got to get out of Wyoming before I make another major mistake, she thought, plastering a smile on her face as they turned the corner and found the teeming hordes of people who'd once been her friends and neighbors. Before it's too late.

"Bella!" A pair of strong, burly arms enveloped her, a huge wet mouth covered hers and the scent of musky after-shave swamped her nostrils. Using knees and elbows she managed to dislodge him, stumbling back for a moment and tugging her sundress up around her.

"Hi, Davey," she said somewhat breathlessly, knowing Luke would be smirking. Davey Granger had put on a good sixty pounds since she'd last seen him, most of them around his gut. He still tended toward flashy clothes, and his flushed face and slightly bloodshot eyes suggested a fondness for hard liquor.

"You look fabulous, Bella," he said, slurring slightly. "I was disappointed when I first saw you, until I realized it wasn't really you at all, but your cousin. I should have known age couldn't tarnish the incomparable Bella."

She glanced over her shoulder, wondering how Luke would react to such fulsome praise. He'd disappeared without a word.

"You look wonderful, too," she said, taking his arm in hers. "Luke tells me you're head of the bank now. I think that's terrific."

Davey's cheerful moon face suddenly looked downcast. "Luke," he said. "I wish I knew how to help him."

"Luke doesn't strike me as someone who needs anybody's help," she said, trying to keep the asperity out of her voice.

"The ranch needs an infusion of money and he doesn't have it," Davey said, grabbing two glasses from a passing waiter and downing half of his.

"It's not his problem," Isabelle said. "It's not his ranch. It belongs to me."

Davey spewed whiskey in front of him in a sudden coughing fit, catching an unsuspecting matron on her beige silk back. By the time he'd finally managed to stop choking, his pink color had turned florid red and his bloodshot eyes were bulging. "Still the same old Bella," he said obscurely. "Let me get you something to drink." And he vanished into the crowd, leaving Isabelle to stare after him in sudden consternation.

"Right glad you decided to show up, Miss Bella," Charlie muttered in her ear.

She turned to him in honest relief. "I'm not. What the hell is going on, Charlie? Where's Luke disappeared to?"

"Marcy Parker's got him cornered. He was hoping to hide out playing poker, but that woman's got more determination than a dozen others put together. Want to rescue him?"

"Not me," she said firmly. "It's only what he deserves." She let herself be drawn into a welcoming embrace and a brief conversation with an old friend before turning back to Charlie. "How long do we have to stay?"

"That's up to you. Maybe just till the dancing starts."

"I don't want to be here for the dancing," she said mutinously, glaring at the musicians as they were tuning up at the far end of the barn.

"'Fraid you'll be a wallflower? Don't worry, I'll ask you to dance," Charlie said with a chuckle.

"You've never danced in your life."

"Hell, fifty-five ain't too old to learn."

"You're sixty-nine," she corrected him absently. "And I have too much respect for my feet to subject them to torture. I'm getting out of here as soon as the music starts. Tell Luke I got a ride home."

"And how are you getting home?"

"Hitchhike."

Charlie shook his head. "He'll have my gizzard if I let you."

"When have you ever been able to stop me from doing what I want?"

"Never."

"Bella!" A good-looking man with a familiar expression in his eyes swept her into his arms. "I got dibs on the first dance," he said just as the music started. And she allowed herself one brief, furtive glance around the crowded barn before she smiled back at her partner and moved with him onto the dance floor.

There was no escape. One after another, the boys she'd known through high school appeared, some paunchy, some better looking, all of them determined to renew her acquaintance, to share a dance, a drink, a few moments of idle flirtation and memories. She was vaguely aware of a few glares from the women, including Becky as she waltzed by in Davey's arms. But Luke stayed carefully away from her, even when the perfectly preserved Marcy Parker appeared by the bar.

Her feet hurt, stuck in shoes that had been too small when she was seventeen. Her face hurt, stuck in a phony smile, trying to remember people, trying to be kind and friendly, unable to forget that these were her father's friends, Luke's friends, not hers. Her eyes hurt, searching the crowds for Luke, her heart hurt, and she didn't know why.

She was barely aware of the men she danced with. Only aware that they weren't Luke, and that they never would be. The compliments, the flirtations, blended together as she was passed from one set of strong arms to another, and she stopped paying attention, content to drift.

The band was playing "Your Cheating Heart." She'd just managed to spot Luke, over by the bar, looking bored as Becky clung to his arm and chattered at him with dauntless determination, when a new set of arms enfolded her, and soft, gentle hands touched her.

She gave her best, absent smile as she continued to stare at Luke, willing him to cut in even though she knew he'd rather eat cactus spines that dance with her, when a sudden sense of foreboding filled her. The hands were too soft for a Wyoming man, the suit beneath her cheek was too expensive, the scent too subtle. Dammit, the haircut was too perfect. She pulled back in sudden dismay, to find herself looking directly into Martin Abruzzi's flat brown eyes.

"What are you doing here?" she whispered, both furious and frightened.

"Looking for you, my little peach blossom," he said, flashing his perfect teeth. "Did you really think you could hide out from me?"

"Not particularly," she snapped. "But where there's life there's hope."

"Then we'll assume you'll continue to be hopeful."

"Is that a veiled threat?"

"Not at all. It's more in the nature of reassurance. I've told you, I don't want you dead. I simply want to negate your danger to me."

"You'll be pleased to know I've decided to give you what you want." She squirmed in his arms, but he continued to hold her just as tightly as he moved her with smooth perfection around the sawdust-littered dance floor.

"You'll marry me?"

"Hell, no. I'll give you the photographs."

"How can I be sure you haven't had copies made?"

"You could take my word for it."

"Do you think I've gotten where I am today by taking people's word for things?" Martin countered lazily. "I really don't think that's good enough."

"Well, what do you want?" she demanded irritably.

He smiled down at her. "I thought I made that more than clear. You."

"You can't want a woman who isn't interested. You'd be miserable."

"Oh, I don't know. I think I might manage to change your mind. I'm considered to be quite good in bed."

"Sorry, not interested."

"How do you know? You haven't tried it yet."

"I'm not going to." She glanced around her in sudden frustration. Why did she have to be surrounded by men who failed to understand her? Luke was finally watching her, just when she didn't want him to, his eyes narrowed and thoughtful.

"Why not?"

"Because I'm in love with someone else."

Martin grinned. "I'm not interested in love, Bella. I'm interested in sex and marriage. A business partnership."

"You don't want to marry someone who's in love with someone else."

"Why not?"

"Martin..." A sudden, brilliant thought entered her devious mind. "Martin," she began again. "Have I got a girl for you!"

"Matchmaking? No thanks, Bella."

"How about someone who looks just like me, but with a touch more larceny in her soul?" She could see she'd gotten his interest, and she persevered. "Someone with a little more laxity when it comes to matters of morality?"

"Your sense of decency and honor can be tiresome at times," Martin admitted.

"Martin, I'm talking about the person you've always wanted me to be," she said, warming to the subject. "Someone sneaky, devious and grasping. Someone properly appreciative of the finer things in life, and totally uninterested in who she has to hurt to get to them."

"Sounds like my kind of woman."

"Where are you staying?"

"Where do you think I'm staying?" he demanded with his first show of irritability. "This two-bit town has one motel."

"I'll send her to you," Bella said somewhat breathlessly. "She'll bring the photographs. The rest is up to you."

"And who is this paragon?"

"My Cousin Becky."

"Cousin, eh? You say she looks like you?"

"Close enough to be twins," she assured him.

"We'll see, Bella. I might let you off the hook after all."

The hand on her shoulder was heavy, familiar. She didn't need to turn around to know it was Luke behind her, cutting in. She turned to him with relief as Martin let her go, moving into his arms as if she belonged there. The music had shifted to another Hank Williams oldie, this time "You Win Again." She rested her head against Luke's shoulder with a sigh of pleasure, vaguely aware that she was trembling. She'd never been fool enough to underestimate Martin Abruzzi, and she had no illusions that her troubles were over. She might have found the solution to her situation, or she might have just dug herself in deeper. For now all she wanted to do was lean against Luke's body and move in time with the music.

She felt him stiffen when her head touched his shoulder, and his hands on her body were brisk and uncertain. A second later he relaxed, shifting her against him, moving with her. He felt so good against her, hard and strong and solid, warm and real. Nothing could touch her, nothing could hurt her while his arms were around her. She danced with him, as she'd danced with him so long ago, and nothing else existed, not the curious eyes of her neighbors, not the past, not the future.

"Was that your mobster?" he whispered in her ear.

She was too relaxed even to answer, but she forced herself to. "How did you guess?"

"He stands out like a sore thumb. Is he going to have you killed?" The question was casual, just vaguely curious.

"I don't think so. I bribed him."

"With what?"

"Becky," she murmured lazily.

She could feel the sudden start beneath her, then the shaking of silent laughter. "Izzy," he said, "you are incorrigible."

"I try," she said, giving in to temptation and nuzzling against his shoulder.

Night had fallen. He danced her through the broad double doors at the end of the barn, out onto the terrace. The stars were bright overhead, the Tetons jagged spikes in the distance, surrounding them with protective menace. Other couples had taken advantage of the night air, other couples were dancing, closely, whispering.

But Luke was no longer dancing. He stopped, moving her far enough away so that he could look down in her face. "I want you to leave, Izzy," he said, so softly she almost couldn't hear him.

She didn't need to look around her to know they were in the same spot they'd been when he'd first kissed her. The Grangers had fixed everything up, made it all neat and clean and citified, but the back of a barn still remained the back of a barn. She looked up into his green eyes, and they were still wild and mad and hungry, as they'd been thirteen years ago. "Why?" she asked, quite clearly.

"Because if you wait much longer I won't be able to let you go," he said quite simply. And then he kissed her.

He laced his long fingers through her thick mane of hair and pulled her face up to his. His mouth slanted across hers, purposeful, demanding and tasting of whiskey. She put her hands on his wrists, maybe to pull him away, but she found she'd tipped her head back beneath his, and opened her mouth to him.

She'd never been kissed like that before. Not with such passion, such raw hunger, such expertise. He seemed to know just how to touch her, just how to move his lips over hers, how to entice her with the rough presence of his tongue, how to demand a response that she would have thought she'd be too wary to give.

She heard a faint whisper of helpless desire, and knew it came from the back of her throat. She heard a moan of anger and longing, and knew it came from him. The stars were dazzling overhead, and then she closed her eyes, giving herself up to the magic of his mouth.

A moment later he released her, pulling back, wiping his arm across his mouth, a dazed, furious expression on his face. The crowded terrace was now deserted.

He was swaying slightly, and Isabelle realized with belated regret that he was drunk. "I guess we drove everyone away," she said lightly, not moving. "At least it's better than last time. No one's come out to defend my honor."

"I guess they don't think there's anything worth defending." The harsh words fell between them like knives.

"Well," Isabelle said after catching her breath from the sharpness of the pain. "I guess that's the end of that. Just tell me one thing, Luke. If you despise me so much, why do you want to kiss me?"

"Because I had too much to drink."

"That's it?"

"That's it," he said flatly. "Now you can answer me one thing."

"Of course," she said with studied politeness.

"If you despise me, why did you kiss me back?"

"Oh, I always liked kissing," she said blithely.

Something in her tone of voice caught his notice. "You always liked kissing," he echoed. "What the hell does that mean? Is that all you like?"

Hell and damnation, Isabelle thought, backing away into the shadows, hoping her expression would be hidden. "No, Luke. I'd also like to see you take a little visit to Morris Draper's."

He laughed then, a harsh sound in the night air. "You want me to visit the local gelder? Hell, lady, you've already done his job for him." And without another word he walked away, back into the barn, leaving her alone in the warm night air.

IN THE END she didn't need to hitchhike. When Isabelle skirted the barn, heading toward the parking lot, she ran smack dab into her Cousin Becky. The feel of Luke's mouth on hers was still too strong in her memory, the imprint of his hands still lingered. She cast a brief, curious glance at Becky's furtive expression, and then dismissed it.

"What are you doing out here?" she asked.

"I thought I might see if I could find a ride home. I've got a headache." She was clutching an overly large handbag, one that didn't match the ruffled pink dress she'd deemed suitable for a barn dance.

"Come on. We'll find Charlie and have him take us."

"What about Luke?"

"I don't want to run into Luke right now," Isabelle said flatly. "I've seen enough of him for one day."

"Your makeup's smudged."

"I'm not wearing any."

Becky's mouth dropped open. "Don't be ridiculous. Of course you are. Your eyelashes can't be that color naturally."

"Luckily for me, they are. If my makeup looks smudged it's because I'm sick and tired of everything around here."

"Me included?" Becky suggested with a smug smile. "Don't worry, I don't intend to hang around much longer. As soon as I find a way out of here I'll be long gone."

Isabelle's mood lightened a bit. "Speaking of which," she said softly, "there's a man I want you to meet."

## Chapter Ten

Isabelle ducked her head under the feather pillow, trying to shut out the early-morning sunlight spearing through her brain. It was no use. Somehow or other her unquestionable talent for sleeping until noon had vanished, maybe with the enforced regimen of the meditation center, maybe with the fresh mountain air of Wyoming. Either way, she hadn't slept past seven o'clock in the five days since she'd been back at Rancho Diablo, and it was usually closer to six when she dragged her weary body out of bed.

This morning was no different. She squinted at her watch, groaned at the five forty-seven in green liquid crystal and swung her feet onto the old pine floor.

The old ranch house was still and silent, but the smell of coffee wafting up through the open window assured her that at least one person was already up and about. She sincerely doubted that person was Becky. For all her saintly housewife act, Becky was as devoted to sleeping late as Isabelle had been. Besides, she seemed more than ready to cut her losses. There was nothing for her to gain at Rancho Diablo, and no need for her to continue trying to impress anyone with her industriousness.

And it couldn't be Luke. She didn't even know if he'd made it home last night, and she didn't care. Maybe Marcy Parker finally got what she wanted from him, maybe he'd spent the night on someone's couch. It was none of her business. And if he had made it home he'd be so hung over he wouldn't show his face until noon.

She pulled on her jeans and an old T-shirt, ran a brush through her hair and headed downstairs. She'd taken a long shower last night before going to bed, in the vain hope that she might wash the taste of Luke from her mouth, wash the feel of his hands from her body. It hadn't done a speck of good, and repeating the experience would be a waste of time. Time was one commodity she didn't care to waste. She wanted to grab her coffee and something for breakfast and be out of there before either of her two housemates appeared to ruin her appetite and her tentative feeling of optimism.

The kitchen was deserted. Whoever had made the coffee had already drained one cup of it, leaving the empty mug sitting on the scarred wooden counter. Isabelle peered out the window into the yard, but no one was in sight. Probably Charlie, she thought, with more optimism than real hope.

For the first time in days she was hungry. More than hungry, absolutely famished, enough so that she was going to do the unthinkable. Sipping at her strong black coffee, she started prowling through the refrigerator, pulling out milk, eggs and butter. She was actually going to attempt to cook something.

At least she'd have no witnesses to her debacle. She was entirely capable of eating anything she put together, no matter how ghastly. She'd had years of experience, living with her own lack of culinary skills, and she'd grown inured to it. Right then she she had an absolute craving for something warm and fresh from the oven.

Muffins couldn't be that hard. There were some blueberries in the freezer—surely with a little care she could whip up something akin to those big fluffy muffins she found in Boston delis.

It took her a while to find a cookbook. Apparently most of the cooking done at Rancho Diablo was accomplished through trial and error, but Isabelle had more than enough experience with her own trials and errors to know she couldn't rely on common sense.

Lighting the old gas oven was an experiment in terror, one that singed her eyebrows and took ten years off her life. Finding the ingredients was equally challenging, but by the time she'd beaten the muffin dough within an inch of its life, poured in the frozen blueberries and watched everything turn a purplish-green, she was feeling reasonably optimistic. She even remembered to butter the old iron muffin pan before filling it to the top, and as she poured herself another cup of coffee and prepared to await her first cooking triumph she was feeling very pleased with herself.

"What are you doing up so early?" Luke's voice broke through her temporary smugness, wiping it away.

She waited long enough to take another sip of coffee. "Waiting for breakfast to cook. What are you doing up?"

"I never went to bed," he said, and he looked it. He headed into the kitchen, directly to the coffeepot, and refilled the abandoned mug. "We've got a problem with one of the horses."

She'd been about to come out with a nasty crack about his probable evening's activities, but that shut her up quite effectively. "What's wrong?"

"Old age, basically. She hasn't been much good for the past few years, but she hasn't been in any pain, and I haven't wanted to put her down. I guess it's being taken out of my hands."

"Poor old thing," Isabelle said.

"What the hell do you care?" he snarled. "You haven't even cared enough to see her."

Isabelle held herself very still. "What are you talking about? Why should I go visit one of your horses? I mean, I know they're actually all my horses, but nevertheless..."

"Don't start on me!" he roared. "I've had too damned much in the past twenty-four hours, and I don't want to start on who owns this place or not. A great horse is dying, one with more heart and soul than most of the horses I've ever known, and there's nothing I can do but watch. And I'm not about to stand around arguing with a coldhearted witch who doesn't give a damn about a horse who used to mean more to her than just about anything else. A woman who's so self-centered she couldn't even be bothered..."

"Shut up!" Isabelle shrieked, desperate to stop his torrent of words. "Are you telling me it's Crescent?"

"Who the hell else would it be? Where are you going?"

But she was already gone, racing across the packed dirt of the corral in her bare feet, half-blinded by tears, running straight to the west barn that she'd avoided so assiduously.

Crescent was already down, her sides scarcely moving, her eye dimmed and closing. Through her tears Isabelle recognized Doc Martin, his head bowed. After close to forty years in practice Doc still hated to see an animal die.

Isabelle sank to her knees beside Crescent, her hands gentle on the old mare's side. "Poor baby," she crooned softly. "I didn't know you were here. I thought you'd gone long ago, and I couldn't stand the thought of coming in here and finding you gone."

Crescent's eye opened, and for a moment she lifted her weary head, greeting Isabelle with a soft whirrup of pleasure. And then her huge body shuddered in pain, and she dropped her head back down again.

"She's right glad you came to see her, Miss Bella," Charlie said from somewhere behind her. "It's eased her. Best come along now."

Doc had moved toward his back, a bleak expression on his face, one that Isabelle had seen before. "No," she said, not moving. "There must be something you can do for her..."

"She's twenty-three years old, Bella," Doc said. "She's got pneumonia, and she's not responding to any antibiotics. She's choking to death, and the only thing I can do is help her along."

"No," she said, her voice raw with tears. "I want to be with her..."

Two strong hands reached behind her, hauling her up unceremoniously. "You can't do anything more, Izzy," Luke said gently. "She knows you were here, and that's enough."

"I don't want to leave her..."

Luke ignored her protests, dragging her away from the stall. "You'll only make it harder for everyone, Crescent included. You don't need to put yourself through all this." They were out in the blinding sunlight, and Isabelle yanked her arm out of his iron grasp.

"You're not going to take her away from me," she said, half-wild with pain and denial. "You already took everything else, you can't take Crescent from me, you can't, you..."

"It's not up to me, dammit," he said. "She's old and she's dying. She's..."

A sudden, high-pitched whinny broke the early-morning air. Isabelle held herself very still, trying to control the shudders that were threatening to shake her apart. A moment later Doc appeared in the shadowed doorway of the north barn. "She's gone," he said in a rough voice. "Damned fine horse."

She wanted to run, but she couldn't move. She wanted to shriek and rage and moan, but her mouth was still. She wanted to cry, but suddenly her tears were gone, leaving nothing but a dry, desperate ache inside her. An ache so deep nothing could heal it.

Doc moved off, his shoulders bowed, and a moment later the sound of his pickup broke the unnatural stillness. Charlie appeared from the barn, followed closely by the two wranglers. "Miss Bella," he said gruffly, "I'm real sorry..."

"Get out of here, Charlie," Luke said softly, still not moving, his green eyes never leaving Isabelle's pale face.

She heard the start of protest, and then it faded, and the men headed toward the ranch house kitchen, leaving the two of them standing alone in the bright morning sunlight.

"You didn't know she was still alive," he said, a statement, not a question.

She forced herself to speak. "Of course I didn't. Don't you think I would have been out here sooner...?"

"You were always afraid of horses."

"I was afraid of riding. Not the horses themselves. Crescent was one of the sweetest, gentlest creatures on God's earth. She wouldn't have hurt anyone." Her voice wavered, then strengthened. "Dammit, why did it have to happen now?" She could feel her mouth tremble, and she bit down on her lip, hard, trying to force the anguish back inside.

And then it was no longer her choice. He reached out and pulled her into his arms, tucking her against his warm, hard body, and she was too surprised to protest. Suddenly the dam of tears broke, and she began to sob, harsh, ugly sobs, all over his clean, dry shirt.

"Let go of it, Izzy," he murmured in her ear, his hands unconscionably gentle. "If you don't it'll eat you up inside."

She didn't know whether he was talking about Crescent, or talking about all the pain and anger she'd been swallowing for almost half her lifetime. She didn't care. All that mattered was the heart beating steadily beneath her, the arms holding her, the comfort, as she cried out her sorrow and misery.

It was a long time before her tears began to fade. A long time before she realized, with sudden shock, that she was standing in Luke Cassidy's arms, receiving a comfort she'd never accepted from a human being in her entire life. She pulled away quickly, rubbing her forearms across her tear-blotched face, and managed what she hoped would pass for an ironic smile.

"Sorry," she said. "That won't happen again."

"No," Luke said gravely. "I suppose it won't. You coming in for breakfast? I think you could do with something to eat."

"I don't really...oh, my heavens, the muffins," she gasped, breaking away from him and heading for the kitchen door at a dead run.

The men were sitting around the table. Becky was there, looking pert and charming in a gingham apron, looking far more like the incomparable Bella than Isabelle did. There was just the faintest suggestion of a smirk on her mouth as she set out a plate of small, dark pellets in front of the dubious-looking men.

"Bella made muffins," she said. "Usually she knows better than to try cooking, but I imagine she was still hung over from last night."

"Shut up, Becky," Isabelle said, sinking down on one hard chair and taking the cup of coffee Charlie passed her. The other two men eyed her with wary sympathy, young Jimmy managing a shy smile. That sympathy almost set her off again, if it weren't for the smarmy expression on her cousin's face.

"My, my, aren't you testy today?" Becky chided. She looked up as Luke appeared in the doorway. "Luke," she said, that husky note still sounding impossibly phony, "I've made your favorite for breakfast. Blueberry muffins. Sit down beside me and have some." And to Isabelle's mingled shame and horror she whisked out a plate of huge, beautiful muffins that looked and smelled even better than anything she'd ever seen in a bakery.

Becky plopped herself down beside Luke's chair at the head of the table, all gracious-lady-of-the-manor, and waited for Luke to join her. A dead silence reigned, one that even penetrated Becky's armored self-involvement.

Without a word Luke took the straight-back chair beside Isabelle, spun it around and straddled it, too close for Isabelle's comfort. With silent accord the men passed him his coffee, their eyes moving from Becky to Isabelle to Luke, waiting.

"Heavens." Becky laughed, her discomfiture apparent. "I thought you had a craving for blueberry muffins, Bella. It had to be something pretty desperate to get you to cook. I thought you'd appreciate my making them for you."

"I'm sure she does," Luke drawled, reaching his long arm across the table, reaching for one of the blackened little pellets that had once been Isabelle's muffins. He buttered it lavishly, ate it in one bite without flinching, and reached for another.

Without a word Charlie followed suit, ignoring Becky's plate, reaching for the disasters with obvious relish. Johnson and Jimmy did the same, and if the room was filled with a crunching noise not quite in keeping with muffins, somehow no one felt like laughing.

"Well," said Becky, reaching for the untouched plate of perfect muffins. "I gather there's a lesson to be learned in all of this, but I have no idea what it is."

"Some people learn faster than others," Luke drawled, draining his coffee and pushing back from the table. "We got work to do, men."

"Yeah, we've got to get rid of...that is, we've got to see about...er..." Jimmy started blushing.

"That's all right, Jimmy," Isabelle said softly. "I lived on a ranch long enough to accept the facts of life. Dead horses are difficult to get rid of."

"Did a horse die?" Becky asked brightly.

"Crescent," Isabelle said briefly.

"Oh, you had me worried," Becky said. "I was afraid it was part of the breeding stock. I know what a disaster that can be. That old mare wasn't good for anything but eating her head off. You're better off without her."

"That old mare—" Johnson, who seldom spoke, broke his own unwritten rule "—had more heart, more bottom, than a skinny, spoiled little brat like you ever dreamed of. She gave birth to some of the best horses in this county, and she deserved to spend as long as she damned pleased eating her head off." Throwing down his napkin, he stormed out of the kitchen, slamming the door behind him.

The other men followed, each of them stopping long enough to place a comforting hand on Isabelle's shoulder. When it was Luke's turn she stiffened, wondering if he was going to touch her again, with Becky watching out of narrowed, hostile eyes, or if he was simply going to move off.

To her surprise he rumpled her hair, in a gesture both friendly and endearingly tender. And then he left them, and Isabelle was too much of a coward to turn and watch him go.

"So that's the way of it, is it?" Becky inquired silkily. "I should have seen it coming. But for some reason I believed you. I really believed you were innocent enough to think Luke and I could make a match of it."

"I did..."

"Then you're not as clever as I always thought you were. But then, this entire episode has been most illuminating. You're not at all what I thought you were, Bella. To me you were always glamorous, in control, able to manipulate things to your own advantage, time after time after time. Hell, I even let you manipulate me. But you're not nearly as ruthless as you had me believe. Beneath that haughty exterior you're just a scared little girl. No match for me at all."

"Why should I be a match for you?"

Becky shook her hair. "I don't know. I always thought I had to compete with you. Now I know it's just a waste of time. You don't have anything I want. You don't realize that now, but you will soon enough." She rose from the table, taking her plate of muffins and dumping them in the trash. "I'm out of here. I've cooled my heels long enough in this one-horse town."

"You're leaving?"

"That's what I said, isn't it?"

"Would you do me a favor before you go?" Isabelle asked. "Drop something off for me?"

"Why should I?"

"Because it'll be to your advantage."

"Why should I believe you? You got me out here promising that it would be just what I needed, and where did it get me?"

"It got you out of Vermont when they were getting ready to arrest you. You really did embezzle that money, didn't you?"

Becky smiled. It was the smile of a cat who'd just caught a particularly juicy mouse, and once again Isabelle wondered how she could have been so naive. How she could have thought Becky was shy and innocent.

"Do I really even have to answer that?" she purred. "The damnable thing is, my partner really did run off with the money. I can't get my hands on it, or him."

"I know someone who can help you."

"And I've got some swamp land in Florida I can sell you."

"I mean it, Becky. Martin Abruzzi can take care of your little problems. He has the experience and the manpower to handle such things. He'll want a sizeable cut, of course, but half of something is a sight better than all of nothing."

"How come you know someone with that sort of expertise?" Becky demanded suspiciously.

"Let's just say I got involved with the wrong crowd. I've decided to return something to Martin and hope he'll let bygones be bygones. But I need a courier."

"And you want me to be that courier? Forget it."

"He was at the barbecue last night, Becky. He was the man in the perfect suit who danced with me just before we left."

Becky was already halfway out the room, but she stopped. "The one who was followed everywhere by two goons? I thought he was a politician or an evangelist."

"He's a gangster, Becky. Almost the same thing."

Becky stepped back into the room. "This is beginning to sound interesting. Where is he now?"

"At the Blue Moon Motel. All you have to do is show up there with the papers I'm going to give you. After that it's up to you. But I imagine he'll be so pleased to get what I'm sending that he'll be more than amenable to any business suggestion you might offer."

"He was very handsome," Becky mused out loud.

"Un-huh," Isabelle agreed.

"Is he any good in bed?"

"I wouldn't know. I expect so. Or at least he's generous enough so that women don't complain."

"Generous?" Becky's contact-lensed eyes lit up.

"Where do you think I got my Ferrari?"

"And you didn't even sleep with him?"

Isabelle shrugged. "Chances are I only would have gotten a Corvette if I'd gone to bed with him. He liked the chase."

For a moment Becky didn't move. Then she nodded, a short, succinct motion. "I'll do it. Bring the stuff to my room in an hour and I'll be ready."

"Just like that?"

"Just like that. Don't tell me you don't appreciate it. This way you'll be able to crawl into Luke's bed without any distractions."

"I'm not going to..."

"Sure you are, Bella. You're just too naive and stupid to know that. For all your sophisticated exterior you have the soul of a seventeen-year-old."

Isabelle watched her go, absorbing the casual cruelty, the devastating honesty of Becky's parting words. Much as she wanted to deny it, she knew she couldn't. Deep in her heart she was still a miserable, lovesick teenager, at least where Luke was concerned. She might as well face it, she wasn't going to get over him. Her only alternative was to get away from him.

Her hands were trembling, probably the result of three cups of wickedly strong black coffee and nothing to eat. She put the mug down, and looked at the plate of muffins. There were two blackened pellets left, and even half a pound of butter wasn't going to make them palatable, particularly without an audience to appreciate her sacrifice.

"To hell with honor," she said out loud, rising from the table. A moment later she was fishing muffins out of the trash, dusting off the coffee grounds and biting into one with blissful appreciation. At least Becky had one redeeming feature. The woman could cook.

Maybe, she thought, she could make more of an effort. Maybe in the past few days remaining, before Mr. Takashima made his final offer, she could manage to improve on her cooking skills. After all, if the men could make such a sacrifice, all for the sake of a woman who scarcely deserved it, then she could at least find a way to repay them. Particularly when she was about to put them out of a job.

No, that wouldn't happen, she reminded herself. Mr. Takashima's offer had to include the written guarantee that everyone would be kept on at equal or better than their current wages. She wasn't betraying the men who'd just championed her. She was helping them. Wasn't she?

Suddenly the muffin didn't taste so good. She dropped it back in the trash, covering the evidence with an empty carton of milk. The sooner she was out of here, the better, she thought for the hundredth time. She was getting as soft, as naive, as Becky had accused her of being.

By the end of the day she'd have Martin off her back and Becky long gone. Maybe things were looking up after all. All she had left to do was wait for Mr. Takashima and find that long-lost diary. If she could just manage to remember that things were going pretty darned well...

If it weren't for Crescent. If it weren't for the way Luke had held her, gently, when her heart was breaking. If it weren't for the fact that no matter what she did to destroy Rancho Diablo, no matter how far she ran or how fast, she was never going to escape. Not for the rest of her life.

# Chapter Eleven

Becky was as good as her word, at least for once in her life. Within an hour she was gone, the incriminating photographs tucked in her Hermes leather handbag, and, as Isabelle later discovered, she also had with her Hoyt's silver cigarette lighter, Isabelle's gold necklace, several pieces of jewelry she'd found on a dressing table at the Grangers' and an unspecified amount of cash lifted from every possible source she could find, including neglected purses at last night's barbecue, Luke's bedside table and even Charlie's stash underneath the sagging bunk.

Isabelle stood on the back porch, watching her drive away in the elegant black Lincoln, Vito's impassive figure at the wheel. That had been a last-minute inspiration on her part, calling Martin up and asking for transportation. It had worked on several levels. For one thing, she hadn't had to drive Becky herself, or risk lending her the Ferrari or one of the decrepit ranch vehicles. There was no telling if they'd ever see them again.

For another, it was the carrot in front of the horse. A taste of the finer things Martin might be enticed into providing, and a not-so-subtle warning, in the person of Vito's stolid persona, that she hadn't better get any ideas about using those photographs to her own advantage. Isabelle had sealed the package tightly, but she no longer had illusions about her sweet, shy cousin. Becky would have the package neatly opened in a matter of minutes.

More power to her, Isabelle thought, leaning one hip on the railing and watching as the black car disappeared in a cloud of dust. She'd need all the edge she could get if she was going up against someone like Martin. For a brief moment Isabelle wondered whether she'd been dangerously manipulative. Was she sending Becky into a dangerous situation, all because she liked to arrange people's lives?

No, Becky was going of her own accord, and Becky could hold her own quite nicely. The two of them would make a perfect couple, much better suited than Luke and Becky. Luke needed another wife like Cathy, someone shy and quiet and housewifely. Someone who'd adore him, someone who knew how to make blueberry muffins.

Not, however, Marcy Parker.

She pushed herself away from the railing, heading back into the spotless kitchen. Becky was gone. It was past time she started making her own plans, too.

The office was cool and dark, even at midday, and the leather seat molded itself to her body like an old friend. She rested her head back against it for a moment, thinking of the years that chair had cradled Hoyt, the years Luke had sat there. It had even belonged to her grandfather—a chair with more history in it than most people had in their entire lives. Mr. Takashima would probably replace it with something new and pneumatic.

She stared at the old black telephone on the littered desk. The same telephone, with its antique dial. She used to sneak in here and call her boyfriends on that telephone, when Hoyt wasn't around. At least, she had until Luke had moved in, and she hadn't been able to think of anyone else.

She leaned forward and picked up the heavy telephone, pulling it closer to her, and for a moment tried to think of someone she could call. Surely in thirteen years she must have met a man she could call and flirt with.

She couldn't think of a one. Her few relationships had been brief and unsatisfying, and there wasn't a single human being she wanted to turn to. She was trapped, just as surely as she had been when she was seventeen, and she had no options but to run, as fast and as far as she had back then.

She stared at the black phone for a long moment, then began dialing. It took her half an hour to reach Mr. Takashima's personal secretary. The Japanese, she'd learned, were amazingly polite but astonishingly inflexible. Even the industrious Mr. Takashima wasn't at work at four-thirty in the morning, and wasn't expected in for another two hours. Would she care to leave a number?

She wouldn't care to. The thought of Luke answering the phone sent chills down her spine. She was about to arrange a time to call back when she heard a telltale footstep outside the door.

"Who were you calling?" Luke pushed his Stetson back on his head and leaned against the doorjamb.

"My therapist," she said.

"I believe it. Why did you hang up so quickly?"

"I didn't want you to overhear all my girlish secrets."

"You don't have any from me," he said, moving into the room and dropping down into the chair opposite her.

"That's a horrifying thought."

He smiled briefly, dumping the hat on the floor and running his big hands through his slicked-back blond hair. "Enough to keep you awake at night," he agreed. "Where's Betty Crocker?"

"Becky? She's gone."

He straightened in the chair, his green eyes narrowing. "Don't toy with me, Izzy. Has she really left?"

"For good."

"Well, this day isn't a complete loss after all," he said, lounging back.

It took all of Isabelle's self-control to keep her eyes riveted on his left shoulder, rather than the faded, body-hugging jeans, the flat stomach, the somber, sensual face. "Why did you hate her so much?" she asked, letting her curiosity get the better of her. "I thought the two of you would make a perfect couple. She could be a sweet little housewife, cook you muffins and wear little aprons, and you could be the big, strong man of the family."

"When are you going to learn not to interfere in other people's lives?" he asked lazily. "I'd think you might try to get your own life in a little better shape before trying to rearrange mine. Unless you think there's a connection?"

She kept her face impassive, ignoring the painful truth of that barb. "I just like to see people happy," she replied. "You haven't answered my question. What do you have against Becky? It seems to me you would have been perfect together."

"For one thing, Becky was a lying, sneaking, thieving little cheat. She was phony through and through, and anyone with any sense could have seen that a mile away."

"I didn't see it."

"That's my point. You saw what you wanted to see, not the truth. A long-term failing on your part, Izzy. You have trouble seeing things for what they really are." He leaned forward, across the desk, and she had no choice but to meet his gaze. "For another thing, even if Becky had been the perfect little hausfrau she pretended to be, she wasn't what I wanted. I'm not in the market for gingham and muffins and sweet domesticity."

"What are you in the market for? Marcy Parker?" The moment the words were out of her mouth she could have bitten her tongue. She sounded like a jealous teenager. She sounded like what she was.

She was unprepared for his reaction. For one of the first times since she'd returned home, his eyes crinkled in amusement, and his wide, sexy mouth curved in a smile completely devoid of mockery. "No," he said, and nothing more.

Like a fool she didn't know when to leave things well enough alone. "Why don't you want sweet domesticity? Weren't you happy with Cathy?"

The humor left him, abruptly, his green eyes turned hard as emeralds and his mouth turned into a thin, angry line. "That's none of your damned business."

"No, I suppose it isn't," she admitted, hating to apologize. She left it at that. "What's for lunch?"

"Speaking of sweet domesticity? I was about to ask you the same question." The tense moment had passed, at least for now.

"Why ask me? Just because I wasn't stuck with an extra $Y$ chromosome doesn't mean I have any talent in the kitchen."

"Amen to that. I ate one of your muffins this morning."

"You ate two of my muffins," she corrected him. "Are you seriously asking me to do something about meals?"

"No," he said. "On second thought, you can be on permanent dishwashing detail, and the men can take care of the cooking chores. You might think twice about packing Becky off."

"Missing her already?"

"I'd live on a diet of your moose pellets rather than have her back here," he said devoutly. "You still haven't told me how you got rid of her."

"I found the perfect man for her."

Luke's response was short but obscene. "Which means she'll be turning up like the bad penny she is."

"I doubt it. I sent her off with Martin. I think they'll be perfect together. Neither of them have any scruples, morals or anything else that would stop them from getting exactly what they want out of life."

He didn't move for a moment. His mouth twitched, and then he exploded in laughter. "You, Izzy Romney, are downright evil," he said finally, wiping his eyes.

"It seemed perfectly logical. Besides, he wanted me. I thought Becky would be the next best thing."

"Is that why you sent her to me?"

"Don't be absurd, Luke. We both know perfectly well that you never wanted me. You made that clear on several occasions."

"So I did."

She didn't want to have this conversation. "So with any luck I will have engineered at least one happy ending."

"Just don't start interfering in my lovelife. I can manage my own happy endings just fine."

"Can you?" The words hung between them, an almost tangible reminder of all that lay unanswered. She couldn't look at him anymore, and instead her eyes dropped down to the messy desk, to the jumble of papers that made little sense to her untrained eyes. She had the sudden, uncontrollable urge to confront him, to tell him what she'd planned behind his back. She didn't need to feel guilty about selling the ranch. He'd stolen her father from her, he'd stolen the ranch from her in fact, if not in the full legal sense of the word. But for some reason she wanted to confess, to make him understand what she was doing, what she needed to do, for her own future.

"What is it, Izzy?" Luke demanded suddenly, leaning forward.

She backed off, suddenly frightened. "What do you mean?"

"You were about to tell me something. What is it?"

"I wasn't about to tell you a thing," she denied it instantly. "Except maybe to suggest you can go to..." The shrill old-fashioned ring of the telephone broke through her uncharitable suggestion, and she stared at the phone with disconcerted enmity.

"You want to answer that?" Luke drawled lazily. "Since you seem to have coopted my desk, you might as well take the phone calls, too."

Warily she reached for the receiver, her voice huskier than normal when she said, "Hello?"

"Mr. Takashima calling for Ms. Isabelle Romney," a clipped voice greeted her. Mr. Takashima's too-efficient assistant had clearly not only awakened his boss, but somehow managed to trace her phone call. Or maybe it was simple guesswork—the phone number of the ranch was listed if anyone cared to try information.

"Wrong number," Isabelle barked, slamming down the receiver and fixing Luke with a guileless smile.

He didn't smile back. "Who was it?"

"You heard me. Wrong number." To her horror the phone rang again, its shrill insistence like razor blades on her nerves. Luke reached for it this time, but she got it ahead of time, her voice shaky.

"Mr. Takashima calling for Ms. Romney," that damnably efficient voice said again.

"Wrong number," Isabelle said again. "If you don't stop bothering me I'll call the police." This time when she slammed the phone down she yanked at the cord.

It pulled from the phone with a dying jangle, leaving bare, multicolored wires exposed. Isabelle stared at it foolishly, wondering what Luke's reaction would be.

"That wasn't a modular phone," he said mildly enough. "Don't you think you were overreacting?"

"It was an obscene phone call."

"I thought you said it was a wrong number."

"It was both."

"How do you know? Maybe the obscene call was meant for you. You have some pretty odd friends."

"Not that odd. It was probably Marcy Parker."

"You have a thing about Marcy Parker, don't you? What has she ever done to you?"

"Absolutely nothing," Isabelle said, wishing she'd learn to keep her mouth shut. In the distance they could hear the kitchen phone ring.

Her eyes met Luke's, blue eyes into green, and once more she was tempted to confess. "I bet you want me to let it ring."

"Yes." She knew there was a horrible pleading note in her voice, she knew that Luke Cassidy would never consider doing a blessed thing for her sake. But still she asked.

Together they sat there, listening to the phone ring, half a dozen times or more. "Okay," he said finally. "On one condition."

"What is it?" she asked warily.

"That you tell me about it. On your own terms. Before you leave here, you tell me what you were about to tell me. And what it has to do with that phone call. Don't bother denying it. Just promise."

It was easy enough to do. Though in the long run she'd be happier just running out once more and letting the banks and the lawyers do the dirty work, she knew this was one time she had to face up to things. "I promise."

He nodded, rising. "Then maybe you might consider clearing out and letting me get some work done. Unless you've decided to take over the bookkeeping."

"You think I couldn't?"

"I hope you'd do a better job than you do of cooking. Scratch that. You have to do a better job than you do cooking. Nevertheless, I don't want you messing with the ranch accounts."

Their fragile, tentative moment of amity vanished abruptly. "Why not? What have you got to hide?"

His very stillness reminded her of a wild animal, one ready to strike out in utter fury. "Is that why you're here, Izzy? I haven't been sending you enough, and you want to see whether I'm skimming money from the top?"

"The checks are smaller," she pointed out, refusing to back down.

She'd managed to push him too far this time. He was out of his chair in a flash, grabbing her across the desk and pulling her halfway across the litter of papers. Sheaves of them fell to the floor, the telephone tumbled over with a noisy crash and Luke's angry green eyes glittered into hers.

"You're hurting me," she said quietly. His big hands were like vices around her upper arms, and his anger would have been awe inspiring indeed if she weren't certain that he wouldn't really hurt her. That his self-control was too absolute to allow him to give in to temptation, either in rage or desire.

He released her, abruptly, and she sank back to her knees on top of the desk, the accounts in a welter around her. He flexed his hands for a moment, as if forcing the tension out of them, and he met her wary expression with a grim smile.

"Izzy, you're enough to drive a saint to murder."

"You're no saint." She didn't move. She was afraid to. Afraid of what would happen if he put his hands on her again. Afraid, not of pain, but of moving past a point of no return. Things were bad enough, but if he knew his power over her she'd be totally, eternally lost.

She felt his eyes brush her tremulous mouth, down to her heaving chest beneath the cotton T-shirt, then back up. "Don't look at me like that," he said roughly. "I'm not going to beat you."

"What are you going to do?" She was level with him, eye to eye, mouth to mouth, chest to chest, and only inches away from him. If she had any sense at all she'd scramble back off the old oak desk, away from him, away from temptation.

But when in her life had she ever shown any sense?

"What am I going to do?" he echoed, watching her out of hooded eyes. "I haven't made up my mind yet. Maybe just keep as far away from you as I can." And without another word he walked toward the door, leaving her kneeling on the desk, waiting for him.

The telephone was out of reach, but there was a heavy brass vase full of dead flowers, no doubt a lingering example of Becky's domesticity, near at hand. Without pausing to think, Isabelle grabbed it and hurled it at Luke's head with full force.

It missed, of course. It clanged against the side of the door, rolled across the floor and ended in a sodden mess of dead flowers, brackish water and dented brass under the window.

"What the hell was that for?" Luke thundered.

"Target practice."

This time it worked. This time she'd finally pushed him far enough, and now she was regretting it. She was halfway off the desk when he caught her, and his hands were hard as iron as he hauled her up against his chest.

For a moment she went with the fear, the sudden panic, that swept over her as she felt the fierce anger vibrating through him. She struggled, trying to push away, but it made no difference at all.

"You should have told me you were into kinky little tricks, Izzy," he growled in her ear. "I would have been more than happy to oblige."

"Luke, let go of..." Her words were swallowed as his mouth covered hers, hard and painfully. He pulled her against him, roughly, his hips against hers, and she could feel the undeniable evidence that she'd somehow managed to arouse him. His mouth was too hard, and she felt her lip split beneath them, and to her shame and horror tears filled her eyes.

"Is this what you like, Izzy?" he demanded breathlessly, his mouth inches from hers.

"Luke..."

He wasn't listening. He kissed her again, hard, and she no longer struggled. The more she fought him the more he seemed to think she wanted it. And she found herself wondering whether she was willing to take him this way, if it was the only way she could have him.

She didn't have to make that choice. With a shocking suddenness, he released her, so that she fell back against the desk, banging her hip, and his eyes were shuttered and unreadable as they swept down her undoubtedly pale face, her trembling, swollen mouth and her tear-filled eyes.

She knew she should say something. Something dramatic and prosaic, along the lines of "How dare you!" But she knew very well how he dared. She'd egged him on, and had only herself to blame for the less than comfortable results.

He reached out a hand, and she flinched away from him, but he wouldn't let her dodge him. His rough fingertips touched her cheek, and came away wet with tears.

He took a deep, shuddering breath. "Damn you, Izzy," he murmured. "Why do you make me so crazy?"

There was no answer she could make to that. She stood, silent and unmoving, as he reached out and touched her again, touched her mouth, and this time his fingers held a drop of blood from her cut lip.

His eyes never left hers. He brought his hand back, touching his own mouth, placing the drop of blood on his own lip. She stared at him, mesmerized, aching for him to touch her again, this time gently, this time with love.

Instead he whirled around and headed for the door. "I'll be back tomorrow," he said gruffly. "Charlie'll know where to find me." And he slammed the door behind him.

It had been so long since anyone had bothered trying to close the office door that the wood was warped. The door lodged about three quarters of the way closed. Isabelle stared at it stupidly, not moving, until she heard the distant sound of the decrepit pickup truck starting up. She reached a shaking hand to touch her mouth, but when she brought it away the blood was gone.

LUKE DROVE like a madman. At least he could be glad of one thing—he wasn't likely to run into some fool tourist this time of year. They didn't tend to wander too far off the beaten track anyway. They were probably congregating around Jackson Hole and Yellowstone, and if any of them were daring enough to wander up this way they wouldn't get much farther than the tiny town of Devil's Fork.

He'd trust any other Wyoming-born native to be able to get out of his way when he was in a mood like this. Not that the ancient pickup had enough power to give vent to his rage and frustration, not to mention his overpowering self-disgust. Even on a flat stretch the old speedometer needle only managed to inch its way up toward sixty, and he was bound and determined to drive ninety.

Of course, if he pushed it even further it might mean the end of a faithful old vehicle he couldn't afford to replace. Slowly, carefully, he edged his booted foot off the gas pedal that had long ago lost its rubber covering, letting the truck settle down to a sedate forty-five. He should know better than to take out his temper on inanimate objects.

Hell, he should know better than to take out his temper on that most animated object of all, Izzy Romney. He knew perfectly well he'd been just looking for a reason to touch her, to kiss her. Damn, he wanted an excuse to do more than that. She was like a fire in his veins—he doubted if half an hour passed each day without him thinking about her, aching for her. And she'd goaded him beyond bearing, practically accusing him of stealing from her. He'd either had to kiss her to shut her up, or tell her the truth. Somehow kissing her had seemed far more sensible.

But that didn't excuse the fact that he'd hurt her. He'd frightened her. He'd used his brute strength and his sexual attraction to her to overpower her, and he didn't like to see his stalwart Izzy overpowered.

Hell, who was he fooling? She wasn't his Izzy, and she never would be. He'd known that from almost the beginning. Once Hoyt put his trust in him, he couldn't betray that trust. And once Hoyt had made his decision, a decision that couldn't be reasoned with, Luke had known it had ended any possibility of a future with her. He hadn't

# Chapter Twelve

Isabelle offered to make the men dinner, but they all responded with unflattering haste, assuring her they could manage for themselves. It was just as well, she thought, sitting on the back porch in the late-evening twilight. She'd made do with a mixing bowl of Cheerios, and probably ate better than anything more traditional she could have concocted. She'd brought Fannie Farmer out on the porch with her, and everything sounded positively heavenly, and absurdly easy.

But she knew what liars cookbooks are, and she knew it took a lot more than a flick of the wrist to perfect an omelet. If she was going to stay, at least for a while longer, then she'd have to make a foray into town and see what passed for a supermarket in Devil's Fork. Surely even rural Wyoming came equipped with gourmet frozen dinners.

A soft breeze had come up, tossing her shower-damp hair around her face, ruffling her ankle-length cotton nightgown. Becky had left behind all her gingham-and-lace outfits, and Isabelle had moved them into her room without a second thought, heartily glad to be out of her slightly outgrown teenage wardrobe. Maybe if she stopped dressing like a seventeen-year-old she'd stop feeling like one.

She hadn't gone so far as to move into the big upstairs bedroom, despite its closet space and comfortable double bed. Even though nothing of her father remained, it still seemed as if it was his room. Besides, she wasn't going to be there that much longer.

The moment she'd had Charlie's assurance that Luke really wouldn't be back until morning, she'd tried to call Mr. Takashima back. As fate would have it, she'd had no luck whatsoever, and when she finally got through to the complex corporation she found that both Mr. Takashima and his assistant had left for overseas, and weren't expected back for several weeks.

Isabelle had had to content herself with the hopeful belief that he was on his way to the States to put his offer in writing. She'd been careful not to appear too eager, in the hope of having him raise his ante, but she could no longer afford such niceties. She needed the sale to go through, and quickly. Before she suffered anything as suicidal as second thoughts.

She'd been sipping at Luke's bottle of Jack Daniels, hoping the liquor might help her get a better night's sleep than she'd enjoyed since she'd been there. She might even sleep past six in the morning. After all, she was going to be blissfully alone in the house—she didn't need to worry about Luke prowling around downstairs.

A streak of lightning split the sky, one of many, and Isabelle forced herself to view it with a sanguine air. She'd never been crazy about thunderstorms. As a kid she used to crawl into bed with her mother, cuddling with her as the storms shook the mountains around her. As an adult she'd learned to ride the storms herself, knowing there was no one to hide with, no one to hold her and comfort her.

Except for Luke, that morning, she thought. She hadn't turned to Luke, he'd simply overridden her objections and given her the comfort she'd needed so desperately and been unable to ask for. The loss of Crescent, who'd already been mourned for years, was a wound she didn't care to examine too closely. As far as she could see, life had a habit of doing that to her. Taking what she loved once, and then ripping it away again.

Luke had taken her father's love, then death had taken him completely, even after she'd already lost him. Every time she thought she'd let go of Luke, there was some new twist, some new pain tearing her apart. What she had to learn to do was take what she needed and get away from Wyoming, from old memories that wouldn't stop hurting. And she had to stop worrying about what Luke was going to think when he found out what she'd done.

She'd promised she'd tell him herself, but she'd broken promises in the past. This was one she might have to break, if she was going to get away with any part of her composure intact. She'd been dealing with Luke from a distance for years. She could deal with his rage easily enough over the telephone. As long as he wasn't in touching distance.

The first fat, cool drops of rain splatted onto the dirt in front of the porch. Isabelle watched it lazily, secure under the porch roof. It was going to be quite a blow—the wind had picked up, swirling the dust across the yard before the rain began to tamp it down. The temperature had dropped suddenly, and Isabelle shivered, hugging her bare arms. She'd had more whiskey than she was used to, and there was nothing to stay awake for. She might as well head up for bed, and hope to God she didn't dream about Luke.

"HELL'S BELLS," Luke muttered as rain splattered him directly in the eye. He sat up, cursing even more fluently, and shoved his sleeping bag down. Wouldn't you know it, the one night he decided to go up into the mountains, away from everyone, and sleep out in the cool night air, would be the night nature decided to have one hell of a thunderstorm.

It was raining with a vengeance. He crawled into the cab of the pickup, dragging his sleeping bag with him, and slammed the door behind him, glowering at the sodden landscape, illuminated all too well with the frequent strikes of lightning. He'd been hoping it was just heat lightning, but he should have known better. He'd lived all thirty-two years of his life in these mountains. But he'd held out, just in case he was wrong.

He could always sleep in the cab of the pickup. He'd done it before, though not in half a dozen years. It smelled of horse manure and sweat, and it was too damned short for a man well over six feet tall. If he didn't find somewhere better to sleep he'd end up grumpier and more ready to fly off the handle than when he'd started, and he didn't want to risk that.

That left several options. He could go find a motel. Considering that the nearest motel was at least thirty miles away, over rain-washed roads, and that he really didn't fancy shelling out thirty bucks or more for a bed when there were plenty of free ones around, he found that the least appealing alternative.

He could head back to the ranch and bunk in with the men. He could just imagine the questions he'd run up against if he did that, none of which he was in any mood to answer. Scratch that alternative.

Or he could go back to Marcy Parker's. He certainly had a welcome there—Izzy was right. He'd just been too absorbed to notice that Marcy's affection wasn't strictly that of a mother-in-law.

Sliding down the sagging bench seat of the old Ford, he thought back to this afternoon's uncomfortable little scene. He hadn't been in a particularly good mood after storming away from Rancho Diablo. He kept seeing Izzy staring at him, tears in her eyes, blood on her lip. And he kept remembering how he felt, dismayed, guilty and wanting the smallest excuse to keep going, to push her down on that cluttered desk and take her there and then, burying his aching flesh inside her, listening to her cries and whispers and knowing they were just for him, feeling her tight around him, taking everything from him and giving it all back again.

"Damn," he muttered, shifting his long legs. He certainly didn't need anything else to add to his physical discomfort in this cramped pickup, and fantasizing about Izzy's long, strong legs was doing just that.

Thinking about Marcy Parker should cool him off, he thought with a wry smile in the darkness. He'd headed straight over to the Parker place, and right now he couldn't even figure out why. Maybe because he'd gotten used to thinking of Marcy as someone he could turn to for sympathy and conversation when he was feeling bedeviled. Maybe because he knew nothing would bother Izzy more than to think of him over there. And maybe, just maybe, he wanted to prove to himself that Izzy's suspicions were crazy.

Whatever his tangled reasons, it had been a major mistake. He'd found Marcy in the living room of her suburban-style ranch house, curled up on a sofa with a fat novel, and the expression on her carefully made-up face when she'd first seen him had been naked with longing.

She'd covered it quickly enough. And there was no way he could run out of there, as he desperately wanted to. So he sat, and drank a beer with her. And all he could think of was Izzy.

"I expect Bella's been giving you a hard time," Marcy had said in her cool, pleasant voice.

He'd laughed. "How'd you guess? The crazed expression in my eyes?"

"You and Bella have a history of fighting. It doesn't seem as if she'd changed much in the past...what is it, fifteen years?"

"What about me?" he demanded, affronted.

"Oh, you've changed," she said with an intimate little laugh. "You're a mature, attractive man, the kind who knows what he wants and sets about getting it. I just wondered whether there might not be a little bit of the wild Cassidy boy left inside. The one who was determined to be just as wild, just as bad, as everyone said he was. The one who set his sights on Bella Romney when she was a high-spirited virgin used to getting everything she wanted, used to having all the young boys eating out of her hand. You weren't going to eat out of anyone's hand, and you set out to prove that by going after Bella."

"You have a good memory," he said gruffly. "Better than mine."

"I was older. And more observant. You were involved in the fray, I was beyond it. Besides, I knew my stepdaughter had a terrible crush on you. I got to hear all the details."

"There weren't any details. I kissed Isabelle at the Grangers' cookout, Davey and I got into one hell of a fight and Hoyt came looking for me the next day with an offer I couldn't refuse."

"And that offer included keeping your hands off Bella? We always wondered."

"The whole county wondered," Luke said bitterly. "They underestimated Hoyt, and they underestimated me. No one had ever given me a chance in my entire life. Hoyt did. He trusted me. He didn't have to tell me to keep away from Izzy. I wouldn't have gone near her if my life depended on it.''

"Why did Bella run away when she was seventeen?"

He drained his beer, rising from the sofa, aching to be away from this inquisition, from a history he didn't want to remember and certainly didn't want to share. "She was sick of living in the back of beyond. She's a girl who likes bright lights and big cities and fancy living, didn't you know that? Wyoming was no more than a starting place for her."

"You really believe that?" Marcy swung her tanned legs off the sofa, onto the tiled floor, and her eyes were shrewd. "Cathy didn't think so."

"Marcy, I don't want to talk about Cathy," Luke said, somewhat desperately. "I've got to get going. Thanks for the beer..."

"She thought you were in love with Isabelle," Marcy said ruthlessly. "She thought Bella ran away because of a fight between the two of you, and that you never got over it. That you married her because you had to, but you always really loved Isabelle."

He forced himself to face her. "I'm sorry she felt that way. She knew when we got married that there were no illusions between us. We'd made a mistake, and we got caught. I tried to be the best husband I could to her. Maybe if we'd had more time, things would have worked out."

"I don't think so. Not if you were in love with someone else. Were you, Luke? Are you?"

He paused. "Are you asking for Cathy, Marcy? Or are you asking for you?"

The faint color that stained her high cheekbones was flattering. "I hadn't realized that you noticed. Or did Isabelle point it out to you?" He said nothing, and she gave a jerky little nod. "I'm not surprised. Women recognize these things. That's how Cathy knew you were still in love with her. That's how I knew Bella was still obsessed by you. She's no good for you, Luke," Marcy said earnestly, moving closer. "You said it yourself, she doesn't belong here. She's just passing through, and this is your home. It's your life, it's in your blood. You could no more pack up and follow her than you could fly to the moon. And she couldn't settle down here, you know that as well as I do."

He turned and walked out, not wanting to hear another word, but her voice carried as he reached the carefully planted courtyard. "You need to get over your teenage infatuation, Luke," she called. "A real woman is waiting for you. Don't take too long."

Just remembering that uncomfortable conversation made him squirm once more in the crowded cab of the old pickup. The damnable thing was, he'd lost a friend. He'd counted on Marcy for innumerable things, for undemanding friendship and advice, things he'd given in return.

That was changed now, changed forever. Another thing he could chalk up to Isabelle Romney's list of sins. If she didn't get out of Wyoming soon, things might never get back to normal.

The rain was sluicing down the cracked windshield, sliding in sheets off the faded sides of the old pickup. Luke made a desultory search of the glove compartment, hoping against hope he'd find an abandoned pack of cigarettes. He hadn't smoked in five years, but Izzy was more than enough to drive him back to it. Once she was finally gone he'd quit again. Though right now he felt like crawling into a bottle and staying there for a while.

He wondered what she had up her sleeve. Charlie thought she was going to try to sell the ranch, but he couldn't believe it of her. She had some standards, she had to. She couldn't sell her birthright away, never mind that it was no longer hers. She didn't know that. As far as she was concerned, she reaped the profits of the ranch without having to do a damned lick of work. She wouldn't turn around and shaft all those who labored for her.

And, of course, she wouldn't get very far if she tried. He'd tried to reason with Hoyt about the will—indeed, he thought he had. He didn't find out until it was too late that Hoyt had every intention of doing what he thought was right and fair. And if his idea of right and fair included what amounted to disinheriting his absentee daughter, he wasn't going to be alive to hear about it.

Luke just hoped Izzy never had to find out about it. If she'd just go back to where she came from, he'd do what he could to increase her checks. He didn't trust her to sign papers without reading them first, so he couldn't sell off some of the stocks that provided her income, enough to give her a bigger stake. Still, one good year and profits would increase. They desperately needed a new, bigger pickup, but maybe Jimmy could manage to keep this thing going with spit and barbed wire for a little bit longer. Just until things smoothed out a bit.

She'd be leaving pretty soon. It didn't sound as if she had to worry about her gangster anymore—she'd provided him with a willing sacrifice. He imagined Becky and the darkly formal Martin would live happily ever after. They certainly deserved each other.

So Izzy had no other reason to stay, apart from a monetary one. Somehow or other he'd come up with money enough to get rid of her. If things really hit rock bottom he'd even sink low enough to hit Charlie up for his life savings. Charlie had offered them often enough, and Luke had steadfastly refused. But he was getting to the point where there wasn't anything he wouldn't do, to get rid of Izzy and find some point of normalcy in a once contented life.

There were no cigarettes anywhere in the cab of the pickup, and he drew the line at raiding Johnson's forgotten stash of chewing tobacco. The rain wasn't going to stop, and he sure wasn't going to head to a motel, or back out into the downpour, or spend the night in the truck.

He turned the key, listening to the engine cough and sputter like an ancient tuberculosis victim. When it finally caught, he spun the wheels in the mud as he started up, back toward the ranch. Izzy would be sound asleep—she'd never even know that he'd come back in the middle of the night. Hell, he had no reason to feel guilty about it.

Because when it came right down to it, even though she didn't realize the fact, the ranch didn't belong to her at all. It belonged to him, lock, stock and barrel. He just hoped to God he wouldn't have to tell her that.

ISABELLE SAT bolt upright in bed. That last crash of thunder had ripped her from a troubled sleep, and she found she was covered with a light film of sweat, her hands trembling, her heart pounding beneath the thin cotton nightgown.

The two glasses of whiskey hadn't done what she'd intended. She'd been hoping for oblivion, for an impenetrable mist to cloud her brain, to keep her happily asleep till midmorning. Instead she'd been tormented by nightmares, erotic ones, terrifying ones, until waking had been, in retrospect, a relief.

Lightning illuminated the room briefly, then plunged it back into darkness. She remembered another night, long ago, when she lay curled up in her bed, watching the storm and writing in her diary. She could even remember what she was writing. Nauseating teenage twaddle about how much she loved Luke.

Damn, she'd almost forgotten that diary. If she was going to make her escape, and she had every intention of doing so as soon as possible, she'd leave with a great deal more equanimity knowing that there was no chance of Luke running across such an embarrassing, incriminating document.

Not that she had any intention of keeping it. Or reading it, and relieving those tortured, adolescent emotions. She was going to destroy it, without glancing at a single word. Burn it, and maybe at the same time burn away any lingering feelings for a man who was no good for her at all.

She wasn't going to sleep, at least not for a while. It was half past two in the morning, and she felt wide-awake. Probably because she'd fallen asleep not much after nine. There had been many, many nights in the past when she'd managed on five or less hours of sleep. If she managed to snatch another few hours toward dawn she'd consider herself lucky.

In the meantime, the house was hers, for the first time. No nosy, devious cousin lurking in the corners. No intimidating figure cropping up when she least wanted to see him. If she couldn't find that damned diary by morning then at least she could rest assured that neither would Luke.

She left Luke's bedroom for last. Even though she knew he was miles away, probably with Marcy Parker, she didn't like the idea of wandering in there in her thin cotton nightgown. It didn't matter that the room had been hers, far longer than the amount of time since he'd coopted it. It didn't matter that it was the most logical place she would have left the diary, it didn't matter that no one would see her, no one would know. She didn't want to go in there.

In the end she had no choice. He'd left the windows open, and rain splattered through onto the floor, and the aging curtains flapped wetly in the wind. The air smelled fresh and damp, full of ozone, and she took a deep lungful. She'd smelled that scent before, in odd places and at odd times, and she'd always been able to place it. It smelled like Wyoming. It smelled like home.

She turned on the bedside lamp, glad that the bedroom faced away from the bunkhouse. She didn't want to risk any of the men waking up and seeing a light in Luke's room. They might fancy a middle of the night talk, and she didn't want to start thinking up excuses.

She took a good look around her. It looked very different than when she lived there. Hoyt had indulged her every whim, and her bedroom had reflected it. She'd had a matched set of white-and-gold French Empire furniture, the finest Cheyenne, Wyoming, could offer. She'd had pink chintz ruffles on the bed, on the windows, she'd had a fluffy white rug on the floor and she'd had a collection of dolls and stuffed animals that she hadn't really wanted but Hoyt kept adding to every year anyway.

It was a man's room now. For a moment Isabelle wondered whether Cathy had ever shared such an austere place. If she had, all traces of a woman's occupancy had been wiped clean. The rag rugs on the rough pine floor were serviceable but not particularly attractive, the curtains flapping wetly in the breeze were plain muslin and the walls were unadorned. Not even a picture of Hoyt, she thought grimly. The furniture was sparse—an old pine dresser, a rocking chair and the bed.

She really didn't want to look at the bed. It was huge, unavoidable. Had Luke shared it with pretty little Cathy? Who else had slept in it?

The sheets were plain white, the quilt that covered it had been made by her grandmother. When she left she might very well take that quilt. It didn't seem fair that Luke should sleep beneath her grandmother's handiwork, while Isabelle made do with a thin cotton blanket.

She pulled her eyes away from the bed, dropped to her knees on the floor and pulled back the rag rug. To the casual observer the floorboard looked no different from its neighbors. It took her a few minutes to pry it up, and with it came a relieving amount of ground-in dirt. No one had touched it in at least a decade, probably more. And beneath the loose floorboard, in the shoe box she'd left long ago, lay her diary, and a withered flower she'd almost forgotten about.

She pulled the shoe box up, sinking back against the bed with mixed emotions. She picked up the rose first, watching as the dried petals crumpled in her hand, dropping down onto her lap. The thorns were still there, she realized, feeling a sharp point pierce her thumb. How symbolic of her entire life, she thought. The flowers faded and died, but the pain remained.

She'd worn that rose in her hair the night Luke had kissed her at Granger's barbecue. It had fallen to the ground when he'd held her head still for his hot, demanding mouth, and in the ensuing melee she'd rescued it, treasured it. It didn't make any sense to hold on to a flower she'd given herself. But the faded smell of pink roses had always reminded her of Luke, and probably always would.

She picked up the old leather diary and opened it, knowing she'd sworn she'd never do such a thing, unable to resist. The storm had grown wilder, noisier, outside, the wind had picked up with a vengeance and the windows rattled in their casement.

She ought to get up and close them, she thought absently, as the wind blew a light mist across her shoulders. In a moment, she promised, looking at her own childish scrawl and remembering all that gut-wrenching misery. Remembering the intense pleasure-pain of it.

The next clap of thunder was close, too close. The house shuddered in protest, the lights blinked and then went off, and the room was plunged into darkness, with Isabelle sitting on the floor of Luke's bedroom, clutching her old diary. She didn't move for a moment. With any luck the lights would come right back on again, and she wouldn't have to hassle with finding candles and matches, with replacing that floorboard in the darkness and making her way back upstairs to her tiny bedroom. She waited, her heart pounding, her senses alert.

She saw the glow of the lantern from a distance, filtering from the hallway. She watched its approach, paralyzed with emotions she couldn't begin to define. She wasn't alone in the house, hadn't been.

It was probably Charlie, coming to check and make sure she was all right. Or maybe it was Becky, her flight with Martin aborted for some reason.

But she knew who it was going to be, even before he stepped inside the door to his bedroom and stopped short. He'd shed his boots, and his blond hair glistened from the downpour. He held an old oil lantern in his hand, and she was clearly the last person he'd expected to see. For a moment he didn't move, and in the lamplight his face was dark, even brutal.

And then he kicked the door shut behind them, closing them in together.

## Chapter Thirteen

"What are you doing here?" Luke's voice was low, even, as he set the lantern down on the old dresser. Isabelle couldn't answer. The bed was at her back, unavoidable, the tightly shut door ahead of her, with Luke in between. Inside something else sizzled, and Isabelle was awash with a panic that had nothing to do with the fear.

He stripped off his wet shirt and dropped it on the rocking chair, advancing toward her slowly. She sat motionless, watching him. He wasn't the wiry teenager she remembered. His shoulders were broader, his chest wider and he had hair now, not too much, across his chest, tapering down his flat stomach, curling blond hair, and she wondered how it would feel beneath her fingers. Beneath her mouth.

He stopped in front of her, and still she didn't move. Reaching down, he took the diary out of her limp hands. "What's this?"

She surged upward, grabbing for it, but she came within the circle of his arms, and as he held the book out of her reach she had no choice but to put her arms around him, straining for it.

She came smack up against his naked chest. Barefoot, she wasn't as tall as she'd thought she was. Her eyes were level with his throat, and she could see the pulse beating beneath the tanned skin, beating fast.

"Let go of me," she said quietly, keeping her eyes trained on his throat, his chest, refusing to meet his steady gaze.

"I'm not touching you," he said. "Yet."

She looked up at him, her eyes meeting his. His eyes were smoky and unreadable in the shadowy darkness. He smelled of fresh rain and warm flesh and heat, and she felt like a wild bird, mesmerized by a predator.

"Better run," Luke whispered, dipping his head down. "While you still can." And his mouth brushed hers.

He'd never kissed her like that. Gently, enticingly, with a kiss that could coax her soul out of her. His lips nibbled at hers, softly, teasing them open, his tongue following, running along the edge of her teeth, past them, taking possession of her mouth with a gentle patience and the sure knowledge that she was his.

She made a little sound in the back of her throat, one of fear, one of surrender, one of a desire that she couldn't even begin to comprehend. His hands reached out and caught her arms as they lay limp at her side, and he pulled them around his waist, around his hot, damp skin, as he deepened the kiss.

When he finally lifted his head he was breathing deeply, and she found she was clutching him tightly, afraid to let go for fear he'd stop, walk away from her as he had too many times, afraid she might fall. "No panic?" he whispered. "No running away from what you're too scared to face?"

She tried to speak, but couldn't. He knew her too well. She wanted to run. She'd wanted this, dreamed about this, for so long she was afraid of having it come true. She was afraid of him, afraid of the disappointment that would follow, afraid that she'd disappoint him.

"No running away," she said, her voice nothing more than a breath of sound.

He didn't smile. His eyes searched her face, looking for a lie. Whatever he saw there must have satisfied him, for he nodded, and his strong arms reached under her, scooping her up and laying her down on the big bed, following her down with unexpected grace.

The storm had abated, leaving only the steady beat of rain. The oil lamp was turned low, the pool of light barely reaching the bed. She lay on her back, her thick blond hair spread out around her, and knew a moment's panic. She'd agreed to this, and now she wasn't sure what to do next. What he expected of her, what he wanted of her.

He loomed over her in the shadows, and his big, tough hand was surprisingly gentle as he reached for the tiny buttons that ran down the front of her nightgown. He undid every one, slowly, carefully, leaving the nightgown still pulled chastely around her, and then he touched her chin, forcing her to look up at him.

"You don't have to look so worried," he murmured. "There's no way this is going to live up to our anticipations. Just relax and enjoy it. I'm not going to hurt you."

"I know that." She clenched her fists. "I just...don't know what you want."

He took one fist in his hand and kissed it, forcing the fingers open. "I want what you want," he whispered against her palm. And then he placed her hand against his chest, against the hot skin with its rough covering of hair.

It felt so good to her, the feel of his body beneath her hand. He lay back, letting her touch him, letting her accustom herself to the heat and textures of his body, and with sudden boldness she moved over him, pressing her mouth against his stomach, trailing light, nibbling kisses against his skin.

Her thick curtain of hair flowed over them, and his hands cupped her head, long fingers threading through the silky strands. He didn't push her, didn't hold her, but the hands on her hair was more a gentle request than a demand.

She moved down and kissed him through his jeans, rubbing her cheek against the thick, turgid length of him, brave enough with that barrier of denim between them. And then that barrier was no protection, it was frustration, and she reached for the button, the zipper, wanting to release him.

His hands covered hers, stopping her, pushing her over on her back with gentle force. Her unbuttoned nightgown fell open, exposing her pale body in the dim lamplight, and his hands followed, cupping the sensitive swell of her breasts, the rough-textured fingers learning her, arousing her. She flinched, her nipples unbearably tender, and he gentled his touch, so lightly that she thought she might explode.

She wanted his mouth on her breasts. She wanted to feel him pull and take from her, she wanted to give him everything she had and more. She wanted to merge with him, to cease to exist as an entity at all.

He kissed her mouth, taking his time to thoroughly learn the contours of her. He kissed her throat, the pulse hammering wildly, the cords and tendons of her neck. He kissed her shoulders, her hands, the soft insides of her elbows. And he kissed her breasts, lightly, worshipfully, playing with her until she was ready to cry out. And then his lips fastened on her, drawing her deep into his mouth, and she did, a tiny little shriek of reaction that she felt at her very core.

He pulled the nightgown from underneath her, dropping it on the floor. He pushed the covers from the bed, stretching her out on the pristine white sheet, and she found she was trembling, her hand shaking as she touched his sweat-slick shoulders, clinging to him as he suckled her other breast.

Every muscle in his body was like iron, tense and straining. She didn't dare reach for him again, not when he'd pushed her hands away, but she wanted to. She wanted to touch and feel him, to know him before he became a part of her. But she didn't know how to tell him.

His hands slid down her body, across her smooth, flat belly, her rounded hips, down her legs and then back up again. She closed her legs against him, more out of instinct than denial.

He brushed his long fingers against the tightly budded curls protecting her. He lifted his head, and his eyes were glittering in the lamplight, and her breast was damp and cool in the night air. "Open for me, Izzy," he whispered, his voice little more than a rasp of sound. "Do it."

She couldn't deny him anything, certainly nothing that she wanted so badly herself. She forced herself to relax, and his hand found her, with a sureness and deftness she'd only fantasized about.

She arched off the bed in sudden reaction, and her whole body felt aflame with longing. "That's it," he murmured approvingly, and she barely heard his words. She reached for his shoulders, clutching him, trying to pull him over to her, into her, desire and desperation fighting for control.

He shucked himself out of his jeans, kicking them onto the floor with everything else, and waited for her to touch him. When she didn't, he took her hand, running it down his taut body until she reached his pulsing maleness. She tried to pull back, but he wouldn't let her escape, closing her fingers around him, not releasing her until she'd accepted it, touching him with wonder and ever-growing arousal. She mimicked the action he'd shown her, listening to his groan of delight with a burning delight of her own. He reached into the bedside table for something, but she wasn't paying much attention. A moment later he'd handed her a silver foil packet.

She knew what he wanted. And while the idea sent shivers of desire through her, she hadn't the faintest idea of how to go about it. Her hands were trembling so much she couldn't even tear the packet open, and he took it back from her with a growl that was part laughter, part frustration.

She fell back against the cool sheets, and a moment later he was looming over her, spreading her legs with his big hands, lifting her hips, resting against her, hot, pulsing and heavy. She shut her eyes, waiting, but he made no move, and she opened them again, wide with wanting.

"That's it," he murmured. "I don't want there to be any mistake about who you're in bed with." He pushed against her, and her last moment of panic came and went, so quickly it was no more than a shadow.

One that he didn't miss. "Relax," he said. "I'm not going to hurt you."

He was wrong, but he didn't realize that. She reached up and clutched his shoulders, bracing herself as he moved, deep inside her, and by the time he was in fully she was panting slightly, wondering how long it would take her to accustom herself to such an invasion. She held herself very still, waiting for the pain to subside, waiting for him to finish what he'd started, but he simply held himself deep inside her, supporting the rest of his weight on his elbows, his eyes dark and troubled as they searched her face.

"Are you all right?"

She realized with sudden horror that if she said no, if she gave him any hint that she was feeling anything other than blissful joy, he'd pull away from her. And that would have been a devastation so complete that she might never recover.

But she couldn't lie to him. He'd see through that, too. Instead she simply pulled him down against her, kissing him full on the mouth, with desperation and love and a helpless longing that she couldn't quite understand.

He reached down and caught her legs, wrapping them around his narrow hips. And then he began to move, slowly, carefully, as if he knew she was still getting used to him. And then discomfort began to recede, replaced by a burning spiral of desire. She clung to him tightly, with her arms, her legs, her body, wanting to absorb him into her very pores. She followed his lead, a willing pupil, mimicking his advance and retreat, until she felt him tremble in her arms as his iron control began to slip.

She wanted that control gone. When he tried to pull back, to slow down the headlong pace, she simply tightened around him, until he had no choice.

He was shivering in her arms, covered with a fine film of sweat, and his hands left her hips to cup her face. His mouth covered hers, drinking hungrily, and then his body went rigid, arching against hers, as he gave himself to her, completely.

She held him tightly, cradling him, and never in her life had she felt so alive, so vibrant. He was hers, totally, at least for this lost moment in time, and nothing had ever come this close to heaven.

He collapsed in her arms, and very gently she stroked his face, trailing gentle little kisses against his temple. She didn't want to let him go when he started to withdraw from her, but she did, snuggling down in the bed with a sigh of pure pleasure.

He sat up, turning to look at her, and if his expression was disturbed it was too dark for her to tell. He reached out and touched her face, gently, and she snuggled against it like a contented kitten.

He moved back, leaning over her, kissing her gently, and she opened her sleepy eyes, smiling up at him. "That was wonderful," she said with a sigh. "The best."

"I wasn't looking for compliments," he said, his voice troubled.

"I know. I just wanted to tell you," she murmured, rubbing her cheek against his. And then her eyes opened, focusing momentarily. "You're not leaving?"

"I'm just going to wash up," he said gently. "I'll be right back."

"All right." She snuggled down again, entirely at ease. She could feel him staring at her for a long moment, but she wasn't worried. Nothing in her life had ever felt so glorious, never had she felt so wonderful. She couldn't dredge up even a moment's worth of worry. She couldn't even manage to stay awake.

There was a chill, wet breeze sweeping through the bedroom when Luke climbed back into bed. He was tempted to close the windows, then decided against it. The damp fresh air felt too good to shut away. He needed all the help he could get, to make things clear in his own tangled brain.

She woke for a moment when he slid in next to her, smiling up at him with that innocent expression he'd never thought to see on her face. When he tucked the big quilt around her and brushed her long, tangled hair out of her face she'd simply sighed happily, and he wanted to shake her awake and demand some answers.

But he didn't. She wasn't using a pillow, so he piled them up against the head of the bed and leaned against them, wishing he had a cigarette. And it wasn't a post-coital smoke he needed. It was a work-through-a-contradictory-and-confusing-situation cigarette he longed for.

He looked at the pink leather book on the floor, the one he'd dropped when the alternative had been to hold on to her. It didn't take much imagination to guess that it was Izzy's diary from long ago. He could probably pick it up without wakening her, and he'd left the oil lamp burning with enough light that he could probably manage to read it without too much eyestrain. It might answer a lot of questions that had haunted him for too many years.

But he wasn't going to do that. He had a certain code of honor, one that he couldn't betray no matter how much it suited him. That code had come to him from Hoyt, and it was stronger than if it had been inborn. He wasn't going to contravene it at this point in his life.

Besides, the past had suddenly become a lot less important. What mattered more was the tangled contradictions that made up the woman sleeping so peacefully in his bed.

He never would have thought of his Izzy as an innocent. But that was exactly what she was. What had she said a few days ago, that she'd always enjoyed kissing? He'd picked up on her odd emphasis, the suggestion that that was all she'd enjoyed.

She really hadn't known what to do in bed with him. She'd followed his lead willingly enough, and her body had made it more than clear that she'd wanted him, and wanted him fiercely. There were certain things a woman simply couldn't fake.

But she hadn't known what to do with the condom. She hadn't really known what to do with his body. She hadn't been a virgin, but she'd been so tight that for a moment he'd been horribly afraid that she was. Whatever her sexual experience, it had been brief and unsatisfactory. She hadn't been lying about her pleasure at the end. She really had had the most pleasurable lovemaking of her life, and she hadn't been anywhere close to an orgasm.

It had been too late for him to do anything about it when he realized she was operating on an entirely different level. When he'd fantasized about Izzy he'd concentrated more on his own reactions, not on the kind of partner she'd be. If he'd thought about it at all, the fantasy Izzy had been some fabulously talented woman who only existed to satisfy his sexual whims.

The real Izzy was a different issue altogether. He looked down at her, sleeping so trustingly beside him, and shook his head. He'd thought going to bed with the wanton Izzy would have gotten rid of his obsession. Instead he found himself in bed with a sleeping beauty who didn't even realize what she was missing. And if he'd ever hoped making love to her would have lessened her hold on him, he knew now it had just the opposite effect. He was tied to her, on a more visceral level, than he had ever imagined.

Dammit, he wanted her again. And this time, he wanted her with him, not a passive recipient of his passion, but a willing, active partner. He wanted to watch her eyes widen with shock when he made her explode. He wanted to see her body convulse and dissolve. He wanted to feel her pleasure and fulfillment.

The oil lamp flickered and went out. The room was plunged into a velvety darkness, one that covered a multitude of secrets, a multitude of sins. Luke slid down in the bed, moving next to Izzy's sleeping body, and very carefully wrapped himself around her.

Her sweet little rear was tucked up against his renewed hardness, her long hair tickled his nose and her breathing was deep and even. He slid his arms under hers, stroking her gently, noting with satisfaction how her nipples hardened at his light touch, how her flesh seemed to warm beneath his.

He kissed the back of her neck, under her jaw, behind her ear, as his hand moved down, over her flat stomach, between her legs, to find her.

She quivered, jerking awake, but he held her still, feeling no qualms as he kept her captive, his long fingers tracing deft, intricate patterns at the damp, heated center of her femininity.

He felt her breathing quicken, her heart begin to pound. He felt the tension ripple through her, and he knew he should release her, give her some choice in the matter. But he wasn't going to. He increased the pressure, touching her with just the right amount of force, his fingers delving deep inside her, and she suddenly struggled.

"Luke, no..." she murmured, trying to turn in his arms.

"Yes, Izzy. Absolutely." She was shivering, shaking apart in his arms, and a moment later she was there, exploding against him with a strangled shriek of shock. He wanted to bury his hard, aching flesh in hers, he wanted to drink in her cries, but he couldn't, intent on prolonging the moment for her almost past bearing. She was clutching the sheet, sobbing into the mattress, and he waited until the last wave had hit her before releasing her, gathering her into his arms with a tenderness belied by his own fierce need.

She wasn't even aware of it. She wept against him, clinging to him tightly, and that was a triumph all its own. She'd forgotten she was the passive recipient. For the moment she'd forgotten everything but her own pleasure, and that was exactly what he'd planned.

With shocking suddenness the power came back on, and the dim bedside light seemed to flood the cavernous bedroom. With a muffled cry she buried her face against his shoulder, clinging tightly. "Don't leave me," she gasped, her voice a mere thread of sound.

He moved just far enough to switch off the light, then folded her carefully into his arms, brushing back her hair, feeling the wetness of tears on her face, the lingering shiver in her muscles. He kissed her wet eyelids, her cheeks, her mouth, and she managed to kiss him back, just barely.

He knew she couldn't take any more, not at that point. He wished there was a way he could stop time, lock the doors and windows and keep the world away from them. In the morning too many things would come between them. The past, the present, the future, and too many lies would drive them apart as he'd always known they would.

Maybe it wasn't hopeless. Maybe when she woke up in the morning he'd tell her about what Hoyt's will had really said, and she'd accept it. But he didn't think so. She'd already accused him of stealing her father. How would she react when she found he'd taken her birthright, too?

Dammit, it wasn't his fault. He'd told Hoyt not to do it, but Hoyt hadn't listened. He'd tried to cover it up as best he could, with the unwitting complicity of Davey Granger at the bank and Hoyt's lawyer. With Izzy half a world away there was no need for her to know her regular checks were coming from a small trust fund Hoyt had left her, and not from the ranch he'd left to Luke.

But she was here now, in his bed where he'd always imagined her to be, and he didn't know how much longer he could live the lie. The longer she stayed the more likely she was to find out, and hate him. His only choice was to let her go, to drive her away, and she'd hate him anyway. It was a no-win situation, and all they had were a few stolen moments that were more intimate, more binding, than his three years of married life.

Maybe if he stayed awake the sun wouldn't come up. Maybe if he kept alert he'd have a chance to make love to her, completely this time, before reality came crashing through. Maybe...

THE ROOM WAS FLOODED with sunlight when Luke finally awoke. Izzy lay snugly in his arms, her long hair wrapped around them both, her eyes still shut. He could see the traces of dried tears on her cheeks, and the memory of what had caused those tears made him instantly hard. She had mauve shadows beneath her eyes, and her lips were faintly swollen, her cheeks slightly reddened from his beard. He wanted to kiss her awake, slowly, carefully, arousing her until she was too far gone to let reality intrude. He wanted to kiss her entire body, from the tip of her nose, along her wise, generous mouth, down her delectable, sensitive breasts. He wanted to kiss the thatch of curls, he wanted to kiss her between her legs, behind her knees, her toes. He wanted every square inch of her body, so that when she left, as she had to, when she ran away, as she always had, she'd take the memory with her. And no one else would ever measure up.

It wasn't a kind, loverly wish. It was a cruel, possessive one, but he was feeling possessive. Threatened, knowing he was going to lose her, when he wasn't sure he'd ever had her at all.

He was going to make love to her at least one last time. And this time they were going to do it right. Not for him. Not for her. For both of them. He moved his mouth down, to gently touch her swollen lips, when the door to his bedroom slammed open with a shocking smack.

Charlie stood there, a big grin on his face. "What the hell are you doing, sleeping in . . . ?" The words trailed off as he realized Luke wasn't alone in the big bed. Isabelle stirred, opened her eyes and saw Charlie staring at them, his mouth open wide in shock.

With a miserable little whimper she dived under the covers, and Luke began to curse.

"Don't use that language in front of a lady," Charlie snapped, looking more fierce than Luke had ever seen him. "Just get up and tell me what the hell is going on."

## Chapter Fourteen

Isabelle must have had worse moments in her life, but right then she couldn't imagine one. She wanted to stay beneath the covers, away from Charlie's accusing glare, away from Luke's too-observant eyes, away from the merciless brightness of the early-morning sun.

The bed smelled of sex. It smelled of her perfume, and it smelled of Luke. Burying her face in the mattress and hiding didn't solve any of her problems—it just brought them home more forcibly.

She felt the sag of the mattress as Luke left the bed, the rustle of clothing and the snick of a zipper. "Listen, Charlie," Luke began, but Charlie was having none of it.

"Just tell me one thing," he said, his voice rough and belligerent. "You set the date yet?"

"We're not getting married, Charlie," Luke said impatiently.

Now why should that hurt, Isabelle wondered beneath the covers. Why should she have thought Luke would say anything else?

The silence in the room lasted so long that Isabelle was half tempted to emerge from the covers. Cowardice won over curiosity, and she stayed put.

"In that case," Charlie said finally, "I guess I'm going to have to teach you a lesson. She ain't got her daddy around to defend her, so you're going to have to make do with me."

"Charlie, I'm not going to fight you."

"The hell you ain't, boy. Just because I'm fifty-five doesn't mean I can't teach you a thing or two."

"You're sixty-nine," Luke said wearily. "And I'm not going to fight you over something that means absolutely nothing."

Rage almost won out over cowardice. She started to throw back the covers, then thought better of it. She still couldn't face Charlie's accusatory eyes.

It hadn't been the most politic thing to say to the old man. "Hell, I ain't going to fight you," Charlie snarled. "I'm going to take a horsewhip to you. Out behind the barn. Now."

She heard the slam of the door, the thump of Charlie's old boots as he left the house. She still didn't move, so awash with contradictory emotions that she was afraid she might shake apart.

It would have been all right if he'd finished getting dressed and left. But Luke wasn't showing much sense that morning. She felt his hand on her arm, his voice low as he started to ask her if she was all right.

He didn't get very far. She erupted out of the bed in sheer bone-shaking rage, hitting at him in a tear-filled, mindless fury.

He subdued her, quickly and effectively, but not before she managed to connect a good one on his cheekbone, one that made him reel. A moment later he had her back down on the bed, wrapped in the sheet, his body holding her in place.

She tried to bang her head against him, but he dodged, and his hand came out to hold her face still. His long fingers were painful against her soft flesh, and she considered spitting at him. Looking into the merciless depths of his green eyes, she wisely decided not to.

"Get the hell off me," she said through her teeth.

"What's gotten into you?" he demanded. "Charlie seems to think you're the poor wronged virgin, and I've either got to shame him in front of the other men and refuse to fight him, or let him whip my tail. All you have to do is look pathetic."

"It'll be a stretch," she snapped. "But I'll manage it. Get off me."

His eyes narrowed for a moment, but he controlled his own temper with an effort. "This isn't how I imagined this morning would go," he said.

"Why should this morning go any particular way? After all, last night meant absolutely nothing." She threw his words back in his face, waiting for something. An apology, a denial, anything.

But Luke wasn't a man she could back into a corner. "I'm not going to argue with you. Charlie's probably dragging out a bullwhip, if I know the old man. I suppose I'd better get this over with. But first things first. I always kiss my ladies in the morning." And he dropped his mouth down on hers.

She kept her lips tightly closed, outraged that he'd even try such a thing. If he attempted to force her she'd bite his tongue, she promised herself, holding herself still in a righteous rage.

He didn't force her. He brushed his lips across hers, lightly, dampening them. His tongue touched the tight seam of her lips, teasing at them, but she kept them shut, her eyes glaring up into his.

He lifted his head just a fraction, and his breath was warm on her face. She wanted to drink in his breath, she wanted to take his mouth with hers, she wanted his head on a pike outside the west barn. She didn't move.

"I'm going to stay right here until you let me kiss you," he said amiably enough. "The longer you fight it the longer it'll take. Charlie'll probably come looking for us, and who knows what he'll do. You might as well . . ."

She crossed the few inches between them and kissed him, hard, her mouth open beneath his, yanking away before he could complete the kiss.

He shook his head. "Not good enough. I want a real kiss. A slow, wet one. And I'm not moving until I get it."

She made a futile effort with her knee, hoping she might manage to connect with a vulnerable part of him, but he was way ahead of her. "Nasty, nasty, Izzy. You don't really want to do that, do you? After all, we only got started last night. Seems to me you're in need of a little more experience in that area, and I'm more than happy to provide it. Until you get bored with country life and run away again. You always run away, don't you? Never face up to the messes you cause. Well, face up to this one." And he set his mouth on hers, hard, his tongue deep in her mouth, forcing a response she wished she could deny him.

Somehow she managed to get her arms free. She should have used them to push him away, to fight him. Instead she reached up and threaded her hands through his hair as her mouth slanted beneath his, her tongue touched his, her body softened and pooled beneath his.

He was hard. She wanted that hardness, wanted it desperately. His hands were on her breasts beneath the tight sheet, and the restriction was another point of arousal.

When he finally broke the kiss he was breathing hard, his pupils little pinpoints in his hard green eyes. His mouth was wet, she knew hers was, too.

He cleared his throat. "I'd better go cool Charlie down," he said finally, still not moving.

At that moment she hated him, almost as much as she hated herself for reacting to him. "You might have a hard time doing that," she said, ignoring the weight of him along the length of her, ignoring the unavoidable evidence of his arousal, ignoring her own liquid reaction to it. "He seems to think my honor's something worth defending. I don't know if you're going to be able to convince him it's worthless."

He stood then, a fluid, graceful gesture. "Charlie always had a weak spot where you were concerned. But we've been friends for years, while you were off jet-setting around. I think I can make him see reason. Sorry if that disappoints you."

She sat up, pulling the sheet up around her, ignoring the telltale discomfort in her body. "I don't want to see Charlie hurt. I'd rather somebody else beat the living crap out of you."

He leaned down, his face close to hers. "Honey, you weren't seduced and abandoned. I never heard you saying no. Even if it was a momentary aberration, you weren't trying to run away last night." He stood back, and if his eyes were shadowed she wasn't interested in delving into the reasons.

"You better be prepared to deal with Charlie," she said, her voice cold and controlled. "You might think you can reason with him. That he'll choose his friendship with you over loyalty to me. But you'll be wrong. You may have gotten my father to favor you. But it won't work every time."

He headed toward the door, his expression grim. "And you'd be damned sorry if Charlie calmed down. Since you're so hungry for blood, why don't you get your clothes on and come watch? Maybe you'll get your wish and Charlie'll manage to draw some blood. Maybe I'll end up hurting him instead, but hell, you won't care. As long as you get to see blood you'll be well-satisfied."

He slammed the door so hard as he went out that it bounced against the jamb, swinging open again, and for a moment Isabelle didn't move, heartily ashamed of herself. Luke was right, in her desire to see him humbled she would have been willing to goad an old man who wouldn't stand a chance against him. And part of the appeal had been Luke's guilt, if he actually hurt Charlie.

She had to stop them. Luke was so angry he'd only make things worse. She had to get down to the barn and assure Charlie it had been mutual. She'd take full responsibility if that would make things better. She should have known not to go traipsing around the old ranch house in nothing but a thin cotton nightgown, whether she thought Luke was gone or not. She shouldn't have made herself at home in his bedroom, awash in nostalgic memories of hopeless teenage passion.

That passion had been fulfilled now, she thought, racing upstairs without a stitch of clothes on and grabbing the first thing she could find. She didn't have to think about teenage lust, or hopeless passion, or Luke Cassidy, anymore. She knew what she'd been missing, and it had been . . .

It had been quite wonderful, she had to admit to herself, throwing an old T-shirt over her jeans, not bothering with underwear. Better, far better, than anything she'd ever experienced. She wasn't quite sure if she'd dreamed what happened next, and she didn't really want to find out. That part of her life was over. The mystery was gone. At least she knew that lovemaking was more enjoyable than she'd ever thought. She'd enjoyed it immensely last night. She could do so again.

All she had to do was find another man she loved as much as she loved Luke Cassidy. Piece of cake, she thought miserably, racing back down the stairs on bare feet, speeding through the house and out toward the west barn. She'd been looking for the past thirteen years. Maybe by the time she was fifty...

She came to an abrupt halt when she reached the barn. The tableau that met her eyes couldn't have been more horrifying. While Jimmy and Johnson watched, their expressions set with that odd kind of blankness that meant they were looking for the first decent chance to either intervene or run, Charlie circled Luke, his banty legs stumbling slightly in the dust, his weathered old face creased with grief and fury.

Luke didn't move. He stood his ground, arms at his side. He'd pulled on a shirt, but hadn't had a chance to button it. He'd pulled on his boots, and his eyes were cool and unreadable above his unshaven jaw. His dark blond hair was slicked back, his jaw firm, and he looked dangerous.

But he wouldn't be a danger to Charlie. She knew that as well as she knew just how perilous he was to her own well-being. "I'm not going to fight you, Charlie," he said steadily, and it was clearly a litany, one that wasn't penetrating Charlie's fury.

"You lily-livered coward. What the hell are you afraid of? What do you think Hoyt's doing right now? Whirling in his grave, that's what! He trusted you, he gave you everything, and you turn around and betray him by bedding his daughter. Someone needs to teach you a lesson, and it looks like I'm the only one who's man enough to do it."

"No, Charlie."

"It's a damned shame Hoyt's sense of decency didn't have any effect on you. Like they say, bad blood always tells."

"Watch it, old man."

"The hell I will. You haven't got a spit of sense, you don't give a damn for anything beyond your zipper. You take advantage of a girl who..."

"I didn't take advantage of anyone," he said coldly.

"Then what was she doing in your bed? You gonna tell me she sashayed in there on her own?"

Isabelle could watch Luke try to control his rising temper with a real effort. "I don't think we're going to accomplish anything arguing like this..."

"You tell me she means something to you, boy," Charlie demanded. "Tell me you didn't just take her to scratch an itch, and maybe I'll listen."

Isabelle didn't move. For a moment it seemed as if her entire future depended on what Luke said. She could see through Charlie's rage now, to the real reasons behind it. He was trying to make Luke admit to something, some kind of commitment. But she had the horrible sense that Charlie had overestimated his old friend. That Luke wouldn't admit to something that didn't exist.

And Luke was a man who knew he was being manipulated, and wouldn't stand still for it. His green eyes were narrow slits in the early-morning sunlight, his mouth was a grim line. "Nothing wrong with scratching an itch, old man," he drawled. "Especially when it's wrapped up in such a willing package."

Isabelle drew her breath in sharply, the pain a tangible thing. He'd known she was there, said it for her benefit, but it didn't make the hurt any less.

He'd overplayed his hand this time. Charlie turned white. And then he charged, full force, his banty legs churning up the distance as he barreled full force into Luke's much larger body, knocking him to the ground.

Isabelle raced forward, determined to stop it, just as the other two men were galvanized forward. But it was too late. Charlie had collapsed on top of Luke, his face a hideous ashen color, his breathing shallow. Very carefully Luke placed him on the ground, tearing open Charlie's old shirt and feeling for a heartbeat.

"Call an ambulance," he snarled, breathless.

"Is he . . . ?" Jimmy began, clearly horrified.

"No. But if we don't get him to the hospital, and damned fast, he will be," Luke said. "On second thought, forget the ambulance. We'll get him there faster ourselves." His eyes fastened on Isabelle, and she'd never felt anything so cold in her life. "Where are your keys?"

"In the car. I'll drive . . ."

"You'll get back in the house and call the hospital. We don't need your help. We just need your car." He turned his back on her, the frail burden in his arms seeming to weigh nothing. "Johnson, you come with me. Jimmy, follow in the pickup. Don't try to keep up—you won't be able to." He strode off toward the ranch house, toward the dust-covered Ferrari.

She knew better than to try to follow. She turned to Jimmy, who was staring at her with a mixture of confusion and misery. "What hospital?"

"The only one around, I guess. Gifford Memorial . . ." His voice trailed off and Isabelle remembered how very young he was.

"You go on now," she said gently. "Charlie'll be okay. It'll take more than . . . than whatever happened to stop a tough old buzzard like him. You'll see."

"I hope so. I never seen anyone look so bad in my life."

"I have," Isabelle said. "And they've all recovered. Go along now, Jimmy. I'll call the hospital."

That phone call took exactly four minutes. And then she went out on the back porch and sat, her hands in her lap, and waited.

IT WAS CLOSE to midnight when Luke finally got back to the ranch. Johnson and Jimmy had returned hours earlier, with instructions to tell Izzy that Charlie was going to be just fine. He might be looking at bypass surgery a few months down the road, and he was cantankerous as all get-out, but for now he'd stabilized and was doing just fine.

Which was more than Luke could say for himself. He was consumed with guilt, not just for Charlie, but for Izzy. Charlie had been absolutely right, he should have known better than to touch her. There was no way, given their history, that they could have a night of mutual pleasure and leave it in the morning. Hell, it hadn't even managed to scratch the itch he'd taunted Charlie about. That itch had become a rash, one that was eating him alive.

The kitchen was spotless when he stepped inside. For a moment he didn't realize the significance of it, used to Becky's domesticity. But Becky was gone, thank heavens. And that left Izzy to exercise talents he hadn't realized she'd possessed.

She must have cleaned nonstop. The place smelled of wax and ammonia, and bustling energy and tears. She must have worked herself into a state of advanced exhaustion. Probably the only way she could stop herself from thinking.

He hadn't had that luxury. He'd been trapped at the hospital, by the side of a sleeping old man, and there'd been nothing to do but relive the past twenty-four hours, hell, the past twenty-four years, and regret the things he'd done. Not to mention the things he hadn't done. What would have happened if he'd taken what Izzy had offered that night in his old bedroom under the eaves? Would it have been any less of a betrayal, of Hoyt, of himself, of Izzy?

He'd been so angry with himself for the situation this morning that he'd blamed her. Accused her of feeding off Charlie's rage, of wanting blood. He knew perfectly well she was horrified, probably more so than he was. He'd seen fights, plenty of them, over the years. He lived a rough life, with rough men, and been in his share of dust-ups.

The damnable thing was, part of him was relieved that Charlie had collapsed. Charlie had been possessed this morning—he wouldn't have stopped until one of them was a messy little pile in the dust. It had been a no-win situation—either he'd flatten a man almost twice his age, or shame the old man by refusing to fight. The minor heart attack had stopped that whole, hideous scene quite effectively.

He wondered where Isabelle was. Was she lying curled up in his bed, awaiting him? He doubted it. She was probably lying upstairs, having cried herself to sleep. Unless she'd already run.

No, she wouldn't have done that. For one thing, he had her Ferrari. For another, she hadn't accomplished whatever she'd come home to do. And until that happened, she was probably going to stay put.

He poured himself a tall, dark glass of bourbon, neat, and headed toward the bedroom. He told himself he wasn't disappointed when he saw the neatly made bed, with no telltale shape beneath the fresh sheets and warm quilt. The floorboard was back in place, and he didn't even bother to glance toward it. She would have removed the diary along with every speck of dust in the room.

He sank down on the bed and began to pull off his boots. Dammit, he didn't want to sleep alone in this bed. He hadn't been able to keep his mind off Izzy; even as he sat by Charlie's bed his mind and body had betrayed him, teasing him with the memory, the feel and sound and smell of her.

Hell, he was going upstairs to get her, drag her down by her hair if he had to. She wanted him as much as he wanted her. Even if they couldn't get anywhere out of bed, they were making better progress with their bodies than they had in years of talking. If Charlie hadn't barged in this morning there was no telling how far they would have come.

He rose, ready to head upstairs, when the phone beside his bed rang. He reached for it, stifling the sudden panic that swept through his gut. Charlie had been in good shape when he'd left that night, the doctors had assured him he faced a full recovery. Surely nothing could have happened . . .

He listened with relief and then disbelief to the overseas operator. He listened with growing anger to the voice on the other end. And then he calmed down enough to answer the questions put to him, briefly, succinctly, factually, before hanging up the phone again.

It was no more than he suspected. It hadn't taken a genius to realize that Izzy was out for the main chance, for herself and herself alone. That selling the ranch out from under them all would cause her no more than a moment's qualm, if that.

Charlie had been ready to die for her honor. He'd tried to tell the old man that she had none, and it had only inflamed him more. Tomorrow, if he was well enough, he'd explain to him exactly how low Isabelle could sink. And if that wasn't enough, then he'd point out a few home truths to the little princess herself, right before he kicked her off his ranch.

He drained the whiskey in one gulp, shuddering as he sank back on the pillows. And then he cursed.

The room smelled of furniture polish and fresh linen and the lingering scent of the whiskey he'd just downed. But beneath it all, a torment straight out of hell, was the faintest tease of scent, and all the ammonia and furniture polish in the state of Wyoming wouldn't get rid of it. Beneath it all, the scent of Compulsion still lingered. And he knew it was in his blood.

ISABELLE WAITED. Lying alone in the narrow bunk, the freshly laundered nightgown pulled down to her ankles, she waited for Luke to climb the stairs and haul her down.

She couldn't wait for him in his bed. Knowing that was where she wanted to be, where she belonged, wasn't enough. There was too much between them, too much left undecided. If he wanted to claim her she'd follow. But she couldn't reach out. Not with Charlie and Hoyt and Mr. Takashima standing between them.

She'd tell him tomorrow. The first chance they were alone, she'd tell him about Mr. Takashima's offer. Maybe he'd agree it was the best thing they could do. If there was ever going to be any future for them, it would have to be in some neutral place. Not the emotionally charged environs of Rancho Diablo.

He didn't climb the stairs. She thought she heard the faint sound of the phone ringing, but she couldn't be sure. She lay still, waiting for him. By the time she would have realized he wasn't coming, she was sound asleep, worn out by the sleepless night before, the emotions of the morning, the physical exhaustion of cleaning the house from top to bottom. Her last conscious thought was that Luke might have a hard time waking her up.

## Chapter Fifteen

"Hey, Charlie," Isabelle said softly, hesitating just inside the door to his private room in the cardiac care unit in the small local hospital. It was only a little after seven in the morning, hours before visiting was officially sanctioned, but she'd lived in that small town in Wyoming the first seventeen years of her life, and been born in that very hospital. There was hardly a person there who didn't know her, and not a soul who'd stop her as she made her way up to the second floor to see the man who'd been a second father to her.

She'd hoped to get there before he woke up, but she immediately saw that she was too late. He was staring out the window, and he looked so old Isabelle wanted to cry.

But he turned at the sound of her voice, his expression so welcoming that the tenuous hold she had on her emotions shredded, and she rushed across the room, bursting into tears.

He reached out for her, enfolding her against his frail chest as she sobbed out her guilt and misery.

"There, there, Miss Bella," he said, his gnarled old hand gently brushing her tangled hair. "No need to cry about an old coot like me. It'll take more than a dicey ticker to slow me down. Just give me a few days of decent food and I'll be raring to go."

"But it was my fault," she wailed. "If I hadn't come home, if I hadn't . . ."

"No such thing," Charlie protested. "I was interfering where I had no cause to interfere, and it served me right. If I could just learn to mind my own business."

Isabelle lifted her head. "But Charlie, you were defending my honor."

"Not exactly," he admitted wryly. "I don't think a woman's honor has much to do with who she cares to sleep with. As far as I'm concerned it's up to you, and if you make a mistake, then you're the one who'll have to live with it. No, I was just looking for an excuse."

"An excuse for what? For hitting Luke?" She was aghast.

"Nope," Charlie said, looking sheepish. "I just wanted to see if I could push him into admitting something he should have admitted years ago. But he's so blind pigheaded stubborn that he wouldn't recognize it if it came up and bit him in the behind."

"What are you talking about?"

"The dang fool's in love with you. Always has been. I 'spect he always will be."

For a moment Isabelle's own heart stopped, then lurched and jerked back into motion, and she shook her head. "No, Charlie. I wish it was true, but it's not. It's just wishful thinking on your part, because you care for us both. But we're poison for each other, you should know that by now. The night before last was a mistake, just as you thought it was, and it's something we'll both have to live with. But it won't happen again, and it shouldn't. I don't love Luke, and Luke sure as hell doesn't care about me."

Charlie's faded blue eyes didn't even blink. "Wanna try that again?" he suggested affably. "Maybe with practice it'll start to ring true."

"Charlie, he doesn't love me." Her voice was edged with tears.

"I suppose only Luke knows for certain," he allowed. "How about the other part? You want to tell someone who used to change your diapers, who put you on your first horse, picked you up after you fell and stood up to your daddy when he tried to make you climb on again, that you aren't in love with Luke Cassidy?"

"I'd like to tell you that," she said weakly. "But I never could lie to you. Not for long. I love him, Charlie. And it won't do me a spit of good." With that she dissolved again into long-overdue tears, dampening the crisp white hospital sheets and Charlie's gnarled old hand.

By the time Luke arrived at the hospital, three hours later, she'd managed to pull herself together. She didn't know what she expected from him. The last time she'd seen him he'd practically accused her of inciting Charlie into his heart attack. He'd avoided her ever since, but she couldn't help hoping he might apologize. That there might be a trace of tenderness in his glance.

He loomed in the doorway, cowboy hat in his hand, dark blond hair slicked back, away from his face. His eyes were flinty, looking through Isabelle as if she wasn't even there, and his mouth was grim.

"Why the hell do you look like such a thundercloud?" Charlie greeted him. "Did the doc tell you something he was keeping from me?"

"Since when has Doc Horsley been able to keep a secret?" he countered, his forbidding expression lightening somewhat. "He tells me you can come home in less than a week, more's the pity. We were just getting comfortable without you."

"Don't count on getting too lazy. Once I'm back I'm gonna ride all of you real hard," Charlie said. "Aren't you going to say good-morning to Bella?"

She'd been trying to pull her hand out of Charlie's surprisingly strong grasp and to escape from the moment Luke made his appearance, but he'd been holding on tightly.

"Hello, Luke," she said evenly.

"Hi." He didn't even look at her, his voice brief and dismissing. "You're only allowed one visitor at a time."

"Says who?" Charlie demanded. "Dammit, I'll see who I want, when I want..."

"Listen, old man, you're only supposed to see immediate family. You're lucky we got in at all."

"Don't give me that. Everyone in Devil's Fork knows that you and Bella are the closest thing to kin I've got."

She was finally able to break his grip, and as she moved backward she started to knock over the chair she'd been sitting on.

Luke caught it in time, his other hand steadying her when she would have fallen against him. The moment she regained her balance he released her, as if he'd been forced to touch a particularly nasty varmint.

"I'll be back later, Charlie," she promised, not looking at Luke, determined not to show how wounded she felt.

"There's no need. I'll be here till early afternoon, then Johnson's coming by, and Jimmy's going to do evening shift. You can head back to the ranch and get started on your packing."

She looked at him then, her clear blue eyes meeting his quite fearlessly. He didn't flinch, and she told herself if she didn't know better she'd think he hated her. He had no reason to hate her, at least none that he knew of. And she was damned if she was going to be kicked off her own ranch. Even if she was having second, third and eighteenth thoughts about selling it.

"I don't need to pack. I'm not going anywhere. Not until I decide I'm ready to."

"I think you're about ready to decide. If you want, I'll be more than happy to explain in detail when I get back there." His voice was as cold as ice.

Charlie was following all this, a worried expression on his face, and Isabelle had little doubt that the monitors hooked up to every life function would be showing that stress. "I don't think we need to trouble Charlie with our little disagreements, do you?" she said sweetly.

She managed to get through to him. Luke cleared his throat, casting a worried glance at Charlie. "You're right. It'll be up to you, of course. We'll talk when I get back."

She moved over to Charlie, pressing a warm kiss against his withered cheek. "Don't let him upset you, Charlie. He's a bully, but you can stand up to him, if I can."

"And I know you can, honey," Charlie said fiercely. "Drive carefully, and come back tomorrow morning."

"You bet."

She kept her head high as she exited the hospital room, managing a gracious smile for anyone she happened to pass as she made her way down to her Ferrari, now broiling in the noonday sun. By the time she reached her car all urge for tears had passed. Besides, she'd cried herself out that morning, confessing in tearful, adolescent detail the full, maudlin depths of her obsession with Luke. She no longer felt like crying. Right then and there she felt completely enraged, and she only had to worry about keeping her promise to Charlie and not driving in a white-hot rage all the way back to the ranch.

Luke moved back from the hospital window as he watched Izzy peel out of the parking lot at unsafe speeds. She looked as if he'd slapped her, he thought. It was nothing more than she deserved. After that transpacific phone call last night he'd been feeling as if he'd been kicked in the stomach by Tumult, his most prolific stud. If he got a little of his own back, then he was entitled to just a trace of revenge.

"Spill it," Charlie said. "Someone put a bee in your bonnet, and you might as well air it. What's up?"

He turned back, surveying his old friend with a detached air. He looked a lot better than he had yesterday, the color back in his ashen cheeks, his faded eyes snapping with irritation and curiosity. If he were a decent human being, Luke thought, he'd drop it here and now, take care of the problem on his own. When Charlie got back to the ranch he'd just tell him Izzy took off for Hollywood or Reno or some ridiculous place like that, and sent her love.

But he'd never lied to Charlie in his life, and he wasn't about to start now, particularly over Izzy. "You ever heard of a man named Mr. Takashima?" he asked.

LUKE HAD DUMPED a couple of old suitcases in her room, his not-so-subtle suggestion that she get a move on. She took them downstairs and left them in his bedroom, keeping her eyes averted from the enticingly unmade bed.

He hadn't bothered with the breakfast dishes, but she'd burned out her housecleaning genes the day before. She'd probably washed enough, dusted enough, cleaned enough, to keep her happy for the next five years. She certainly wasn't going to start picking up for a sullen cowboy who didn't know what he had when it was offered.

It would serve him right if she did go ahead and sell the place to Mr. Takashima's corporation. Luke hadn't done anything to make her regret such a rash move, particularly when he'd still be holding down the same job, at probably twice the salary. She'd never paid much attention to any of the financial details of running the ranch, assuming that Luke would resent any interference. But clearly there wasn't much money around. That pickup needed replacing, the west barn needed a new roof and at the Grangers' cookout she'd heard that Luke was in the market for a new stallion, only he hadn't managed to come up with the very reasonable asking price.

If Mr. Takashima were in charge there'd be money to spare. The finest in equipment, technology, the latest in methods, would be at their command. It would be run like a cross between a corporation and a family, and everyone would benefit.

Except Luke. She knew Luke well enough to know he'd walk. He'd rather run the ranch on a shoestring, scraping to get by, than have to answer to anyone about his methods. Pigheaded, that's what he was. And always right. And so damned narrowminded that she felt like spitting nails even thinking about him. It made no sense that she'd love him. He didn't deserve it, and she was a fool and a half to care.

Except that he had a streak of kindness beneath that cynical exterior. And a surprising gentleness when she was hurting. He had his own wounds, too. Growing up with someone like old man Cassidy had to be rotten for anyone, and although Hoyt had done his best to make up for it, he'd only gotten Luke when he was nineteen. Past time for being fathered.

She couldn't do it. She couldn't stab Luke in the back, even if it was the best thing that could happen to him. She couldn't sell out to Takashima, take the money and run. She was going to have to cancel the tentative plans, and start making some plans on her own. Like how she was going to survive without her sizable profits from the ranch.

It was more than clear that Luke needed to plow the profits back into the place for a few years, and she'd tell him that. As she told him off, just as she was about to leave.

She'd tell him a few other things at the same time. Like how she had once thought the sun rose and set with him. How she would have given anything, done anything, if he'd only made the slightest effort in her direction. But that now it was too late.

And maybe she'd convince him. But more importantly, maybe she'd convince herself.

The ranch was quiet that early afternoon. Johnson had already left for the hospital, and Jimmy was in the bunkhouse, mending some harnesses. He always ducked his head and blushed when she was around, a fact that amused her. He hadn't seemed the least bit shy with that nubile young lady he'd been dancing with at the Grangers'. Maybe she'd reached the age where she could be intimidating.

It had been a long time since she'd been alone at Rancho Diablo. She walked through each barn, her sharp eyes checking for needed repairs. Things were in pretty good shape, considering. What could be mended was mended, what had to be replaced had been replaced. There was no sign of waste anywhere, and the only extravagance she could spot was the premium horse feed, a luxury she heartily approved of. If you were feeding pregnant and lactating mares you needed the best food money could buy, even if you had to make do on canned stew and boxes of macaroni and cheese.

It wasn't until she reached the last barn, Crescent's barn, that the inescapable sank in. She knew horses, better than she realized, and it didn't take an expert to realize that the stock was in better shape than it had been when Hoyt was in charge. Luke had taken a decent breeding operation and expanded it, maybe too far, maybe too fast, but the results were undeniably impressive.

She'd been assiduously avoiding Crescent's empty stall, when a flash of movement caught her eye, caught her throat in a vicelike grip of sorrow. For a moment the flash of sorrel tail had looked like her beloved old mare, and she'd been willing to believe...

But no. The mare in Crescent's stall was young, maybe two years old, smaller than Crescent, and better formed. She was looking across at Isabelle with patent curiosity, and as she caught Isabelle's eye she tossed her head, her thick mane flying in what seemed a perfect imitation of Isabelle's own patented gesture.

She found she was smiling, the tightness in her throat easing. She crossed the barn, her sneakered feet quiet, and came up to the horse.

"Hi, there, lady," she said softly, using the tone that had always managed to tame wild beasts and left men like Luke Cassidy unmoved. "What are you doing in here? What's your name?"

A new card had been neatly typed, typical of the efficiency of the operation. "Half-moon," Isabelle read. "Out of Crescent by Wayfarer." She looked up at the horse again. "You're Crescent's daughter?"

Half-moon nodded in agreement, bringing her beautiful head close to Isabelle and searching for a treat. "Sorry, lady," she murmured, feeling the pockets of her old jeans. "I'm afraid I don't..." Her voice trailed off as her hand came in contact with a small, crumbling rectangle. She drew it out, an aging lump of sugar from half a lifetime ago. She held it out, her hand flat, and Half-moon lapped it up eagerly, snuffling her approval.

"She's a real sweetheart," Jimmy said, appearing out of the bright sunlight, saddle and tack in his hands. "One of the nicest mares we've had in a long while, though most of Crescent's offspring were winners. But Half-moon might be her mother and then some. Sweet tempered, beautifully paced, steady and even. It's going to break Luke's heart to part with her." He moved into the stall, saddling the mare, and true to her reputation, Half-moon accepted the leather restraints with remarkable equanimity.

"What do you mean, part with her?" Isabelle demanded sharply. "Doesn't he need her for breeding?"

"Sure he does. But he's got two other mares, and Murphy's willing to work out a deal with his yearling. He's always had an eye for Half-moon, and he's finally going to get her."

"Does he want to breed her?"

"Dunno. I think he wants her for his wife. She's afraid of horses, and Half-moon's the gentlest ride around. Even the most complete coward wouldn't be afraid on her back. Begging your pardon, miss," he added, blushing beet-red as he suddenly remembered that Isabelle could easily be termed a complete coward.

She moved into the stall beside Jimmy, running her sure, smooth hands over Half-moon's sides. It was like touching Crescent again. "He can't do it," she said fiercely. "I won't let him."

"Begging your pardon, miss, but he's got to," Jimmy said. "We're in a bind. You should know he wouldn't do such a thing if he didn't have to. Hell ... I mean, heck, he was there when Half-moon was born. Helped pull her out, was certain she was going to make it even when Doc thought she wouldn't. He loves that horse almost more than any of the rest of them. But he's a realist. He does what he has to do.''

She put her head against Half-moon's smooth side. "He's not going to sell her," she muttered, and the horse moved her head around and nibbled her hair.

"Jimmy!" Luke's voice bellowed, carrying into the peaceful confines of the barn.

Jimmy started guiltily. "I'll be right back. You'll be all right...?"

"Sure. I've been around horses most of my life. I just don't like to ride them."

"You wouldn't mind this one, miss. She's a real treat." He disappeared, following the sound of his boss's voice, and she wondered briefly what was bugging Luke. Whether he was taking his anger toward her out on everyone else, or whether he really had a problem with Jimmy.

"I better go see what's happening," she murmured to Half-moon, who nodded her head in agreement. "I don't want Jimmy taking the brunt of Luke's temper if it's really only me he's mad at. I'll be back."

She could hear their voices before she reached the open door of the bunkhouse. That is, she could hear Luke's voice. He wasn't making any effort to modify his tone, and it took her only a moment to realize his lecture had absolutely nothing to do with her.

"...I want you to be damned careful," he was saying, his voice crisp. "I'm not your mother, I'm not your nursemaid and I'm not your priest. Most of all, I'm not your sex education counselor. But you're a good man, one of the best we've had around here in years, and I don't want to see you get yourself in a mess of trouble because you didn't have the sense to be careful."

"I don't see what business it is of yours," Jimmy said stiffly.

"No, it's not. Except that Ruthann's mother confronted me at the hospital and told me you didn't bring her home until eleven o'clock the morning after the dance. And that Ruthann is just itching to settle down and start a family."

"I know that. I told her I wasn't ready."

"I hope you know how to keep that from happening."

"I know. What's the big deal anyway? If Ruthann gets knocked up she can always take care of it. There are doctors..."

"I don't think Ruthann's thinking that way, and I'm sure her mother isn't. You'll have a ring around your finger and a noose around your neck before you realize it. It's no fun being a daddy at nineteen, and it's not funny marrying someone because you have to, and then trying to live with the mistake."

"How would you know?"

"How the hell do you think I know, boy? Cathy lost the baby she was carrying, but I sure wouldn't have married her if I didn't have to. I lived up to my responsibility, and I'd make it my personal business to make sure you did, if it came to that."

Isabelle must have made some noise, some sound of distress. The two men turned in her direction, Jimmy beet-red in embarrassment, Luke flinty-eyed and furious.

He moved away from Jimmy, advancing on her with menacing grace. "Nosy, as always, Izzy," he snapped. "When are you going to learn to mind your own business?"

She held her ground for a moment. For years she thought he'd loved Cathy, that he'd forgotten about Isabelle the moment she left. And now that image of the perfect marriage was shattered, leaving only the ghosts of unhappy people behind.

"Goodbye," she said, quite calmly. And then she turned and ran, back across the hard-packed yard to the west barn.

It took her two tries to get up on Half-moon's broad back. It took another minute to get her out of the stall, moving briskly through the barn and out into the bright sunlight. The stirrups were down too low, set for either Jimmy or Luke, but she could manage. She was counting on Half-moon to live up to her reputation, to move steadily and surely out into the countryside, to take her away from cheats and liars and coldhearted men who didn't know what they had when it was thrown at their feet.

With unaccustomed bravery she kicked Half-moon's sides, and the mare responded with a smooth, gentle surge. They moved out, toward the foothills, and in the distance Isabelle could see Luke watching her, shouting something after her.

But she wasn't listening. If it was up to her, she wasn't going to listen to him ever again. The jagged spikes of the Tetons loomed ahead, calling to her. She'd come back, eight years ago, to say goodbye to her father. Now it was time to say goodbye to the mountains, to the land, to the place she'd never return to. A place that was both a haven and a threat to everything she ever thought she'd wanted. She'd go alone into the mountains, for one last time. And when she left, she'd never again think of them, or the man that lived there.

# Chapter Sixteen

"She really can ride," Jimmy said, his voice low and admiring as he watched Isabelle canter off toward the mountains.

Luke glared at him. "She's a born liar. Besides, look at the way she holds on to Half-moon. I don't think she knows much about what she's doing, I think it's just a natural aptitude that she's squashed down."

"Why would anyone want to do that?"

"Charlie said she got scared once, after she fell. And Hoyt tried to force her to ride again, and it got her back up. Isabelle isn't someone you can force to do anything." His eyes followed her progress. She must be heading for the old riding path up through the foothills. There wasn't much left to find—no one had had time for recreational riding in the past few years, and the path would be overgrown and rubble strewn. She'd probably hold that against him, too, he thought with a trace of regret.

Hell, it was nothing compared to what he held against her. Of all the sneaking, devious, black-hearted tricks, to try to sell the ranch from underneath the men who'd given it their lives, while she was out gallivanting around like she was the queen of the world.

To top it off, Charlie hadn't even been irritated when he'd told him about her perfidy. "Don't you believe me?" Luke had demanded when Charlie hadn't responded.

"Sure, I believe you, son. I just can't get that riled about it. After all, there wasn't much she could really do. She doesn't own the ranch, you do. So what's the harm?"

"She was going to put you out of a job at age sixty-nine," Luke practically shouted.

"Fifty-five," Charlie corrected amiably. "I doubt it. Did you ask this Mr. Takashima about the terms? I bet they were sweet enough to take care of all of us."

"Are you telling me I should take the offer?"

"Hell, no. I'm just telling you you're a mite too quick to judge, and much too happy believing Isabelle's a snake in the grass. I've never known a man so eager to think the woman he loves is dirt."

"I don't love her!" Luke shouted.

A nurse popped her head in the door and waggled her finger in admonishment. "I don't love her," he repeated in an angry whisper.

Charlie just shook his head with maddening calm. "And here I thought you were a man who knew his own mind," he said. "Guess you still have some growing up to do."

The hospital room door wouldn't slam, no matter how much force Luke had used when he stormed out of there. It closed with a quiet hydraulic thud, and the linoleum floors muffled the sound of his boots as he stalked out. At least the truck door had made a satisfying crash when he'd slammed it with all his force. Unfortunately it had broken one of the rusty hinges and spread the hairline crack on the windshield, one he'd put off fixing because there were always better things to spend the money on.

He'd been ready to lace into the first person he saw, and that person had been Jimmy. He hadn't expected Izzy to overhear, but he should have at least been prepared for that eventuality. Izzy turned up in the damnedest places, and if it was going to be an embarrassment and an inconvenience for him then he could pretty well count on her being there.

He wondered whether he should go after her. For all her natural grace on Half-moon, she really was a novice. And Half-moon, gentle as she was, could get spooked by a snake, a thunderstorm, or the like.

Except there weren't any snakes big enough to scare a horse in that area. And the sky was clear and cloudless, no thunderstorms in sight. He had no reason to ride to the rescue, like a knight on a white horse. If he wanted her out of his life, and there was really no question that he did, then he needed to start letting go right now.

"What are you standing around for?" he snapped at Jimmy, who was still transfixed, staring after Izzy's rapidly disappearing figure. "Don't you have any work to do? We're short one hand, and we have fifteen horses here. I'd think you could find something to keep you busy."

"Yes, sir," Jimmy said, turning beet-red and backing away.

Once more Luke cursed himself. He shouldn't take his temper out on the boy. Just because Izzy was a fire in his soul didn't mean that others deserved to be the brunt of his rage and frustration. If she didn't leave he'd tell her exactly why he wanted her gone.

But he'd rather not deal with that. He didn't want to listen to her excuses about Mr. Takashima, listen to her recriminations when she learned about the will. He'd just like her to disappear, like a bad dream.

No, not a bad dream exactly. A fantasy, an erotic one at that, that had no connection with the hard facts of reality. If he just stayed cold and aloof he'd make it through. Hell, he had more than enough practice at doing just that. He could certainly carry it off for a few more days.

He heard her come in, an hour and a half later. He was in the office, and he'd managed to close the warped door by brute force, but the sound of her footsteps echoed through the old wood house, pounded in his brain. She was moving slower than her usual headlong pace, and for a moment he wanted to rush out of the office and make sure she was all right, that she hadn't fallen and hurt herself.

But he didn't. By the time he'd half risen from the old leather chair he realized it was nothing more than sore muscles making her move so slowly. She didn't hesitate as she passed the office, and a moment later he heard the sound of water running as she filled the rust-stained bathtub.

He sat back, his mind filled with pictures of her stripping off her clothes, slipping into the water and lying there, soaking away her first case of saddle sores. And it was all he could do to keep from following her upstairs and offering to scrub her back.

He managed to avoid her the rest of the day. He ate in the deserted bunkhouse—Jimmy took the pickup in to meet Johnson, and the two of them were planning to eat something in town. When he looked up at the house he thought he could see her moving around, see her in the windows, and he kept strictly away.

The hell with Charlie. He knew his own mind, he knew his own weaknesses. He knew if he were around Izzy he wouldn't be able to keep from touching her, and if he touched her he'd either strangle her or make love to her. Either act would seal his doom.

He waited until ten o'clock, until the sky was inky black, with only the bright, almost-full moon shining overhead, before going back to the house. There was a light on in her bedroom, his old room, but he was counting on her not to come down again. He wouldn't actually go inside until he was certain she'd settled for the night. Or, he might even spend the night outside. At least there'd be no downpour to interrupt him, and send him back into a hornet's nest.

He sank down in the old rocker on the back porch, propping his scuffed cowboy boots on the railing. He wished that Charlie was someone he could talk to. But he never could say much to Charlie when it came to Izzy. The old man had divided loyalties, and Luke sure wasn't about to make him choose.

Tipping the chair back, he closed his eyes, breathing in the scents of a hot summer night. Leather. Hay. The sharp tang of whiskey. And the faint, disturbing scent of Izzy's perfume.

She sat down beside him, not making a sound, and he wanted to slam his chair down and run, like Izzy always ran. He held still, eyes closed, ignoring her.

"I brought you a drink." Her voice was low, self-contained, and he almost forgave her. Opening his eyes, he took the tall, dark glass, taking a healthy swallow.

"Thanks," he said briefly, turning his attention back toward the distant mountains. He didn't want to make small talk with her. He didn't want to make big talk. He wanted to touch her, hold her, kiss her, carry her back to his bed and strip off all her clothes. He took another deep swallow.

"I went for a ride today."

"I noticed."

"I wish you wouldn't sell Half-moon. She's a wonderful horse. She'd have beautiful babies."

"I don't have a choice. We need another stallion more than we need another mare."

"But she was Crescent's last foal."

"And her best," Luke said. "But you can't afford to be sentimental if you're running a horse-breeding operation like this one."

"No one would ever accuse you of being sentimental," she said with a touch of asperity.

"No," he agreed.

The silence between them wasn't a companionable one, it was fraught with tension. He opened his mouth to ask her to go away, then shut it again. He wasn't going to give her that much, the knowledge that her very presence bothered him. Calm indifference was the best defense. If he could just manage to keep it up.

"I wanted to talk to you," she said finally. "Before I leave."

"You've decided to leave?" He didn't bother to keep the pleasure from his voice at the thought.

"It seems best all around. Tomorrow morning. I'm already packed. I'll stop and see Charlie on the way. I'll let you know where you can send my checks."

He made a noncommittal noise. She'd find out soon enough that her big windfall wasn't going to come through, and she'd need those checks sooner than she thought. She was going to have to make do with less than usual, but it should manage to keep her in designer clothes and put gas in the Ferrari. It was enough to solve any number of problems for the ranch, but the money was hers, her token inheritance from her father, and he wasn't going to ask for it.

"I wanted to tell you about something else, so you'd know how to deal with it." The tone of her voice caught his attention, and he turned to watch her. She was staring out at the same mountains he'd been studying so intently, and her profile was deceptively calm.

"You don't have to tell me anything," he said.

"Yes, I do. I came here for a reason. I promised I'd tell you about it myself, and I'm keeping my promise. I was making arrangements to sell the ranch."

"Were you?" He kept his voice cool and noncommittal.

"To a Japanese corporation. They've been buying up ranches all through the northern Rockies and they were interested in Rancho Diablo."

"How'd they find out about it?"

"I heard about what they were doing, and I suggested they might be interested. They were."

"I see. Where does that leave us?"

She still wouldn't look at him. She'd seen the ragged edge of the mountains most of her life, but she still couldn't seem to drink in enough of the sight. Particularly since her alternative was to meet his accusing gaze.

"The offer was generous, I made sure of that. All your jobs were guaranteed, at the same or better salaries, and there'd be plenty of money for upgrading. You need a new roof on the west barn, you need a new pickup..."

"I know what we need," he said harshly.

"It didn't seem like such a bad idea," she said, her voice as distant as the mountains. "It would have severed any ties I still had to the place, and provide me with a comfortable nest egg. If you had any sense at all you would have thought it was a good idea yourself. The only difference would be that you'd be answering to Mr. Takashima instead of to me, and there'd be plenty of money for repairs and expansion."

"Still trying to arrange everybody's life, Izzy?"

She shrugged. "It seemed to make sense. Until I realized that of course you don't answer to me. You don't answer to anyone but yourself, always have and always will.

It would shred your soul to have to take orders or explain yourself to anyone, no matter what the obvious advantages were."

"What about Hoyt? How would he feel about your selling Rancho Diablo to a foreign corporation?"

A small, self-deprecating smile curved her lips. "Well, I have to admit that that might have been part of my less noble motive. If Hoyt took a tiny little spin in his grave then that didn't bother me too much." She turned to meet his gaze then, and her expression was rueful. "You see, I'm as shallow and rotten as you've always said I was. I still hold a grudge against my father, and he really didn't do anything to deserve it."

Luke controlled his own start of guilt. "So where does that leave the ranch?"

"I tried to call Mr. Takashima all day, to tell him that he'd have to talk to you. As far as I'm concerned the deal was off. I never got through to him, but I left the message, and he's got the world's most efficient administrative assistant. He'll get the word. After that it's up to you. You can go through with the deal if you want."

"You think I should, don't you?"

"Yes," she said flatly. "For all the reasons I've told you. Money, security, the chance to expand without having to worry constantly about the bottom line. I don't think you'd even have much interference from the corporation. The Japanese are famous for their business management, and part of that involves getting the best people and letting them go on with things. And there's one even more important advantage."

"What's that?"

"If you agreed to the sale, I'd never have anything to do with Rancho Diablo again."

"Take the money and run, is that it?"

"That's it." Her voice was suddenly raw with strain. "Isn't that an offer you can't refuse?"

"I'll think about it." She was crying. He couldn't believe it, his tough, incomparable Izzy was crying, and doing her damnedest to hide it. He wanted to take her into his arms and kiss away her tears. He kept his face turned away, ignoring her.

She rose, moving behind him, out of his sight if he'd been looking at her. "I'll leave Mr. Takashima's phone number and address on your desk before I go," she said stiffly.

He tipped the chair back again, breathing in the night air and the scent of her perfume. "There's no need," he murmured. "He gave it to me a couple of days ago when he called."

He could sense her stillness. "You knew? You knew all along?"

"Just since yesterday. Not the details, but the bottom line."

"I see. And what did you say to him?"

"I told him to go take a flying leap."

"So this confession was completely unnecessary?" She was beginning to get angry. He preferred that to her tears. It didn't make him want her any the less. It just made the contest a little more even.

He turned and looked up at her. The moonlight was shielded by the porch roof, and he couldn't see her tear-streaked face, but her eyes glittered with rage. "I wouldn't say that," he drawled. "It had its advantages."

"To further humiliate me," she snapped. "I appreciate it, Luke. It makes it all that much easier to leave." She took a deep, steadying breath. "I'm going to bed now. If you have any sense at all you'll sleep late. That way you'll never have to see me again."

She slammed the door behind her as she went, the old wood making a satisfying thwack as it hit home. He heard her stomp through the house, half imagined her muttering darkly under her breath.

Leaning back again, he closed his eyes, drinking in the night, drinking in the sudden feeling of peace. She was a fool, his Izzy. But a surprisingly noble one, at that. He should have known she wouldn't betray the men who'd put their hearts into this place over the years. She couldn't even do it to him, who more than deserved any kind of revenge she felt like dishing out.

She was just too damned busy arranging everybody else's life. She needed to spend a little time on her own.

She'd made her uncomfortable, damning confession. He was going to have to do the same. She'd been kept in the dark for too long. She was clearly more than able to face the truth he'd been so busy shielding her from. And of course, his reasons for secrecy had hardly been that noble. Sure, he hadn't wanted her to feel the hurt of Hoyt's rejection. But he also hadn't wanted to face her rage and blame. She already felt Luke stole her father from her. How was she going to react when she found he'd stolen her ranch, her birthright, from her, too?

He'd have to tell her. Tomorrow, before she left. And there was no question that she'd leave, run away. Even if she had second thoughts, the moment she learned the truth she'd be off. And whether he liked it or not, he really might never see her again.

He drained the glass of whiskey, setting his chair down with a snap. Before she left, there was some unfinished business between them. Charlie was right, he'd used every excuse in the book to hate her, to keep her at arm's length. He couldn't do that anymore. For one more night he was going to give in, to her guileless enticement, to his own burning needs.

He turned off the lights as he moved through the old house, stopping by his room to pull off his boots and rummage through the bedside table. And then he headed upstairs in the darkness.

Her door was closed, with a thin thread of light coming under it. He stood there for a moment, hesitating. And then he opened it.

She was sitting in bed, the sheet pulled up in front of her. It was a warm night, and her shoulders were naked. Her thick blond hair hung around her, and apart from her tear-glazed eyes, she looked exactly as she had on a night thirteen years ago.

He moved into the room, closing the door behind him, flicking off the light switch. For a moment the room was plunged into darkness, and then the brightness of the moon filtered through, shining off Isabelle's shoulders, glistening in her eyes.

"What are you doing here?" she asked, though clearly she knew the answer to that question.

"What I should have done thirteen years ago," he said, unbuttoning his chambray shirt. "Finishing what I started two nights ago." He dropped his shirt on the chair, waiting for her to protest, to argue.

For a moment she didn't say a word. And then slowly, deliberately, she dropped the sheet she'd been holding up against her.

SHE COULDN'T BELIEVE he was there. She couldn't believe there was going to be a second chance, for her, for him, for the future, when she thought she'd destroyed it. She could feel his eyes on her breasts, feel the heat of his gaze. And then he took the straight-back chair and wedged it under the door handle before turning to her.

"I don't want any interruptions this time," he said, his voice gravelly with suppressed emotion. He sat down on the bed beside her, and the thin mattress swayed beneath his weight. For a moment she was afraid he was going to suggest they go downstairs, use the bigger bed. But he didn't.

He reached out his hands and threaded them under her thick mane of hair, pulling her toward him. Her breasts touched the smooth hardness of chest, her arms slid around him and she was the first to kiss him, with a desperation she couldn't quite dismiss.

"Easy, easy," he murmured, his hands stroking down her naked back. "We've got all night. We've got forever, if we want it. I want to do this right, this time." He kissed her eyelids, he kissed her ears, he kissed her mouth, fully, his tongue stabbing deep, until she shivered in his arms, her skin covered with a layer of sweat. Very gently he pushed her back against the thin mattress, drawing the sheet the rest of the way down, leaving her naked in the moonlight. It took all her willpower not to try to cover herself, not to reach for the sheet. But she held still, letting him look his fill, letting him judge for himself.

He put his big hands on her shoulders, sliding them down to cover her breasts. She arched against him, the rough texture of his skin against her burning softness almost unbearably arousing. His mouth followed, taking one erect nipple and swirling his tongue around it, and she felt an answering heat deep within her. His hand cupped her other breast, his thumb teasing the hard nub, and she felt on fire, certain she wouldn't be able to bear any more. And then he moved, trailing kisses down her stomach, across her hipbones, to the silky center of her.

She jumped, startled, and tried to squirm away, but his hands had captured her hips, holding her still, as his tongue found her.

It happened so quickly she didn't have time to protest. In one moment she was making a desultory effort at pushing his shoulders, in another she was digging her fingers in, arching off the bed as an astonished sob escaped her.

He moved away then, up the bed to stretch out beside her, and she could feel the shocking texture of his jeans against her leg. He kissed her mouth, with reckless abandon, and she could feel the sheer joy in him. "I don't want to give you more than you can take," he murmured, his lips against hers. "It's going to be a long night, and we've only just begun." And he moved his hand down, sliding it deftly between her legs.

She caught his wrist, pulling him away before he realized what she was doing. She sat up on the bed, pushing him down and leaning over him, her hair curtaining them both. "My turn," she said, putting her hands on the heated smoothness of his chest, half expecting an argument.

But he simply smiled, leaning back and shutting his eyes. "Be my guest," he murmured.

For a moment she panicked. Her experience hadn't involved much more than passive participation, and she didn't want to disappoint him. And then the momentary uncertainty vanished as his skin seemed to warm beneath her hands. She leaned down and put her mouth against his chest, teasing his flat masculine nipples lightly, feeling the increasing thudding of his heartbeat beneath her ear.

If her hands fumbled with the clasp of his jeans, he didn't seem to mind. The zipper stuck, but she persevered, even though her hands were shaking and her heart was pounding. When she finally released him he was bigger than she remembered, and she knew a momentary panic. One that vanished as she touched him, delicately, with an instinctive knowledge that brought forth a muffled groan of appreciation.

Encouraged, she began to experiment. And then touch wasn't enough, she wanted to taste him, she wanted him everywhere, in her mouth, in her body, all over her. Leaning down, she put her mouth on him, rewarded by his surge of surprise and arousal, his muttered curse that was more a prayer than a profanity, by the hands that cupped her head and gently held her there.

And then he pulled her away, pulled her up and over him, so that she was straddling his fully aroused body. She tried to pull away, to move onto her back, but he shook his head. "No," he whispered, his voice hoarse with strain. "Do it this way." And he lifted her hips, positioning her against his waiting hardness.

She hesitated, feeling him hot and ready against her, and then she sank down, taking him deep within her, and it was beyond anything she'd ever experienced. She shut her eyes, tipping her head back, and her hair rippled down her back. She could feel his hands reach up to touch her breasts, and she thought she'd die from the wonder of it. And then his hands slid back, down her sides, to catch her hips, to show her what he wanted.

She learned quickly. The rocking motion came to her naturally, but the pleasure was so intense she couldn't maintain it. She began to shake all over, and she had to put her hands down on the mattress to support her weight.

He moved then, pulling her down and underneath him without breaking their link, and he was huge and powerful over her, filling her with such unearthly delight that she thought she might die from it. She was reaching for something, she wasn't quite sure what. She wanted to feel that intense explosion of pleasure again, that fragmented moment of delight. It was just out of reach, beyond her in an inky midnight, and no matter how high she reached, she couldn't quite gain it.

He put his hand between their bodies, touching her deftly. He surged against her, filling her hotly, as his mouth claimed hers. And then it happened, beyond anything she'd experienced before, a terrifying sort of madness that convulsed her body in a white-hot flame. She felt him go rigid in her arms, heard his hoarse cry, and knew with a savage delight that he was hers. Forever, in that fierce darkness where no one else could survive.

The moon was shining in her eyes, stinging her eyelids. She knew her face was wet with tears, but she didn't care. Luke had collapsed against her, his face cradled against her neck, and he was slippery with sweat. He was still gasping for breath, and his heart beat counterpoint with hers.

With sudden reckless abandon she slid her fingers through his thick blond hair and yanked, gently, pulling his face up to meet hers. He looked dazed, like a man who's been kicked by a very big horse.

"You're mine, Luke," she said, her voice low and determined. "I'm serving notice. Don't think you can drive me away, don't think you can change your mind and end up with someone else. I'm staking my claim, and it won't do you any good to try to escape. You're mine, for the rest of your natural life."

He didn't say a word for a moment, and she wondered whether she'd gone too far. And then he smiled crookedly. "Izzy, I've known that since I was nineteen years old. What took you so long to figure it out?" And he silenced her mouth with his.

# Chapter Seventeen

She awoke in a tangle, her arms and legs entwined with Luke's longer ones, her hair wrapped around them both. Her entire body ached with a pleasant, mind-numbing glow, and she thought absently that it was a good thing she hadn't really had much of a chance to sleep during the long, adventurous night. It would have been impossible in that narrow, concave bunk bed. While it was definitely the stuff of fulfilled fantasies, crammed together in that tiny, cavernous space, the reality of it had more than its share of discomforts, and she was looking forward to moving downstairs into Luke's big bed.

She had no idea what time it was. Probably not much past six—the sun was just climbing in the clear blue sky outside the narrow window. She couldn't begin to guess how much sleep she'd had the night before, but there was no question that she needed more.

She wasn't going to get it. She looked at Luke's sleeping face, and her heart caught and twisted. He didn't look a day over nineteen, he looked like everything she'd ever dreamed of, and she was suddenly terrified. Was she caught up in some childhood fantasy, one that wouldn't stand the test of time? Was she in love with a nineteen-year-old who no longer existed except in her imagination?

Luke stirred, shifting in his sleep, tucking her closer against him, and she went, willingly, closing her eyes and trying to think of all the rational, concrete reasons why she loved him, why it was the forever-after kind of caring, not an outdated infatuation complicated by wonderful sex. She couldn't think of one. No guarantees, no proof. Only the gut feeling that he always had been, always would be, the one man for her. The rest she'd have to take on faith.

Sleep was out of the question by then. She slipped out of his arms, forcing herself to ignore his murmured protest as he tried to hold her. Once she reached the floor he flopped over onto his back, snoring gently, and it was all Isabelle could do to keep herself from crawling back into bed and covering him with kisses.

It would definitely be a bad idea. Her spirit was more than willing, it was positively eager, but her flesh was definitely feeling weak. She needed a cup of coffee, she needed a long hot bath to soak away some of her delicious little aches.

She threw on an old sundress and carefully moved the straight-back chair from its sentinel position under the doorknob.

"Where are you going?" Luke was barely awake.

"I need coffee."

"You're not going to make it, are you?" He groaned. "Don't you have instant?"

"Instant's not worth drinking."

"Then I'll make the real stuff. Even I can manage a coffeemaker," she said with false bravado.

He just looked at her, skepticism clear on his sleepy face. "Don't burn the house down," he said, flopping over on his stomach and falling asleep.

It took her half an hour to figure out the coffeemaker, and even then she was uncertain whether she dared leave it long enough to take the bath she so desperately needed. In the end she decided that even she couldn't destroy coffee, and she stole a cup from the still-dripping brew before she headed off for the bathroom.

The water was a faint beige as it shot out of the faucet, but it was blessedly hot. She sank into it with a grateful sigh, leaning back and closing her eyes as she listened to the sounds of the ranch, the joking voices of Jimmy and Johnson, the whickers and whinnies of the horses.

When she awoke the water was cold, her skin was wrinkled, and the sun was high in the sky. Even worse, she could smell the acrid odor of overheated coffee, and she cursed under her breath as she jumped from the bath.

Her suitcases were still packed, upstairs in the bedroom. Instead she raided Luke's closet, stealing an oversize white T-shirt and a pair of jeans that were just a bit too snug around the hips and miles too long around the ankles. She rolled them up, then padded into the kitchen to see whether she'd actually destroyed the coffeemaker as Luke had predicted.

There was a thick layer of brown sludge at the bottom of the Pyrex pot, but it was still working. Switching it off, she poured herself another cup, shuddering as she forced herself to swallow some of the desperately needed caffeine. She thought she could hear sounds of life from upstairs, and she was half tempted to go back up, but she knew perfectly well what sort of trouble she'd get into if she tried.

Instead she went out on the porch, sinking down in the rocker and propping her bare feet up on the railing. It was going to be a warm day, breezy and glorious, and it matched Isabelle's mood perfectly.

She saw the dark blue car from a distance, and for a moment she had the horrifying fear that it might be Mar-

tin, returning Becky to the bosom of her unloving family.
She relaxed when she realized it was a BMW that pulled up
beside her Ferrari, spraying it with dust, and Davey
Granger stepped out, thinning hair glistening in the late-
morning sun.

He didn't even see her sitting on the porch. He went
straight to the Ferrari, touching it with reverent hands,
barely restraining the urge to drool all over it.

"Morning, Davey," she called.

With obvious reluctance he pulled his attention from
Isabelle's car, moving toward the porch. "Hi, Bella. Is that
your car?"

"Yes."

"Wanna marry me?"

"No."

"Wanna sell me your car?"

"No."

He accepted his dismissal calmly enough. "Got any
more of that coffee?"

She grinned. "I made it."

Davey shuddered. "Never mind. Is Luke around?"

In the distance she could hear him rummaging around.
"I imagine he'll be out directly. What'd you want to see
him about?"

"Nosy as ever, aren't you, Bella?" Davey said genially.
"Nothing that concerns you. Ranch business."

"Ranch business concerns me, Davey."

"Now don't get your back up. It's just finances. Nothing to worry your pretty little head about."

Isabelle controlled the strong urge to hurl the mug of
black sludge in his face. "My pretty little head is really
quite capable of understanding finances, Davey. Why
don't you try explaining?"

"Bella, it's none of your business. I'm not going to divulge privileged financial information to an outsider."

"What the hell are you talking about?" Isabelle demanded, incensed as she slammed her feet down on the porch. "I own this ranch, and everything on it." She heard the door open behind her, felt rather than saw Luke standing there, taking in the altercation in brooding silence.

Davey laughed. "Don't be absurd, Bella. You know as well as I do your daddy left Rancho Diablo to Luke. Seemed only fair at the time, since you'd run off and hadn't bothered to return."

The world seemed to shift on its axis. She wanted to jump up, to scream in Davey's fat face that he was lying, but she really doubted whether her feet would support her. Besides, everything had the horrible, despairing ring of truth.

"Get out of here, Davey." Luke's voice was cold, implacable.

Davey looked startled. "You don't mean to tell me she didn't know?"

Isabelle raised her head. "Didn't know that my father disinherited me? No, somehow I missed that little piece of information."

"He didn't disinherit you, Bella," Davey said earnestly, finally realizing he'd committed a major faux pas. "He left you stocks, more really than the ranch could afford to lose. And Luke's been sending you a share of the profits, when there've been any. Really, you've made out much better than if your father had left you the ranch."

"Do I have to throw you off the place?" Luke asked gently, and Davey blanched at the threat.

"I'm gone. Gosh, I'm sorry, Bella. Sorry, Luke. I just didn't realize..."

"Get out."

Isabelle didn't move as Davey scrambled for his car. He almost sideswiped the Ferrari as he sped away, leaving the two of them alone on the porch. She waited for Luke to say something. But what could he say? He'd done what she'd always said he had, stolen her father from her, even to the point of her father's final, ultimate rejection. She thought it wouldn't hurt anymore, but after last night the betrayal felt all-encompassing, so devastating that she wasn't certain she'd ever stop hurting.

She wouldn't be able to salvage her heart from the tangled mess. She wouldn't be able to salvage any hope of happiness, either. All she had left was her pride, and in the absence of everything else it took over.

"So," she said, not bothering to turn around. "Mr. Takashima couldn't have bought the place anyway. My noble confession was for absolutely nothing. You must have been laughing your head off."

"I wasn't laughing."

"Were you ever going to tell me?"

"I don't know." His voice was devoid of emotion. She didn't know whether it was because he wasn't feeling any, or if he was simply tamping it down. It no longer seemed to matter.

She rose then, a bright smile on her face. "Well, it's been an education, to say the least. And never let it be said that I'm a slow learner." She met his impassive gaze, her heart crying for something. Something he wouldn't give. "Have a cup of coffee," she suggested affably. "It's delicious."

She moved past him, waiting for his arms to shoot out and stop her, to pull her into his arms, to force the dam to break. But he let her go, moving out of her way as she stepped through the door, and she knew it was futile to hope.

She'd hoped he'd be down at the barn by the time she got back downstairs, but he wasn't. He was sitting on the porch, a freshly brewed cup of coffee in one big hand, waiting for her.

Her suitcases weren't that heavy. She carried them to the Ferrari, dumping them in the trunk and slamming the lid. She hadn't bothered to change out of Luke's baggy clothes—she figured it was the least he owed her. She moved back to the porch, her pink leather diary in one hand. Putting her hands on the railing, she looked at him, her face pale but determined.

"I'll stop and see Charlie on my way out of town," she said. "And I'm going to have Davey put the stocks at your disposal."

That moved him. "It's your damned money," he snapped. "If you think I wanted Hoyt to do this, you're wrong."

"Davey made it clear that I've been bleeding the place dry. You can't separate the two. If you want to, you can call it a loan, just for the next couple of years until things even out. Do me a favor, though. Don't sell Half-moon."

"Why not? Are you coming back to ride her?"

"Never in this lifetime," she said fiercely, some of the hurt and anger breaking through.

"Then what the hell does it matter?" he shot back. "You won't know whether she's here or not. You're running away again, just like you always do when the going gets rough."

"Are you going to give me a reason to stay?"

"Hell, no! You've got to find your own reasons."

"I don't see any around me. Do you?"

He cursed then, briefly, profanely. "Get out of here, then. If you hurry you can make it to a city by sundown.

That's what you want, isn't it? Bright lights and excitement?"

"Whatever you say, Luke. You know me so well." She dropped the diary in his lap. "I thought you might like this to remember me by. Maybe you'll find you've been wrong, at least once in your life." She turned to go, but he shot out of the chair, the diary falling unheeded to the porch, and his hand caught her, whipping her around, the railing between them.

He was in a towering rage, angrier than she'd ever seen him in her entire life. "Go ahead, run," he said. "Maybe sometime in this life you'll learn that a man needs more. Loving someone isn't enough. He's got to be able to trust her not to turn tail when things get nasty. Things always do, sooner or later. Out here you need to be able to stay the course."

She jerked away from him, stumbling backward, and he let her go, staring at her with mute frustration. "Goodbye, Luke," she said emotionlessly.

HE WATCHED HER drive away, his fist clenched around the cup of coffee. He wanted to hurl it after her, smashing her expensive window, denting her expensive car, just as he wanted to break her armored heart. Damn her for breaking through, making him think there might be a future between them, only to turn tail and run.

And damn him for not telling her. For not being man enough to face up to the possibilities. She'd been far braver than he'd ever imagined, telling him about her machinations with the obscure Mr. Takashima. That would have been the perfect time to explain to her just why it wouldn't have done her any good in the first place.

But he hadn't. He'd used the first excuse he could find and gone to bed with her, too concerned with the present, that night in general, than in any chance of a future they might have. He'd blown it, and she'd been true to form, running away from pain, running away from him.

Jimmy was coming up from the west barn, his face red with exertion. "You going to visit Charlie this morning?" he inquired innocently.

How was he going to face the old man? And how was he going to face the next forty years, without her? "He's got visitors this morning."

"That where Miss Bella was headed in such an all-fire hurry?"

"Yup," he said, declining to elaborate. Jimmy would find out soon enough that she was gone for good. Luke didn't feel like making explanations right there and then.

"Sure do like her," Jimmy said soulfully.

Luke glared at him. "I thought you were in love with Ruthann."

Jimmy blushed. "Of course I am. Miss Bella ain't my type at all. But I still like having her around."

Luke shut his eyes against the bright hot glare of the sun. "So do I," he murmured. "So do I."

ISABELLE KEPT HER VISIT to Charlie light and cheerful. He didn't seem to notice that she was wearing Luke's clothes, or if he did, he didn't say anything. He already seemed a hundred percent better, his color improved, his temper sharpening. When she finally left he didn't say anything about the tears in her eyes, the gravel in her throat. He just held her tightly for a moment, his own eyes moist, and then released her.

Davey argued like crazy about the financial arrangements, but he couldn't talk her out of it. With a few dozen signatures she turned over the income from her stocks to Luke. It was up to him what he chose to do with it. She was going to make certain he wasn't able to find any sort of address for her, to send her the money.

She didn't look back when she drove out of town. She knew she'd see Davey, his nose pressed against his office window, drooling over her car. But everyone else would have forgotten about her.

She got as far as Laramie the first night, heading toward Denver. Denver wasn't big enough, so she just kept driving, blindly, heading as far away and as fast as her Ferrari could take her. She made Santa Fe by nightfall, but it was too pretty, so she kept on going, ending in a dingy motel in downtown Albuquerque, too tired to think, too tired to remember, too tired to do anything but lie in the uncomfortable double bed and cry herself to sleep.

The flashing neon outside her window woke her up sometime after three in the morning. She lay there without moving, wondering where Luke was. Wondering what he was doing, if he was sleeping alone. Or if he'd ended up in Marcy Parker's bed, trying to forget her.

Because he'd need to do something drastic to wipe her out of his memory. Despite his treachery, his dishonesty, he really did care about her, at least a little bit.

The knowledge hit her with the force of a stunning blow. She sat up in the uncomfortable bed, the covers clutched around her, as she remembered his parting words. What had he said? Something about "loving a woman isn't enough. He has to be able to trust her not to run away."

And she'd run. She'd run from a man who'd just told her he loved her. She'd been too angry to listen when he'd said the words, too caught up in her own hurt and sense of betrayal to realize it wasn't Luke who'd betrayed her.

It was Hoyt. She'd spent years resenting him, hating him, for rejections that were slight compared to his final will. For some reason she couldn't hate him anymore.

Petty cruelties wounded beyond bearing, but this was different. It brought home to her, in clear, simple terms, how very wrong Hoyt had been.

Not about Luke. Luke deserved his love and respect, deserved the ranch. But his daughter had deserved the same, and in Hoyt's pleasure over finding a son, he'd abandoned the daughter who once would have done anything for him.

It was Hoyt's mistake, not her failing. But it was a mistake she was going to right. She was going to stop running, here and now. Thirteen years was long enough. She wasn't going to be the fool her own father was, turning her back on love that was offered like a perfect rose, thorns and all. She was going back and fighting for Luke. Fighting for a stake in the ranch, for that matter. It had been borne in on her during the past ten days that Wyoming was where she belonged. Not in cities where people didn't even meet your eye, not in countries where people didn't even speak the same language. She belonged in Devil's Fork, at Rancho Diablo. And if she was wrong about Luke, if she'd read too much in his angry statement, she still intended to stay.

She threw back the covers, heading for the bathroom and the rusty, tin-lined shower. The other residents of Turtle Walk Sleep-a-Wee would probably be cursing her through the paper-thin walls as they listened to her shower. Served them right. She'd spent too much time listening to the irritating sounds of other couples finding ecstasy to have much sympathy.

She got herself a cup of coffee in the vending machine outside the motel office, and damned if it didn't taste even worse than the cup she'd brewed her last morning at Rancho Diablo. By dawn she was flying back up Route 25, collecting speeding tickets with reckless abandon.

It was late afternoon when she finally drove back into the tiny town of Devil's Fork. She drove straight to the hospital, making certain Luke's battered pickup was nowhere to be seen in the small parking lot, and practically ran up the stairs to Charlie's room.

He was sitting in a chair by the window, most of the tubes finally unhooked, but he looked hunched over, old and dejected. Isabelle paused there, a sudden panic filling her. Maybe he'd gotten worse, maybe the prognosis wasn't nearly as rosy as his doctor had painted it.

"Charlie?" she said uncertainly.

He turned to stare at her, shock and then joy creasing his face, and his old eyes filled with tears. "Dammit, Bella, I thought you'd gone for good this time." And he held out his arms for her.

She ran into them, kneeling beside him and hugging him fiercely. "I'm not as dumb as I look," she said, her voice a mixture of laughter and tears. "I think I've been running long enough."

He held her back, to look at her, as if he couldn't get enough of her. "Does Luke know you're back?"

"Not yet."

"For God's sake, tell him. He was in this morning, and he looked like holy hell. Bella, I've never seen him so tore up. Not when Hoyt died, not when Cathy was killed. He looks like death warmed over."

"I'm going out there, as soon as I take care of a little business in town. You're sure he wants me?" She couldn't help asking for a little reassurance.

Charlie snorted his disgust. "You're too smart to ask me a question like that, girlie. I don't know how he's made it this long without you. I reckon he told you about the will, and that's what made you run this time."

"He didn't. Davey let it slip."

"Hell," Charlie said, his voice thick with disgust. "I told him he should tell you himself, but he didn't want to. He figured there was no reason to hurt you if you didn't have to know. He tried his damnedest to talk Hoyt out of it, you know. He never wanted to take a thing away from you. And Hoyt promised him he wouldn't do it. But once he died we learned he'd just gone ahead and done it anyways. Always was a pigheaded fool, your daddy."

She shrugged. "It doesn't matter."

Charlie peered at her as if he couldn't believe what he was hearing. "You mean you don't hate him anymore?"

She shook her head. "It's a waste of time. Besides, I may have lost my father to Luke, but I've always had you. It's not every girl who has a second father waiting in the wings when the first one messes up."

Charlie squeezed her hand, his grip frail but determined. "You bet, Bella." He wiped the tears from his leathery cheek. "And I get to be the one who gives you away at the wedding."

"If Luke asks. And if you get out of this damned place. I thought you'd be doing a jig by now."

"The heart just sort of went out of me. Once you left."

"Well, I'm back. And I'm not going anywhere, except out to the ranch."

"What are you waiting for, then?" he grumbled.

"I need to know exactly what Luke needs in a new pickup truck."

"Why?"

"A girl needs a dowry," she said. "And what good is a Ferrari on a ranch?"

## Chapter Eighteen

Driving a half-ton Dodge pickup with four-wheel drive, plowing package, air-conditioning and every accoutrement known to man was a lot different than driving a Ferrari, Isabelle thought as she moved sedately down the dirt-packed road to the ranch. She was going to miss her car, particularly when she saw Davey Granger tooling around it. If things worked out as she hoped they would, she'd have to talk Luke into getting a four-wheel drive station wagon so she'd have some mobility. Something with room for kids in the back seat.

Reed Rathburn at Devil's Fork's only auto dealership had looked skeptical when she'd first driven in with her sleek little car, but after her suggested phone call to Davey down at the bank he became much more enthusiastic. She probably could have gotten more money out of Davey if she'd dealt with him directly, but she was in a hurry to get back to Rancho Diablo, and with Rathburn she could take care of both items of business at one time.

There was also going to be quite a nice piece of change left over after she bought the pickup. Enough to put a new roof on the west barn, enough to pay for Murphy's new yearling and maybe pay a few bills besides.

The ranch was deserted when she got there, sometime before six. She was just as glad. She still wasn't quite certain how she was going to handle the situation, and the more time she had to get nervous, the better. She started to haul her suitcases out of the back of the truck, then thought better of it. She didn't know where to put them.

To put them in Luke's room might have been presuming too much. She certainly didn't want to spend another night alone in that narrow bunk bed, and she couldn't fancy moving into her father's old bedroom. She'd figure it out sooner or later.

The one thing she brought was her *Cooking for Idiots* cookbook. She'd perused it during her brief stop for lunch, and it didn't look that impossible. Maybe if she welcomed Luke back with a home-cooked meal, things might go more smoothly.

"LOAD HER BACK UP," Luke ordered, his voice terse.

"But Luke," Jimmy said. "Why'd we bring Half-moon over here if you're not going to sell her?"

"I've changed my mind," he said shortly. "Sorry, Jeff. I just can't do it."

Jeff shook his head. "Do you want me to give you more? I'm willing to. She's a beautiful horse, with the sweetest temper around, and you know my wife is scared of riding. With Half-moon she'd be able to learn."

"You know me better than that, Jeff. It's not money, though God knows I need it. No, this horse belongs to another lady who's afraid of riding, and I can't sell her."

"I thought Bella had left."

Damn this small town and everybody knowing everybody's business, Luke thought. "She'll be back," he said. And wished he believed it.

It was a long ride home to Rancho Diablo, with nothing for company but his own brooding thoughts and the horse trailer lumbering along behind the old pickup. Jimmy had stayed behind, visiting Jeff's daughter Ruthann, and Luke hadn't known whether to be glad or sorry. Jeff's ranch was only seven miles from Rancho Diablo, but those miles seemed endless.

Once he got back things wouldn't be much better. Johnson had done evening chores before he took off to visit Charlie. He'd have no one for company but the memory of Izzy, the scent of her perfume that still seemed to linger in the old house, the damned diary that he couldn't stop reading.

She really had loved him. Long ago, when he'd been too proud and too angry to open up to anyone but Hoyt, she'd been as obsessed with him as he'd been with her. Beneath her bravado she'd been longing for him, and all he'd done was push her away.

He probably shouldn't be regretting it so sharply. It wasn't time for them. Seventeen was too young for marriage, and if he'd started touching her he wouldn't have been able to stop.

So instead he'd rejected her, and she'd run, run from him, run from Hoyt, and things had been disastrous ever since.

If only he'd found the diary, he wouldn't have viewed her return so warily. If he'd known she'd once loved him, he would have trusted her enough to try to rekindle that feeling, to get through her brittle defenses.

Of course, he'd managed that anyway. But he'd blown it in the end, by being just as sneaky and manipulative as he'd always accused her of being.

He was going to have to come up with another way to pay for Murphy's young stud. He was going to have to figure out a way to stave off the creditors. He wasn't going to touch Isabelle's money, not unless she were there.

He was going to go find her. He knew that now, much as he'd been fighting that knowledge. As soon as Charlie was out of danger he was going to chase after Izzy and drag her back by her glorious mane of hair. If she could be noble, so could he. He was going to sign over the damned ranch to her, and then the next step would be up to her.

He didn't notice the pickup as he drove into the yard and carefully backed the trailer into the west barn. By the time he got Half-moon settled back in her stall he was tired and grumpy and hungry. All he wanted was a frozen dinner and a tall glass of whiskey, not necessarily in that order.

He saw the pickup truck first, shiny red, loaded with options, parked near the kitchen door. He saw the smoke next, pouring out of the kitchen, thick and black and ominous.

He began to curse, and run, coming to an abrupt halt as Izzy staggered out the door, waving the smoke away from her and coughing.

She saw him a moment later, and she managed a wry smile. "Fire's out," she said. "No need to panic."

He didn't move. "What happened?"

She shrugged, not quite meeting his gaze. "I was trying to cook dinner. Pork chops, to be exact. The cookbook was called *Cooking for Idiots* but I guess I'd overestimated my abilities."

His glance dismissed the diminishing smoke. "I wasn't talking about that. What happened to you? Why did you come back?"

Now that the time had come she seemed hesitant. She leaned against the porch railing, looking out toward the distant mountains. "I guess I decided that while this may be the kind of place a girl runs away from, it's the kind of place a woman comes home to. And somewhere along the way I grew up.''

"Did you?"

She met his gaze then, fearlessly. "Yes. I figured out some other things while I was at it. That Hoyt was dead wrong. I needed a father's love and a sense of belonging, and he took those away from me."

"He gave them to me."

"Yes, but it wasn't your fault. I've been hurt and angry for so long, blaming you. But it wasn't you, it was Hoyt."

"So you're staying for a while?" He didn't dare to hope. He was moving closer to the porch, slowly enough so as not to frighten her.

"No."

That stopped him, a few feet away from her. "No?" he echoed.

"I'm staying here forever. No more running." She managed a shy smile, one that looked delicious on her smoke-smudged face. "I thought I explained that to you once already. You're mine, and there's nothing you can do about it."

He took another step, closer to his ultimate and final destination. "Oh, yeah?"

"I've already seen Charlie, and he's going to give me away. You're going to have to marry me, you know. You didn't use anything the last time we were together, and who knows, I might already be pregnant."

He took another step, closer still. "Who says we're that fertile?"

She grinned, sure of herself now. "I bet we are."

"Pretty sassy, aren't you?" He loved the idea of seeing her round and full with his child. He loved the idea of seeing her standing on the porch, teasing him, knowing she was going to be there, forever.

"Yup," she said. "I even brought you a dowry." She gestured toward the pickup.

At any other time in his life he would have been all over the truck. Right then it was the least of his worries. "You traded the Ferrari?"

She nodded. "It was worth a lot more than the truck. We can buy the yearling with the balance, and maybe even fix the barn roof."

"Babies cost money," he pointed out.

"Then the mares better start breeding, too."

He'd reached her by then, but the railing stood between them. Without ceremony he hauled her up and over it, pulling her into his arms. He kissed her, long and hard and deep, and when he lifted his head he saw tears in her eyes.

"God, Izzy, don't cry," he said tenderly, wiping the tears from her cheeks. "Don't worry, you won't have to do any cooking."

She grinned crookedly. "For you I'd even learn how to cook."

"Well, darlin', even for you I wouldn't learn to eat your food," he said solemnly. "I'll find you a cook for a wedding present."

She sighed, happy beyond belief. "I always knew you loved me."

THE WEDDING TOOK PLACE three weeks later, long enough to plan the biggest blowout in Jackson County in twenty-five years, long enough to make sure Charlie was well enough to party up a storm, long enough for Izzy to suspect she was well and truly on her way to being a mother, as well as a wife and rancher.

Johnson spent the festivities flirting with Marcy Parker, who used the occasion to drink just enough to force Johnson to drive her home. He wasn't seen for three days, and when he finally surfaced he had a smile on his usually taciturn face.

Davey Granger drove his Ferrari to the wedding, pulling out half his remaining hair when a cowpoke threw up in it after too much champagne.

Rebecca and Martin Abruzzi sent red roses and a case of Dom Perignon and their best wishes. The Basho Meditation Center sent brown rice.

And Jimmy gave Isabelle the best wedding gift of all. One week before the wedding he eloped with the thoroughly pregnant Ruthann, bringing her back to Rancho Diablo, and by the time the wedding rolled around she'd proven herself to be the best cook this side of the Rockies. Life, thought Isabelle, looking up at her new husband, had happy endings after all.

STEP

INTO

THE

## WINNER'S CIRCLE

## MILLION DOLLAR SWEEPSTAKES
## AND
## EXTRA BONUS PRIZE DRAWING

No purchase necessary. To enter the sweepstakes, follow the directions published and complete and mail your Official Entry Form. If your Official Entry Form is missing, or you wish to obtain an additional one (limit: one Official Entry Form per request, one request per outer mailing envelope) send a separate, stamped, self-addressed #10 envelope (4 1/8" X 9 1/2") via first-class mail to: Million Dollar Sweepstakes and Extra Bonus Prize Drawing Entry Form, P.O. Box 1867, Buffalo, NY 14269-1867. Request must be received no later than January 15, 1998. For eligibility into the sweepstakes, entries must be received no later than March 31,1998. No liability is assumed for printing errors, lost, late, non-delivered or misdirected entries. Odds of winning are determined by the number of eligible entries distributed and received.

Sweepstakes open to residents of the U.S. (except Puerto Rico), Canada and Europe who are 18 years of age or older. All applicable laws and regulations apply. Sweepstakes offer void wherever prohibited by law. Values of all prizes are in U.S. currency. This sweepstakes is presented by Torstar Corp., its subsidiaries and affiliates, in conjunction with book, merchandise and/or product offerings. For a copy of the Official Rules governing this sweepstakes, send a self-addressed, stamped envelope (WA residents need not affix return postage) to: MILLION DOLLAR SWEEP-STAKES AND EXTRA BONUS PRIZE DRAWING Rules, P.O. Box 4470, Blair, NE 68009-4470, USA.

## FAST CASH 4033 DRAW RULES
## NO PURCHASE OR OBLIGATION NECESSARY

Fifty prizes of $50 each will be awarded in random drawings to be conducted no later than 6/28/96 from amongst all eligible responses to this prize offer received as of 5/14/96. To enter, follow directions, affix 1st-class postage and mail OR write Fast Cash 4033 on a 3" x 5" card along with your name and address and mail that card to: Harlequin's Fast Cash 4033 Draw, P.O. Box 1395, Buffalo, NY 14240-1395 OR P.O. Box 618, Fort Erie, Ontario L2A 5X3. (Limit: one entry per outer envelope; all entries must be sent via 1st-class mail.) Limit: one prize per household. Odds of winning are determined by the number of eligible responses received. Offer is open only to residents of the U.S. (except Puerto Rico) and Canada and is void wherever prohibited by law. All applicable laws and regulations apply. Any litigation within the province of Quebec respecting the conduct and awarding of a prize in this sweepstakes may be submitted to the Régie des alcools, des courses et des jeux. In order for a Canadian resident to win a prize, that person will be required to correctly answer a time-limited arithmetical skill-testing question to be administered by mail. Names of winners available after 7/30/96 by sending a self-addressed, stamped envelope to: Fast Cash 4033 Draw Winners, P.O. Box 4200, Blair, NE 68009-4200.

SWP-H3ZD

Fall in love all over again with

_This Time..._
MARRIAGE

In this collection of original short stories, three brides get a unique chance for a return engagement!

- Being kidnapped from your bridal shower by a one-time love can really put a crimp in your wedding plans! _The Borrowed Bride_— by **Susan Wiggs,** _Romantic Times_ Career Achievement Award-winning author.

- After fifteen years a couple reunites for the sake of their child—this time will it end in marriage? _The Forgotten Bride_—by **Janice Kaiser.**

- It's tough to make a good divorce stick—especially when you're thrown together with your ex in a magazine wedding shoot! _The Bygone Bride_— by **Muriel Jensen.**

Don't miss THIS TIME...MARRIAGE, available in April wherever Harlequin books are sold.

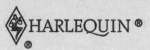

HARLEQUIN ®
®

BRIDE96

HARLEQUIN

AMERICAN ◆ ROMANCE®

*With only forty-eight hours to lasso their mates—*
*it's a stampede...to the altar!*

WILD WEST
*Weddings*

## by Cathy Gillen Thacker

Looking down from above, Montana maven
Max McKendrick wants to make sure his heirs get
something money can't buy—true love! And if his two
nephews and niece want to inherit their piece of his
sprawling Silver Spur ranch then they'll have to wed the
spouse of *his* choice—within forty-eight hours!

Don't miss any of the Wild West Weddings titles!

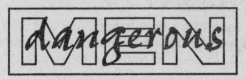

# Yo amo novelas con corazón!

Starting this March, Harlequin opens up to a whole new world of readers with two new romance lines in SPANISH!

**Harlequin Deseo**
- passionate, sensual and exciting stories

**Harlequin Bianca**
- romances that are fun, fresh and very contemporary

With four titles a month, each line will offer the same wonderfully romantic stories that you've come to love—now available in Spanish.

Look for them at selected retail outlets.

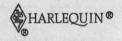

Harlequin invites you to the
wedding of the century!

This April be prepared to catch the bouquet with
the glamorous debut of

*Weddings by
DeWilde*

For years, DeWildes—the elegant and fashionable
wedding store chain—has helped brides around the
world turn the fantasy of their special day into reality.
But now the store and three generations of family are
torn apart by divorce. As family members face new
challenges and loves, a long-secret mystery begins to
unravel.... Set against an international backdrop of
London, Paris, New York and Sydney, this new series
features the glitzy, fast-paced world of designer wedding
fashions and missing heirlooms!

In April watch for:
**SHATTERED VOWS**
by Jasmine Cresswell

Look in the back pages of *Weddings by DeWilde* for
details about our fabulous sweepstakes contest to win a
*real* diamond ring!

**Coming this April to your favorite retail outlet.**

WBDT

HARLEQUIN®

# You're About to Become a *Privileged Woman*

Reap the rewards of fabulous free gifts and benefits with proofs-of-purchase from Harlequin and Silhouette books

# Pages & Privileges™

It's our way of thanking you for buying our books at your favorite retail stores.

PROOF OF PURCHASE

WL-PP113

Offer expires October 31, 1996

**Harlequin and Silhouette—
the most privileged readers in the world!**

For more information about Harlequin and Silhouette's PAGES & PRIVILEGES program call the Pages & Privileges Benefits Desk: 1-503-794-2499

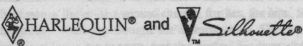

HARLEQUIN® and *Silhouette*®

WL-PP113